AB

David F. Ross was born in Glasgow in 1964, and lived in various
parts of the city until the late '70s. He subsequently moved to Kilmarnock, where he has lived ever since. He was educated at James
Hamilton Academy until being politely asked to leave. (*Expulsion
is such a harsh word, isn't it?*)

Following a frankly ludicrous early foray into sporadic
employment (*Undertakers, Ice Cream Parlour, Tennis Groundsman,
DJ ... he'll save these stories until he knows you better*), David found
himself at Glasgow School of Art, studying architecture.

In 1992, he graduated from the Mackintosh School of
Architecture. He is now the Design Director of one of Scotland's
largest, oldest and most successful practices, Keppie Design.
(*Funny old world, eh?*)

David has worked all over the world, leading his practice's
strategy on projects in countries as diverse as China, Egypt,
Malaysia, India and Libya. He is a designated business leader for
East Ayrshire Council, a Board Mentor for Entrepreneurial Spark
and he was design advisor to Strathclyde Passenger Transport for
their modernisation programme of the Glasgow Subway in advance
of the 2014 Commonwealth Games.

He is married to Elaine and has two children, Nathan and Nadia,
who have both signed legally binding agreements to house him in
the best Old Folks' Home his money can buy. He is a Chelsea fan
– from long before the cash-rich days – and occasionally writes
stream-of-consciousness rubbish for @ByTheMinChelsea and
other @ByTheMinSport feeds on Twitter.

David's most prized possession is a signed Joe Strummer LP.
The Last Days of Disco is his first novel.

Anything else you'd like to know?

www.davidfross.co.uk

THE LAST DAYS OF DISCO

Orenda Books
16 Carson Road
West Dulwich
London SE21 8HU
www.orendabooks.co.uk

First published in ebook by Orenda Books 2014

This B-format edition published by Orenda Books 2015

Copyright © David F. Ross 2014

David F. Ross has asserted his moral right to be identified as the author of this
work in accordance with the Copyright, Designs and Patents Act, 1988.

All Rights Reserved. No part of this publication may be reproduced in any form
or by any means without the written permission of the publishers.

A catalogue record for this book is available from the British Library.

ISBN 978-1-910633-02-1

Typeset in Minion by James Nunn
Printed and bound by CPI Group (UK) Ltd, Croydon CR0 4YY

*This is a work of fiction. Names, characters, places and incidents are either products
of the author's imagination or are used fictitiously. Any resemblance to actual
events, locales or persons, living or dead, is entirely coincidental.*

Sales & Distribution
In the UK and elsewhere in Europe:
Turnaround Publisher Services, Unit 3, Olympia Trading Estate
Coburg Road, Wood Green, LONDON, N22 6TZ
www.turnaround-uk.com

In Australia/New Zealand:
Australian Scholarly Publishing, 7 Lt Lothian St North, North Melbourne,
Victoria 3051, Australia
www.scholarly.info

In USA/Canada:
Trafalgar Square Publishing, Independent Publishers 814 North Franklin Street
Chicago, IL 60610, USA
www.ipgbook.com

For details of other territories, please contact info@orendabooks.co.uk

THE LAST DAYS OF DISCO

OF DISCO

DAVID F. ROSS

ORENDA
BOOKS

For Elaine, Nathan and Nadia

'Sneak home and pray you'll never know,
The hell where youth and laughter go.'

from 'Suicide in the Trenches'
by Siegfried Sassoon, 1917

PART I

A TIME FOR ACTION

'Now that the official figure for unemployment has exceeded three million, is the Prime Minister proud of the fact that she has brought so much despair to so many families in the United Kingdom? Is she proud of the fact that she and the Government have created more havoc in the British economy than the German High Command in the whole of the last war?'

Dennis Skinner, MP for Bolsover
Prime Minister's Questions, January 1982

1

A MAN ON THE EDGE

'Bobby Cassidy was a man on the edge. Monaco was his kinda town ...'
As experiences go, this was a highly unusual one. He had always imagined driving at ridiculous speed through the Nouvelle Chicane with James Hunt and Gilles Villeneuve visible in either wing mirror, unable to pass. But now that it was actually happening, Sean Connery's commentary – *Where was that actually coming from?* – lent the whole thing a strange and distinctly surreal air. And it was becoming much weirder. Attempting to keep his full concentration on the tight, twisting track with all of its ludicrous hairpin bends and various urban distractions – *Was that really Sally McLoy from Hurlford waving at him from the balcony of the Grand Hotel, topless, with those massive tits jiggling away like jellies in an earthquake?* – he was troubled by the fact that he couldn't recall how he got here.

With three million on the dole and the numbers growing by the day, how had he actually become a racing driver in the first place? He couldn't remember the interview, or even filling in the application form. How many races had he completed? Had he met and been interviewed by Murray Walker? Did he still live in a two-storey, terraced council house at 13 Almond Avenue, Kilmarnock, Scotland, Europe, The World, The Universe (school jotters ... old habits die hard) with his mum, dad, sister Heather and prodigal elder brother, Gary? And most disconcertingly, why did he now have three arms?

'*Shurely shome mishtake* ...' 007 was beginning to really irritate Bobby now.

'Shut the fuck up, Sean. I'm tryin' tae fuckin' drive here.'

As he came round the sharp corner at Portier and headed towards the famous tunnel at 180mph, Bobby caught a glimpse of his reflection in the glass barriers surrounding the circuit. The red-and-white McLaren looked like a massive fag packet on wheels. A horizontal line of piercing spotlights caused him to lift his left hand off the tiny steering wheel and up to shield his eyes. As his hand reached his head, two conflicting realisations dawned on him. First, he wasn't wearing a fucking helmet, and second, the third arm wasn't his. It belonged to a woman sitting in a bucket seat behind him. And not just *any* woman; it was the right arm of the lovely Sally James from *Tiswas*, and she was starting to fondle his cock.

'Sean, big man, we're no' in fuckin' Kansas anymer ...'

He awoke just in time. It wasn't Sally who was gripping his hard-on. The third arm belonged to Bobby's elder brother, Gary. That the two were lying in a top-and-tail manner suggested either pre-arrangement or that somebody more responsible had placed them that way. To Bobby, whose recognition of environment and understanding of context was currently diminished, the latter of these two scenarios offered only slightly more comfort.

Bobby retched at this thought. He pulled back instinctively and, amazingly, Gary didn't stir. If Bobby was careful and composed, he could still get out of the situation with his dignity intact. The World Championship dream over for another season, he swiftly but delicately eased his brother's hand away from his dick, then Bobby slid himself out of his own single bed and onto the pile of discarded and dirty clothes that lay adjacent. Gary moaned a bit, but didn't wake up. Bobby had to work hard to stifle an attempt by his stomach to empty its contents right there and then. He edged open the door to his room enough to squeeze through and then made his way along the ten feet of hall to the toilet – arse cheeks and sphincter working overtime.

As he reached the sanctuary of the small bathroom, a new and equally unpleasant sensation began. Motörhead had set up their gear inside his skull and were starting rehearsals for a forthcoming tour.

'Let's turn it up t' a hard fuckin' eleven, lads,' said Lemmy. 'Wake this stupid cunt up proper.'

This rapidly grew into a headache the like of which Bobby could scarcely remember. Worse than when he got his head wedged in old Doris Peters' garden fence when he was eight. Having squeezed through to nick apples from her tree, his head had got stuck on the way back out. He'd only been in the garden for about twenty minutes, but either he'd grown during the robbery, or He'd tried to leave the scene via a smaller opening than the one Gary and his bastard mates had forced him through on the way in. The pain from having Gary drag him out by the legs had lasted about a week.

He sat on the toilet pan like the famous Rodin figure for around twenty minutes. *What a fucking state to get into*, he thought. He hadn't moved since forethought had wisely prompted him to open the small top-hung window just before the deluge had begun. His legs were numb from lack of circulation caused by severe buttock clenching in the early stages. Thereafter, he thought *fuck it*. It sounded like the Brighouse & Rastrick Brass Band tuning up but it was less effort to just leave the sluice gates open.

The cistern – temperamental at the best of times – had given up the ghost around flush six. By the time Bobby felt sufficiently empty to attempt standing, Motörhead was still thrashing away. As he tightly gripped the towel rail, holding on for stability like an OAP, they'd at least decided to try out a few unplugged acoustic numbers. Bobby allowed himself a glimmer of a smile at this ridiculous analogy.

'Thanks Lemmy, ya manky, wart-faced bastard,' he whispered

at the vaguely familiar image staring back at him from above the avocado-coloured sink.

What the fuck had occurred last night? He'd had a few mental hangovers before in his short career as a 'drinker', but, Jesus Christ, this was crazy. He couldn't remember getting home. Truth was, he couldn't even recall going out in the first place. All he knew for certain was that Gary would be central to the reasons behind his amnesia. A pain in his lower back was now also beginning to make itself known.

'Fuckin' hell, you. Get a shift oan, eh?' The gruff, croaky voice jolted Bobby. It had come from the imposter who had recently been trying to ease Bobby's penis into fifth as he accelerated towards La Rascasse.

'Ye'll never believe the dream ah've just had,' it said.

The bathroom door was now opened to the maximum its chain-lock would allow. Harry – Bobby's dad – had fitted it following his sister's impassioned pleas for a bit of privacy following her first frightening steps on the road to womanhood. There hadn't been a working lock on the bathroom door for around ten years. Rather than get the right one for the situation, Harry had rooted around in his shed and fashioned a temporary solution from an old padlock. It had now been temporarily keeping unwanted visitors at bay for nearly fourteen months.

'Ah was in disguise,' declared Gary, his ferret-like features pressed against the two-inch gap like Jack in *The Shining*.

'Dressed up as the Phantom Flan Flinger, so ah was. Sally James comes ower, aw coy an' that – an' mind this is aw live on fuckin' telly, Saturday mornin' anaw. So she tells everybody, *"It's time the Phantom was unmasked".*' Bobby gagged.

Gary's face was now pushed so far into the gap that he looked distorted – like a Picasso, with both eyes on the same side of the head.

'Whit the fucks that smell? Izzat you, Boab? Fur fucksake, yer no deid in there, are ye?' Gary sniffed the putrid air several times before continuing.

'So, as ah was sayin, ah'm aboot tae get unveiled on live telly. But instead of takin' the cape off, Sally fuckin' reaches inside it, an' starts wankin' me off! Fuckin' mental, man.' Gary paused to maximise the effect. Bobby was astonished that they had both been dreaming about the same person.

'Wan ae thae dreams yer absolutely fuckin' convinced is really fuckin' happenin'.' Gary pondered again, inhaled deeply and carried on.

'Then, just as ah'm getting close, she fuckin' stops ... leavin' me hingin'.' A third pause.

'So fuckin' hurry up an' get oota there, tae ah finish masel off.' A few more sniffs.

'Unless you want tae do it, that is ...?'

→-<-

'Ah was fuckin' kiddin', for Chrissake. Ye didnae need tae spew aw ower the door. There's nae way ah'd av been letting you anywhere near ma knob. Ah don't even care that yer a fuckin' bender ... it'd still be like ... incest or something.' Gary was enjoying taunting his younger brother.

Although he could have done without it on this particular morning, Bobby was generally glad his brother was home again. He could be *a total cunt* at times but, on the whole, he'd always looked out for Bobby. He had often taken the full brunt of Harry's anger for things that were actually Bobby's fault.

Bobby lifted his head away from his hands and looked around the room. He still felt as if he was part of a slow-motion replay of incidents that had happened earlier. He watched his elder brother's freckled and impressively muscular frame disappear into the adjacent kitchen. Outside, it was a beautifully crisp late-winter morning: blinding low-level sun and sporadic vapour trails of breath from people out walking. The view from the dining table made Bobby feel slightly better. Regardless of how bad they are, hangovers eventually pass. He looked over to take in his parents' newly decorated living room with its smart woodchip wallpaper *'painted in mongolia'*, as his mum Ethel had demanded. (Bobby called his mum Mrs Malaprop, and while the rest of the family found this highly amusing, the joke was lost on Ethel.) As far back as Bobby could recall, his mum had always been a bit brittle. When he was little, there were regular tense arguments between his parents. Usually they involved Gary. They had become fewer in recent years but her emotional fragility was the apparent legacy.

Bobby looked intently at the picture of a small boy that was hanging above the three-bar electric fire to the front of the room. It was a painting but not an especially good one and most certainly not an original. At least ten other people Bobby knew had the same painting positioned in a virtually identical location in *their* houses. Despite this, there was an undeniably hypnotic quality to the image. Years ago, when she first got it, Ethel had told her daughter that it was a painting of Gary when he was little. The track of a tear that wound its way down the chubby little cheeks came from large, blue, turned-down eyes, just like Gary's. It wasn't ever explained why someone had painted a picture of Gary while he was in such a state of distress. Nor why his parents had then framed it and hung it in a position of such prominence. Familiarity had rendered her mystification obsolete over the years, but neither Bobby nor his sister had ever been able to look at the picture without thinking about Gary. Especially in the months after he had suddenly left home and headed for London.

The 'crying boy' bore no resemblance to other members of the Cassidy family. Neither did Gary. Numerous family photographs were arranged around the principal room of the Cassidy home. On the sideboard; on top of the bloody piano that Harry had 'rescued' from the school where he now worked as a janitor; on the sills of the two windows that looked out onto the front and rear gardens; on the massive wooden cabinet that housed the television – for so long, the dominant voice of the household. (When it 'spoke', *everybody* listened.) Gary appeared in none of these photographs. Bobby hadn't really thought about this before. Gary had always just seemed to be generally absent; a bona fide black sheep. Now, though, with him back home and a real air of détente finally existing between his brother and his father, Bobby found this absence from family events quite strange.

The door of the kitchen opened and the tinny sound of Soft Cell drifted through it, followed by Gary. He was carrying a tray by its large wicker handles. Arranged carefully on the tray was, by Cassidy standards, an extraordinarily decent breakfast. A plate full of toast – carefully buttered and sliced diagonally, continental style; two boiled eggs – one already decapitated – sitting snugly in comedy egg-cups; a pot of tea encased in one of Ethel's knitted and badly fitting woollen cosies; and two cups – one plain white and the other welcoming the drinker to Blackpool – made up the ensemble. Gary wasn't finished though. The giveaway smells of bacon and sliced sausage made this whole exercise even more impressive, considering Gary's former Olympian levels of laziness. *Maybe the Army had done him good after all.* Bobby shuffled about uncomfortably in his seat. He had picked the one that faced the rest of the room only because the base of his back was still sore and its solid canvas back was more appealing than the four hard-panelled chairs that sat around the circular table.

'Some night, eh boy?' said Gary, the lean, bare-chested Scots Guardsman.

'Ah don't ken. Canny fuckin' remember anythin' … an' ah really mean *anything*,' said Bobby, still contemplating which parts of this greasy feast set before him might stay the course following consumption.

'It's yer eighteenth! Fuck's sake, Boab, yer no supposed tae remember anything. It's a well-known fact. Like yer stag do … or the '60s.'

'Is it fuck! Ah don't remember the '60s cos' ah was a *wean*, no because ah was pished. When did we go out?' Bobby tried to turn the focus to questions that would hopefully prompt small fragments of recollection to return.

'About nine in the morning,' Gary said proudly, before adding, 'on Friday.' Bobby's face first recorded emotions of surprise, then shock, then shame and finally – as Steve Wright wished everyone a pleasant Sunday from the kitchen – resignation. A whole day (and night) of Bobby's life had gone AWOL. He asked if they had gone to the Kilmarnock v Hearts game on Saturday. Gary nodded, his soldier's mouth full of toasted equivalents. Bobby enquired if they had gone to Casper's Nightclub at the Cross.

'Friday … and Saturday tae,' Gary replied.

'Where the fuck did we stay on Friday night?' Bobby tentatively asked, not entirely sure if he was prepared for the answer. His head was now firmly back in his hands.

'Picked up three wee lassies fae Galston … went back tae theirs for a party, ken whit ah mean?' said Gary with a salacious wink.

'What, just the two of us?'

'Naw,' said Gary. 'Thommo was wi' us. How can ye no remember any o' this?'

Gary was suddenly aware that Bobby was staring transfixed at his left arm. He was particularly focused on the tattoo on its upper part, running from shoulder blade to just above the elbow. The dark-blue ink on its pale canvas looked a bit like a police badge, but with the words '2nd Battalion' above the crest and 'Scots Guards' below it. The crest lay over a bayonet that had a serpent coiled loosely around it. Sensing the question forming slowly in his brother's head, Gary stood up to break the spell. Bobby looked down at his bare feet, through the absurd glass dining table his mum had recently badgered Harry into buying. All the Cassidy males had simultaneously thought the same thing the first time they saw it: *A glass table! How can you rearrange your balls and give yourself the occasional secret wee fiddle when you're sitting at a fucking glass table?*

Ethel's justification was that it would make the room appear much bigger than it was. Harry considered this to be a typically female attitude: looks over function.

At this precise moment, though, the table's permeability *was* performing a valuable function. It permitted sight of a series of numbers written on Bobby's right foot. While not opening an immediate portal into his *Lost Weekend*, it was nevertheless a clue, since, on closer inspection, it was obviously a phone number. With Gary *playing the cunt,* it was apparent that he was going to have to piece this mystery together himself.

The front door opened and, a full thirty seconds later, closed again. Gary and Bobby stared at the closed door separating the entrance hall from the room they were in. It opened slowly and before either could see him, Harry announced, 'It's bloody freezin' out there.'

Harry had returned from a walk to pick up the Sunday papers – a journey he took and enjoyed every Sunday morning, although this particular morning's jaunt had taken longer than normal. Harry had bumped into Stanley May, who had felt the need to impart his own second-hand knowledge of Harry's sons' activities over the last forty-eight hours.

'So you two clowns seem tae have made a right arse o' yersels then.'

With these words from his father, Gary silently took his leave, pulling a Kilmarnock FC jersey from the radiator as he went. Harry watched him from the other end of the long, narrow room. Harry was of average height and the stereotypical outline for a working-class male in his late forties from the west of Scotland. But, silhouetted against the bright sunlight from the window behind him, Bobby thought he looked like the Michelin Man.

Harry nodded towards the other window behind Bobby, where wisps of smoke betrayed Gary's current location. 'Ah suppose *he* was responsible?' It was more statement than question.

'Ach, ah dunno. Ah can't really remember much. Ah don't think ah can really blame Gary though. No this time at least …'

'That'll make a change then,' mumbled Harry as he unfolded the *Sunday Mail* in the comfort of his armchair.

'Gie him a break, Dad. He's been like a different guy since he came back fae England.'

Harry did have to concede that the Army seemed to have made a decent person out of Gary, and while he didn't quite extend to pride, Harry did now have a modest foundation of respect for Gary.

'So anyway, Dad. He's away back tae Wellington soon. Ah think you should maybe go out for a pint wi' him. Whit dae ye think?' It was unnerving Bobby to be talking to the back of his dad's balding head, but he continued nonetheless. 'Why don't ye take him tae the Masonic next time yer goin' doon?'

No response.

'He kens Stan and he kens Desi O'Neill tae. It's no like he'd be sittin' there like a spare pri ... part in the corner.' Bobby still found it awkward to use foul or coarse language in front of his parents, unlike his best mate, Joey Millar, who positively relished the opportunity.

'Is there no somethin' on the night?'

Still no response. The younger man sighed.

'Look Bobby, jist leave it eh, will ye? Things are better wi' him an' me. That's enough for just now.' Harry was in no mood to expand. He put down his paper, got up and went over to the television. Having flicked quickly through the three channels he settled on *Farming Outlook*.

'Did ye get me the *Sunday Post*, Harry?' Ethel's wavering, high-pitched voice floated through the same door her husband's had twenty minutes earlier.

'Aye.' There weren't going to be any long conversations involving the main man of the house this morning.

Ethel strode towards the kitchen, pausing only to address Bobby. 'When did you two get in?'

'God knows.' Bobby was aware he'd need to get up from the chair soon or face a grilling, but he had a real concern that his legs wouldn't support him.

'Bobby, put a shirt on when yer at the table.'

This prompt from his mum was enough to make him move. More focused interrogation would surely follow if he didn't.

'Bobby, there's blood on ma seat covers!' Ethel had come back in from the kitchen and spotted a small red stain low down on the beige hessian.

'It's no me, Mum. Ah'm no bleedin',' proclaimed Bobby, as he slowly spun around trying to examine himself.

'Whit's that oan your back? Right doon low. There,' said Ethel, squinting.

'Ah can't see anything. Where?' Bobby was still pirouetting.

'It says something about a H-E-A-R-S-E,' said Ethel. 'Hang on. Ah need to go an' get ma glasses.' Harry watched Ethel disappear upstairs to retrieve her glasses from her bedside table and then got up to take a look, already suspecting the worst.

'Ya bloody eejit! You've got a fuckin' tattoo that says "I TAKE IT UP THE ARSE" …'

'Eh? Aw fuck! Away ye go!' Bobby's shock at the tattoo being the source of his back pain made him temporarily forget to whom he was speaking. 'FUCK! Is that *all* it says?'

'Hey. Mind yer language, and naw, that's no everythin'.' Below that there's a line sayin' "THIS WAY FOR A GOOD TIME", an' then there's an arrow pointing tae the crack o' yer erse! For fuck's sake, Bobby, that's a real bloody tattoo! That's no washin' off!'

Split between hunting Gary down and avoiding his mother's return, Bobby headed for the back door. Needless to say, his brother was long gone.

'Fuckin' bastard, Gary,' mumbled Bobby, as he pulled a white Adidas T-shirt – *Gary's, fuck him* – from the line and pulled it on to cover the lightly bloodied artwork. It was bitterly cold and hung like frosted cardboard, having been left out overnight.

'Where's Mum?' said Bobby to Harry, who had joined him in the crisp, clear air of the garden.

'Sadie Flanagan's at the door. She'll be there for ages. Yer bloody lucky, boy. She'll have forgotten by the time they're by bletherin'.'

Father and son sat on the damp timber bench. They stared out across the garden towards the school where Bobby intermittently showed his face as a sixth-year student, but where Harry went every weekday throughout term time, and the odd Saturday.

'What are ye doin' wi' yer life, son?' Harry had posed this question many times to his middle child – mostly over the last five months and always with no tangible reaction.

Bobby shrugged. He was always irritated by this line of questioning. He had just turned eighteen. The ink on the cards in the living room had barely dried. He just wanted to *fanny about*. When his dad used that term, it was with disdain. When Bobby said it to Joey Miller, it sounded aspirational.

Joey was slightly younger than Bobby. Not eighteen until October, Joey could be really intense and the *lassies* thought he was a bit strange, verging on creepy. A lot of them called him Jeeves, because he always seemed to be in Bobby's shadow, and that really irritated both of them. But Bobby saw the other side – Joey was really witty, heavily into music and completely on the same wavelength as Bobby was. Joey wouldn't have gone to the Killie match. Bobby knew that much. Joey was a Rangers fan, but he'd at least grown up on the south side of Glasgow, so he was entitled. Kilmarnock was full of fucking Old Firm glory-hunters and Bobby hated all of them.

'What are ye thinking about after leavin'?'

Bobby's protracted hangover made it feel like he was hearing his dad from underwater. It wasn't a good feeling.

'Are ye listenin' tae me?' Harry shook his son's shoulder.

'Och, Dad, ah dunno. Ah just ...'

'Just whit? Ye'll need tae dae well wi' yer English this time if yer goin' tae university after the summer.'

Bobby couldn't bring himself to admit that he'd virtually given up on the English higher. His prelim only a few weeks earlier had been a disaster. His mark had been of a level that only Norway's entrant for the Eurovision Song Contest would've considered acceptable. He'd concealed this from both parents so far, but truth was he was heading for expulsion. The Beak had already warned him twice that if he was asked to leave English, he'd be out of school altogether. This situation also applied to Joey, although maths was his particular nemesis. Bobby was fully aware of the creek into which he was drifting – and also the paddle that he had dropped overboard about half a mile back. The last thing he had on his mind now was to jump in, swim back and retrieve it. *Fuck that.* If the waterfall was just around the bend, he'd continue just to drift towards it, lying back and soaking up some rays en route. *Waterfalls are way more exciting than fucking creeks.*

'Look Dad, I'm sorted. Joe and I are gonna start up something. Just don't ken whit yet.'

'Jesus Christ, Bobby, he's the same as you! If brains were dynamite, he widnae have enough tae blow his nose.' After he'd

WENTZL
H O T E L ★★★★

Rynek Główny 19, 31-008 Kraków, Poland
T: +48 12 430 26 64, F: +48 12 430 26 65 • hotel@wentzl.pl, www.wentzl.pl

t guilty. Joey was undoubtedly clever – he

that Harry had never heard before. Harry

s stupid; he meant that he was perhaps the

person in the Northern Hemisphere. He

appropriate gag to illustrate that.

about something tae do wi' music,' said

imism to inflect the tone.

mpted Harry. 'Record shop? Studio work?

re was a softly sarcastic edge to Harry's

ncealed enough to avoid his son's impaired

anythin,' announced Bobby, as if this was

for the older man. 'We were thinkin' more

ssy Regal packet between the thumb and

l. He had no option – a couple of years ago

been sliced off by a loom in the BMK Carpet

he after leaving school. With his other hand,

he pulled a cigarette carefully out of the newly opened pack of twenty. Bobby watched how effortlessly his damaged hand performed the lighting of the cigarette with a Swan Vesta. He genuinely admired his father for the way in which he had coped since the accident. There had been no anger, no bitterness; simply an acceptance that it was a big pothole in life's bumpy road that he hadn't been able to swerve. Initially, Bobby hadn't been too enamoured that his dad's only offer of employment following his recuperation had been as a janitor at the school that Bobby attended. But Harry was a well-known and well-liked guy around New Farm Loch, and, as a consequence, nobody took the piss. In fact, given the number of Mitre 5 footballs Harry had brought home during the last few years, Bobby had to concede that the arrangement had *some* advantages. Today was just about to be one of those occasions where the same held true.

'Well, if you are serious about it, there's a note on the staffroom noticeboard,' said Harry, following a long period of making his 'little stick of heaven' vanish into perfectly constructed smoke rings.

'Sayin' what?' A suddenly attentive Bobby turned for the first time to look directly at Harry.

'A wee lassie's lookin' for a mobile disco for an eighteenth birthday party.'

'Where?' asked Bobby.

'Ah telt ye! It's on the noticeboard in the teach—'

'Naw, naw … where's the *party*?' Initial exasperation diminished as Bobby realised his dad was gently pulling his leg.

'The Sandriane. In about three weeks' time. Her name's Lizzie. She's no at the school so ye might need tae be quick. She's probably stuck the same note up oan other noticeboards tae. There's a phone number at the bottom.' There was another pause in the conversation as Harry could almost visualise the wee technicians in Bobby's overheated brain working hard to compute the information he'd just been given. Harry laughed as Bobby's eyes darted backwards and forwards. He pondered the idea of pressing Bobby's nose to see if a piece of ticker paper would have come out of his mouth with the words 'Get number please' written on it.

'Will ah get ye the number then?' said Harry, jumping ahead.

'Eh, em, aye. Ah think so …' Bobby had moved onto rehearsing the conversation he would have with Joey later that afternoon. The

Brain Trust techies had also started formulating some pertinent questions of their own: *Where are you getting the equipment? Do you have enough records? What about lights? A van? A driver?*

The wee bastards were asking too many questions now. They were supposed to be coming up with the fucking answers. That was their job. Bobby got up and headed for the stairs. He was shivering a fair bit, having just realised how long he'd been outside in the January air of a Scottish morning. He was planning to go and run a hot bath then get ready to go and get Joey. Probably contact Hamish May as well. Although he did think it might be better to have something more concrete to tell them. He should call this *Lizzie* and get the details. Make sure the job was actually still available. There was a lot to be done, but he had to acknowledge feeling a lot more vibrant than he had half an hour ago. Even Lemmy's mob had fucked off.

'Hullo, Bobby, son.' Mrs Flanagan's voice was as deep as a Cumnock coal mine and twice as dangerous. 'Ah see ye hud yersel a wee time last night, spray paintin' yer name oan the side ae Viviani's shop wa.'

Ethel turned to look at Bobby, her mouth partly open.

'Oh, ah'm sorry. Huv ah said too much?' Mrs Flanagan put her hand over her mouth theatrically.

Auld fucking cow, thought Bobby as he edged past his *tut-tutting* mother and headed for the comparative safety of the bathroom.

'There was something else ah wanted tae talk to you about, Bobby. But ah can't remember whit though.' Bobby and his dad were often concerned about Ethel's increasing forgetfulness, but, today, and with the blood not yet starting to steep through Gary's white T-shirt, he was grateful for it.

When Bobby got to the top of the stairs, he could hear the Sunday morning sound of the Human League coming from the small transistor radio; a sure sign that his sister had taken up residence in the bathroom. He'd be going nowhere soon. Bobby stealthily moved back down the stairs past his glowering mum and auld bag Flanagan who – just to rub it in – said a second cheery 'Oh hullo, Bobby, son.'

Rot in Hell, you piss-stained auld cunt, he thought. Bobby hunted for the telephone. They had recently bought a new 'mobile' handset, which was absolutely fucking brilliant. It didn't have much of a range and, at the size of a brick, it was bigger than the Bakelite one it had replaced, but with the aerial fully extended, you didn't have to sit out in the hall – or in the same room as everybody else – when phoning your pals.

He inclined his foot forward far enough to see the slightly faded number. After five rings, a voice hoarser than auld 'smelly cunt' responded.

'Hullo? Hullo?' The voice said this with such timing that it was all Bobby could do to avoid replying '*We are the Billy Boys …*' He didn't, and the sandpaper sound snapped back at him.

'Hullo! Who the fuck is this?'

'Em, ah'm Bobby Cassidy. Who's this?'

'You phoned *me* ya cunt!'

'Aye, but ah think ah might've been given the wrong number.'

'Ah'm Franny fuckin' Duncan. Noo whit dae ye want. Ah'm in ma fuckin' scratcher.'

Franny Duncan. Jesus Christ. What was he doing with Fat Franny Duncan's number written on his foot? Bobby's brainiacs were running about in a panic. Words like 'gangster', 'dealer', 'doings', 'big', 'fat' and 'bastard' all ricocheted around like the steel balls in a multi-play pinball game.

'Ah'm thinking of becomin' a DJ.' Bobby stumbled over the words, all too aware that he'd already volunteered his name.

'For fuck's sake. Phone back later on, at about four. Ask fur Hobnail. He'll sort ye oot.' *Click.* The phone flatlined, with a constant droning sound.

Bobby stared at it for a few seconds. *Hobnail? Was that a fucking code word?* Along with all those words that sprang to mind when thinking of Fat Franny Duncan came another two: 'mobile' and 'DJ'.

It was a big risk, but at least Franny Duncan would know where to get equipment, and might even have some for hire. Bobby Cassidy had taken one wee step back from the edge.

2

MEN MAKE PLANS AND GOD SMILES

Fat Franny Duncan loved the *Godfather* movies, but he did not belong to this new band of theorists who reckoned *II* was better than *I*. For Fat Franny, original was most certainly best, although, given the success of the films and the timelessness of the story, he was staggered that there hadn't been a *III*, like there had been with Rocky. He also couldn't comprehend why there had been no book spin-off, although, even if there had, he would certainly not be wasting his time reading it. He knew the dialogue from both films pretty much by heart, and used their most famous quotes as a design for life. Particularly the lines of Don Corleone, who Fat Franny felt certain he would resemble later in his life. He was, after all, fat. There was no denying this. Bulk for Brando's most famous character helped afford him gravitas and – as a consequence – respect; a level of respect that Fat Franny felt was within his grasp. Michael was a skinny *Tally* bastard and, although he undoubtedly commanded reverence, it was driven by fear.

Fat Franny was intent on pursuing a line of legitimacy with his business that would bring him universal veneration. The burgeoning entertainment venture was the vehicle for this. It had started reasonably well. The mobile DJ-ing had begun slowly, but over the last year and a half had branched into more lucrative gigs such as weddings and anniversary parties. There was money to be made in *functions*, of that there was no doubt. As a consequence, Fat Franny had assembled a *roster*: a collection of acts for every eventuality. From kids' parties, to coming-of-age celebrations right up to charity do's – Fat Franny Duncan had it all covered. So, as he surveyed his *talent* – sat at the kitchen table for their twice-weekly meeting in his expansive ex-council house – why did he feel like he wanted to stab a butcher's knife through each of their hands?

'Franny.' A sheepish Bert Bole broke the silence that had engulfed all present for the last fifteen minutes.

Everyone at the table eyed their black-clad leader nervously. He ran chubby fingers through the thinning, greying hair on the top of his head and then tugged at the black hairband that was holding the rest of it in a tight ponytail. Finally, he teased at the slim moustache with his forefinger and thumb. To Bert Bole, it looked like a ritual before a slaughter.

'*Franny*! Boss …?' Bert had raised the level of his voice – but only slightly – in an attempt to get a reaction from the fat man with the faraway look in his eyes at the end of the table. Fat Franny often thought of the Don at times like this – and there had been a few too many lately. Surrounded by his subordinates, he imagined what Corleone would have said to Bob Dale – Fat Franny's *Luca Brasi* – if these morons had told *him* what they'd just announced at the meeting.

Bob Dale responded, barley audible.

'He hearths ye. He just disthnae *belief* ye!' Bob Dale didn't speak often. A hair-lip and ill-fitting teeth gave his speech a very pronounced lisp, which had been ridiculed mercilessly at school. As a consequence, Bob had found it more productive to retaliate with his fists than with his broken voice. His stature grew, along with a reputation that he was *not to be messed with*. But by that time the lasting damage was done. The legacy of those early brutal days was a nickname – Hobnail, which was the sound he made when trying to tell people who he was.

'Nae tips? At a fuckin' Cumnock wedding?' By contrast, Fat Franny's vocals were loud and, for the assembled entourage, all too clear. 'Ye must be fuckin' jokin'! Even the bastard minister usually comes awa wi' a fifty spot.' Don Franny spread his arms wide, then placed them at the ten-to-two position, palms face-down on the table top, before continuing, ' … and a go on at least two ae the bridesmaids!'

Bob Dale smirked at this but was careful not to let Fat Franny see it. Almost everyone else remained silent with gazes averted. Only Jill Boothby – one half of married DJ duo *Cheezee Choonz* – indicated a wish to contribute, but her raised hand would remain unrecognised by the Chair for the rest of the meeting.

'It's like this …' Fat Franny's deep growl seemed to come from way down in his gut, reverberating around the bare walls of the cold, twice-extended kitchen. Again there was another long pause as Fat Franny visualised Hobnail clipping Bert Bole and then dumping his weighted body off the pier at Irvine Harbour. He refocused.

'Like it or no, you fuckin' clowns are part ae a business. Ah'm funding aw yer fuckin' gigs here. Ah'm providin' the equipment. Ah provide aw the security tae stop ye gettin' a kickin' at shiteholes like the Auchinleck Bowling Club.' Fat Franny looked around the table at them all, one at a time, in a clockwise direction. 'You lot – an' ah can't believe ah'm fuckin' sayin' this – are the fuckin' talent.'

The Cheezees were motionless. Bert Bole had his hands outstretched, as if appealing for permission to speak. Mr Sunshine, the former children's entertainer, appeared to be asleep.

'Hoi … Sunshine!' Fat Franny threw a cream doughnut, hitting the older man on the side of his face and dislodging his Dr Crippen-style spectacles. 'Fuckin' wake up, ya auld prick! This is for your benefit as well.'

Hobnail could tell Fat Franny's mood was worsening and thought better of indicating the dollop of cream that was still attached to Mr Sunshine's bizarre ginger beard.

'You lot are just no bringin' in enough, an' it better fuckin' change, a'right?' Fat Franny pointed to Hobnail. 'He tells me yir aw holdin' oot on the tips.' The talent all turned as one to look at the standing Bob Dale, who calmly folded his arms, shut his eyes and nodded.

'So here's whit's gauny happen. Each ae ye needs to come up wi' a gig of yer ain in the next month or yer out an' ah'm gauny get other acts in.' Fat Franny stood up quickly, causing his chair to fall dramatically behind him. 'Ah'm away for a shite. Huv a good think about whit ah've just said.'

'For God's sake, put yer haun' doon, he's away,' said Bert to Jill, once both Fat Franny and Bob Dale were well out of earshot. Although not the oldest of the four, Bert was generally their mouthpiece on the odd occasion when they felt a collective need to raise an issue with the fat man. Bert had been involved with Fat Franny's crew for nearly three years. Back when they were both in their late thirties, Bert's wife, Doris, had developed a serious gambling addiction. It had started pretty casually. A few nights at the bingo with friends from the BMK had progressed to include daytime visits to William Hill's after she lost her job at the carpet factory.

Bert had ended up working extended shifts as a janitor at the James Hamilton Academy. He was well regarded by teachers and pupils alike, mainly due to an unshakeably optimistic outlook. He had a belief in human nature, which led him to attempt to do things for others even if it involved disadvantaging himself. His good nature helped Harry Cassidy to get a job as a fellow janitor, when a more selfish man – and especially one in his financial situation – might have been tempted to keep the additional shifts for himself. In the early part of 1979, things had started to become markedly worse for Bert and Doris Bole. Even though they both knew Doris had a significant problem, it wasn't easy for them to talk about, and they dealt with it by effectively ignoring it. When they got into serious arrears with the rent and their growing utility bills, Bert took some well-intended advice and went to see Fat Franny Duncan over in Onthank. Nearly three years later, Bert was still working as a pub singer under an alias – Tony Palomino – paying off what had originally been a manageable £150 loan to clear a three-month rent backlog. A month after Bert had made this arrangement, Doris was dead.

A favour called in by Bert's doctor to a fellow Mason in the Fiscal's department ensured a verdict of 'death by misadventure'. It was a convenient way of avoiding a verdict of suicide, by claiming that the overdose of anti-depressants that had *actually* killed her was accidental. It didn't ultimately make a great deal of financial difference to Bert, but it did at least secure the pitiful insurance policy payout to cater for a decent cremation. His mates at the Hurlford Masonic Club paid for the wake. Fat Franny's weekly compound interest calculations made sure the closure of the debt was always out of reach, so while Bert was somewhat imprisoned by history, he never quite understood the motivation of the others.

Mr Sunshine was a fifty-two-year-old bachelor, whose real name was Angus Archibald. He used to be a children's entertainer, performing magic tricks and doing puppet shows. Despite a few criminal investigations relating to 'improper activities' in his past, he now worked under Fat Franny's banner as a DJ for children's parties. Two of Fat Franny's minders – Des Brick and Wullie the Painter – constantly persecuted Mr Sunshine, calling him a 'kiddy-fiddlin' paedo', amongst many other lurid things. The erstwhile Angus Archibald rarely got flustered by this, simply drawing on his pipe, tapping his nose and saying quietly, 'Not proven.' Mr Sunshine's bizarre appearance also caused many a second look from parents who'd hired him. He was a heavy, but small man, and he didn't carry the weight well. He looked a bit like the television magician, the Great Soprendo, but with a wispy ginger, partly combed-over hairpiece, pallid freckled face and trademark *Wishee-Washee*-style beard. It was a resemblance Mr Sunshine traded on, appropriating the 'Piff, Paff, Poof' catchphrase for his own performances. Given his 'look' and a suspect past, perhaps operating under Fat Franny's wing was the only place he *could* get hired.

Cheezee Choonz were far harder to fathom. They were a married couple in their early thirties who only worked at weddings. Jay Boothby was reasonably talented. Unlike Bert Bole, he could actually sing, although, strangely, the Cheezees worked for Fat Franny as mobile DJs. Bert couldn't really understand why, when there was an opportunity to earn more money by having a DJ-plus-singer offer for weddings, he was sent along with the Cheezees. Bert began to wonder if Fat Franny even knew Jay was a decent singer. He only became aware of it himself when he heard Jay testing out the microphones in an empty hall, a few months ago.

Jay was from Cumbria and Jill was from Cumnock. They 'met' through CB radio in the summer of 1980 and married six months later, moving to Kilmarnock in the hope of pursuing Jay's dreams of becoming a club entertainer. Jill could take it or leave it frankly, but she had no real circle of friends and, as Fat Franny's most prolific earners, being out with Jay almost every weekend left her with little time to spend with anyone else. Bert was equally uncertain how they had come to be part of Fat Franny's Union, but, if he was honest, he had never really bothered to find out.

'Have any of you three got any leads here?' asked Bert.

'Yer jokin', aren't ya?' replied Jay Boothby. 'Where are we gonna find the time to look for gigs? I hardly know anyone up here.'

'Whit about you, Sunshine?' Bert wasn't hopeful, but felt that he should be inclusive.

'Oh aye … the Cub Scouts have lined up a jamboree and the Crosshouse Mothers 'n' Toddlers Group have called for a bookin' … and … and … whit the fuck dae you think? If ah could get gigs of ma own, d'you think I'd be here in this fat cunt's freezin' hoose?'

Bert sighed deeply. At least he'd asked.

'Well, ah've got one. At least it's somethin'. It's a note on the school noticeboard. Some wee lassie's looking for a DJ for her eighteenth. If we can tell Franny we've got that wan, it'll maybe dae for noo. Ah'll let him ken that I'll phone an' get it sorted the night.'

'Hullo, can ah speak tae Lizzie ... eh, please?'

'Aye, son. Wait an' ah'll get her. Whit's yer name, pal?'

'Eh, it's Rob ... *Boaby* Cassidy. Ah'm phonin' about the disco she's havin' ...'

He was only kept waiting for perhaps a minute, but, for an anxious Bobby, it seemed like half an hour. He imagined Lizzie's house; the man who answered as a butler who had to make a journey to the east wing to alert the demure Miss King that a gentlemen caller was holding for her.

'Ah'm Lizzie King. Whit ye efter ...?' Illusion shattered.

'Eh, hullo ... hi. Sorry tae bother ye, but ah was phonin' about the party. Ken? Yer eighteenth?'

There was no immediate response, but the heavy breathing from the other end indicated to Bobby that she had indeed run from a remote part of the house or – more likely – that she was a fat lassie.

'Ye put a notice up at the Jimmy Hamilton, lookin' for a mobile DJ,' Bobby continued, hoping to make a connection.

'Aye, that was me. Are you wan ae Duncan's mob?' rasped Lizzie King, sounding like a seventeen-year-old Ayrshire Bonnie Tyler. *Aye, fat* and *a smoker,* thought Bobby.

'No, well, not really. Ah'm borrowin' some gear, but that's all.' Bobby wasn't quite certain of the relevance of the question, but there seemed to be an edge to it nonetheless.

'Whit's the name of yer disco?' When he'd rehearsed this phone call in his head, all Lizzie's questions had been about his musical taste, his DJ influences and – most importantly – the price. With the benefit of hindsight, this was an obvious one and he felt a bit stupid that he couldn't immediately answer her.

'We've just started up ... but don't worry, we're great. Folk have been phonin' non-stop lately. Phone's been ringin' off the hook, so it has.' Bobby searched vainly around the room for some inspiration. 'We're kinda booked solid for the next month, ken?' he lied, looking at the discarded copies of *Playboy* and *Razzle* that lay around his room and then at the VHS tape in his left hand. *Big Juggs Disco* …? Nah, wouldn't work. *Disco Deep Throat* …? Nope, that would rule out the church gigs.

'It's a mixture of parties like yours and …'

'For God's sake, ah'm no Eamon fuckin' Andrews. Ah don't gie a fuck about yer life story. Just gies the name ae the disco!'

A Rickenbacker riff provided the answer. In just over four years Weller had never let Bobby down and here he was again, just in the nick of time.

'Aye, sorry. It's Heatwave. Heatwave Disco.' Bobby looked at the cover of the *Setting Sons* LP with a mixture of pride and relief. He felt as if he'd just been told he'd passed a polygraph test.

'Ah'm no payin' more than £40, an' ye'll get it on the night, at the end,' said Lizzie with a force that firmly established the offer's take-it-or-leave-it status.

'OK. That's grea … eh, fine. Yeah, we'll see ye on the night then?'

'Don't be fuckin' late or ah'll be dockin'.' *Click.* There it was again – that monotonous dialling tone. It was in sharp contrast to Lizzie's vivid accent, but Bobby listened to it – hypnotised by it – for several minutes. When he finally pressed the big button and re-holstered the aerial, he allowed himself to laugh out loud. He was now a DJ.

3ᴿᴰ FEBRUARY 1982: 10:25PM

'An' now … comin' ride atcha, it's the wan und only Adam and his Ants with "Stan an' Doliver" …' Fat Franny was giving them his best lines, but the twins' twenty-first birthday party was lifeless. No shock to the heart could revive *this* turkey. The Broomhill Hotel was an awkward venue. A narrow winding stair made the journey from car park to dancefloor with heavy speakers one to avoid. The plan of the function area worked against the generation of any atmosphere. The dancefloor was square, but too close to the bar, where people queued. The DJ had to set up behind a column and adjacent to the door to the toilets, which meant that half of the L-shaped room and a corner of the dancefloor wasn't even in the DJ's line of sight. The upper floor of the Broomhill didn't need a lot of people for it to appear full which, on the evidence of tonight, was just as well. But it was a Tuesday night – the dead zone for mobile DJs – and of the thirty-odd partygoers, more than half looked like a SAGA Tours mini-bus would be returning them to an old folks' home in about five minutes; just in time for *Late Call*.

A lot of nights were like this. If it wasn't for the fact that the money was the same, regardless of whether the hall was full or not, Fat Franny would've found it all pretty depressing. He often wondered what the main motivation was for people holding a party for *themselves*. A hopeful public display of their popularity? The desire for an event, which – with Kodak's assistance – they might be able to recount forever? Or simply an opportunity to maximise the *presents* count?

Fat Franny could tell almost instantly into which category people fell. Within half an hour he had Deirdre and Donna Dunlop – the twins for whom this particular celebration was in aid – firmly in the first grouping. Their furtive glances towards the door and the slight drooping of their shoulders as another elderly relative came through it were a dead giveaway. But there was an additional edge evident here. The twins were apparently in a self-esteem struggle with each other, and the result on this particular evening was a dull, dreich, no-score draw with a third of the match still to play.

'An' a very highly 'propriate one for y'all now. It's Dave Stew-Heart and Barbara Cat-Skin with "It's My Party" …' Fat Franny chuckled to himself at this jokey pronunciation before continuing, '… and I'll bloody cry if ah want tae …' No-one looked up, far less laughed. He faded the music down again and flicked the mic switch. 'We'll be cutting the cakes after this wan.'

'Fuck's sake, Bert. Get us a pint, will ye?'

Bert Bole had been downstairs in the bar, building up the courage to come up and tell Fat Franny the bad news. As he stood at the bar watching Pearl Fisher pour the golden liquid into the pint glass, he thought it could maybe wait another day. Fat Franny didn't seem to be in a good mood, and this damp squib of a party was clearly the principal cause.

'That'll be 75p, luv,' said cheery Pearl, whose surname since she'd married Andy Fisher had required her to be almost constantly upbeat. The number of times she'd had to smile cheerily, as some drunken prick had asked stupid questions about her name badge. Still, it could have been worse. Andy knew a guy who knew a guy called Colin Curtain, and *he'd* married a girl named *Annette*.

Bert walked back over to the decks and put the pint down on a three-foot-high Marshall amp. Cliff Richard was singing about exultations and telling everyone that he was in love with her, or him. The assembled well-wishers surrounded the blushing twins, and an impromptu Hogmanay-style, crossover-arm-linking began, giving the whole scene a surreal air. When the circle started rushing in towards the girls, Fat Franny pushed on 'The Stripper' by the David Rose Orchestra, just to witness the confused looks on the faces of those on the dancefloor.

Thirty minutes later, and, entirely predictably, the twins' dad approached the decks.

'We're goin' tae call it a night, big man,' he said. There were now less than fifteen people in the room, but four of them were being paid to be there and another was Bert Bole.

'Fair enough pal,' said Fat Franny. With a bit of luck he'd be home before midnight. An unexpected bonus.

'Let's say we call it thirty quid, eh?' said Mr Dunlop.

'Whit? Ah don't fuckin' think so!' Fat Franny had had this exact conversation many times before.

'Come on. We booked ye til one o'clock but yer stoppin' at eleven.' Mr Dunlop's arms were widespread in demonstration of the reason behind his argument.

'Aye, but ah'm only stoppin' cos' you asked me tae. Ah'll play on tae one in the morning if ye want me tae.' Fat Franny had recently read a book on mind games, which had suggested mirroring and matching as a tactic of positive negotiation. Accordingly, his arms were also now opened out with hands facing upwards.

'Ah'm no sure that's entirely fair.' Mr Dunlop now had one hand on his hip and the other was scratching the top of his balding head. Fat Franny knew this looked ridiculous, but since it had been highly recommended to him, he mimicked as the book decreed.

Bert Bole watched this bizarre ritual from the comparative safety of the bar. He observed both men looking like teapots, saluting like Hitler and then – most curiously – both standing on one leg. Whatever it was, Fat Franny looked to have emerged triumphant. The other guy had just slapped money down on a box of records, leaving Fat Franny with that recognisable, thin-lipped smile, which only seemed to happen when he came into contact with money. Bert reconsidered his earlier trepidation and decided that having just been paid was as good as it was going to get to let Fat Franny know he had been usurped.

5TH FEBRUARY 1982: 2:47PM

'So whit did Gary end up gettin' ye?' said Joey Miller.

'Eh? Ach, bugger all,' replied Bobby. 'Cunt got me a magnifying glass an' a satsuma. He told me to look through the glass. When ah did, he says, "*Look, ah got ye a Space Hopper*".'

Joey laughed and folded his arms. 'Aye, ah've got a family like that as well. For ma sixteenth, ma dad got me "Hide and Seek".'

Joey was sitting on a three-foot-high, red-facing-brick wall. It had been around twenty minutes since his best friend had started speaking, and he'd taken advantage of the first available pause in Bobby's pitch to try and change the subject. Bobby's constant pacing back and forth had almost created a curved groove in the black tarmac in front of him. They had been friends for more than five years and this current scenario was a familiar one: Joseph Miller, the logical ponderous *Hutch* to Robert Cassidy's hyperactive and relentlessly optimistic *Starsky*. But it was a good combination. Bobby was the 'ideas' man and Joey the pragmatist, the one who was left with the task of turning Bobby's various dreams into some form of reality. A sort of Butch Cassidy and ... Jeeves!

There had been the money-making scam from a year ago that had almost resulted in a school expulsion for the pair of them. Bobby had envisaged an alternative tuck-shop where crisps and chocolate could be sold at a discounted rate. Joey had access to the goods through his part-time shelf-stacking job at the local Safeway. It operated successfully for three weeks before various interfering prefects detected a strange downturn in the revenue from the school's four official outlets. Another piece of entrepreneurial hustling had the fifteen-year-old Joey searching for a ten-foot ladder as a key part of the new Cassidy & Miller window-cleaning company. Having established a client list and a local rota, which would bring in £23.50 a week, Bobby established the rules of engagement. They would work solidly through the glorious summer of 1980, pay off mental Mogga McManus for getting the ladder *and* nobbling main competitor, Tam Cooper's van, and then save their cash for a week on Arran in September. Bobby's latent vertigo meant Joey being constantly lodged at the stupid end of the ladder, from where he fell five days into the venture, breaking an arm and killing the dream in the process.

But on this miserably wet February morning, Bobby seemed to have a far greater sense of purpose than before. He had barely come up for air in the rollercoaster tale about an eighteenth birthday party, the Sandriane Bar, Paul Weller and mobile discos, Lizzie King and, most significantly of all, Fat Franny Duncan. It had been a promising venture up until *his* name had been associated with it. Joey Miller knew all about Fat Franny. Both he and the Fatman lived in Onthank on the other side of town. Onthank was Fat Franny's personal *fiefdom*. The repetitious sprawl of semi-detached, two-storey grey boxes grouped in actual – and metaphorical – cul-de-sacs was where he earned a living. There wouldn't be many who would testify to the fact, but Joey was convinced that drug-dealing and money-lending would be as much a part of Fat Franny's empire as the ice-cream vans and this new mobile-DJ scam about which Bobby was currently so energised.

'Don't worry about Fat Franny,' said Bobby, right after Joey had said he was worried about *anything* that involved Fat Franny. 'We're only hiring the gear off him,' reasoned Bobby. 'It'll be just for one night.'

Joey's expression hadn't changed since the start of the story, but secretly he was just as enthusiastic about its infinite potential as his friend. Joey really loved music; in fact, probably more than Bobby did. Joey immediately pictured himself running Mod nights at the Henderson Church Hall; The Jam, Secret Affair, The Who – all blasting out at such volume it could be heard at the Cross. Fat Franny Duncan, though. That was a major spanner.

'He's a fuckin' mental case, Boab. Is there naebody else tae get gear from? Like a band or something?'

'Listen, it'll be a'right. One night. In and out. Nae need to go back tae him once we're up and runnin',' reasoned Bobby, in trademark bottle-half-full mode. 'Ah must've been speakin' tae somebody that kent him, that night of ma birthday. Ah got hame and his fuckin' hoose phone number was written on ma foot.'

'Lemme go an' speak tae Jeff McGarry,' said Joey, using his frozen hands to lever himself off the wall. 'Ah'm sure he kens a guy that gets lights and stuff for heavy-metal bands. They both work out at a farm near Hurlford.'

Bobby looked puzzled. 'Izzat no that cunt that's got the thing aboot cows'? Did he no get put away fur it anaw?'

'Aye, but he's a decent lad, Jeff. Get ye whatever ye want for nae mair than twenty quid. You name it, he'll get ye it. A toaster, a fridge, second-hand motor …!'

'Whit, aw for twenty quid?' asked a disbelieving Bobby.

'Naw, twenty quid's his mark-up,' replied Joey.

'So if his mate at the farm … y'know, Bon Scott's roadie … can get us the gear, we're payin' Jeff twenty quid jist for the introduction …? Fuckin' hell, Joe, she's only payin' *us* forty!'

'But like ye said, once we're up and runnin' we'll be away … and this way, we'll still have the use ae wur legs if anythin' goes wrong.'

Bobby had to contend that, with this last point, Joey made a compelling case. So they agreed to follow the recommendation of a convicted cattle fetishist and made the call to Hairy Doug, the nomadic biker and Grateful Dead fan, and – according to Jeff McGarry at any rate – owner of the biggest cock in Scotland.

3

LAUREL & HARDY MEET THE HAIRY GUY

'Ye know the only downside tae spending time in here? Listenin' tae *this* shite every day.' Joey stretched his legs out until his body lay flat across three of the softer sixth-year common-room seats.

'Get up an' switch it off then,' said Bobby.

'These stories must be aw made up. That fuckin' depressin' theme; a tragic story ... "We fell in love, then I had to have my leg cut off, then we were separated by a ragin' storm and never saw each other again" ... Whit a loada fuckin' horse manure. And then ye find out that their *tune* is fuckin' "Lady In Red".' Even lying down, Joey was capable of a level of animated exasperation that Bobby found impressive.

'When Heatwave gets goin', ther'll be nae *middle-o-the-road* pish gettin' played. That's got tae be rule number one.' Joey folded his arms.

Bobby laughed. Since Joey had embraced the dream and put the spectre of Fat Franny Duncan to the back of his mind, there had been around twenty-three 'rule number ones'.

'Right. Got it,' said Bobby. 'Nae *Christy Burgh*. Nae *Goombay Dance Band*. Nae *Flocks o' Fuckin' Seagulls*.' Bobby sighed. He feigned irritation, but he secretly loved these exchanges with his best friend.

'Did yer man Jeff say the biker guy would be there all afternoon? Mibbe ah should go tae economics today.' Bobby looked up at the monochrome clock above the double doors into the common room. It recorded the time as 10:32 p.m. – just as it had for every minute of the last thirty-six days. 'Whit time is it? Dunno why ma dad can't get that bloody thing fixed.' Neither of them wore a watch and therefore relied on the numerous clocks, which were located at department boundaries all around the James Hamilton Academy.

'Dunno. Half-eleven, mibbe,' said Joey, eyes now closed and giving the impression that only an earthquake with a north-east Kilmarnock postcode as its epicentre would move him.

'Right. Ah'm goin' tae auld Fowler's class at ten to twelve an' then we'll fuck off tae the farm after dinnertime, eh?' Bobby really didn't want to go and listen to Kondratieff's cyclical theories of economic expansion, stagnation and recession. Although he broadly understood it, and could appreciate why an economist might find it important, it said nothing to him about his own current interest: The *Black* Economy.

Bobby actually quite liked school – or rather the freedom its flexible sixth-year structure afforded him. He had to be careful, though. Having a parent working in the same building wasn't ideal. But he had accumulated a decent level of 'O' grades and Highers in the two previous years and – as with Joey – this allowed him the comparative freedom of coasting through his final year on the assumption that he would progress on to university. For this to happen, though, Bobby needed a pass in the subject that had become his tormentor.

Joey had no intention of going to university. His dad worked for British Rail in Glasgow and felt that it was a man's duty to leave school as soon as possible and earn, in order to help pay his keep at home. Joey's dad left school at fourteen and proudly belonged to an era that considered *that* to be more than enough education for the essential tasks in life: enough reading to be able to laugh along to John Junor's rancid, bullying 'Angry from Auchtermuchty' columns about 'poofters'; enough writing to be able to fill in the betting slips at the bookies; and, enough arithmetic to instantaneously add up the exact accumulator payouts. Some – but not all – of that ethos had rubbed off on his son.

Joey actually *was* asleep by the time Hamish May came into the common room at twenty-five past twelve. Hamish came in with two others and, on seeing Joey, quickly put a forefinger to his mouth. The 'shushing' was to remove background noise to allow him to deliver his trademark farting-in-someone's-face routine. Hamish May's farts were the stuff of legend. It wasn't clear exactly what his daily diet was. but when he recently ate two tins of catfood to win a £1 bet in this very common room, it was apparent to all present that there wasn't much at which Hamish turned up his nose. In fact, the environment still stank of that very event because one girl – who hadn't been party to what was going on – caught sight of the big man polishing off the cat food and promptly brought up a few Meaty Chunks of her own.

'Shoudnae be sleepin' at the school anyway,' reasoned Hamish, in justification of a punishment dealt out to a wayward pupil by a prefect. Yes, Hamish May was a sixth-year prefect and, more incredibly, given his involvement in a number of Bobby Cassidy's money-making schemes, he was Deputy Head Boy.

'Fuck off, you,' gasped Joey, once he had finally stopped gagging. 'Help me open aw the windaes. Jesus Christ, mate. Whit the fuck have you been eatin?'

'At break earlier, ah had fourteen boiled eggs. Ah won three quid ower behind the gym block. Boaby Kerr said that bit in that Paul Newman film couldnae be done,' said Hamish, proudly.

'An' he'd have been right as well then. Paul Newman ate about fifty,' said Joey.

'Boaby Kerr's a prick though. Made a bet without havin' seen the film. He thought it was *fifteen*, no fifty … and when he wisnae lookin' ah drapped one intae ma bag.'

'Just like the one ye drapped in here?' said Joey.

'That was a fuckin belter, eh?' The two others who had come in with Hamish laughed their approval.

'So whit ye up tae later then?' said Hamish. He sat down next to Joey and pulled out a ten-pack of Embassy Regal, from which two were already absent. He turned the pack upside down and two sticks fell onto his palm. Hamish put both in his mouth and lit them before handing one to Joey. Joey didn't smoke much, but he rarely refused a cigarette when offered.

'Me an' Boab are headin' out tae a farm near Hurlford. He's got this plan tae start up a mobile disco, an' auld Harry's gied him some cash tae buy lights and stuff.'

Joey drew deeply on the cigarette anticipating a barrage of questions about this new information. There was none, though. Hamish blew smoke rings – a skill Joey had never mastered – and then stood up briskly.

'Fair enough' he said. 'The two o' ye buggerin' off for the day then?'

'Aye. Ah'm no comin' back *here* later,' said Joey.

'Ah'll turn a blind eye then,' said Hamish, pointing to the yellow badge on his dark-blue blazer. 'Ah'll see ye later. Ah've got dinner duty so ah need tae go.'

'Aye, Hammy. See ye.' Joey felt he'd got off lightly from this encounter. He felt sure Hamish would have been wondering what *his* place in Bobby's plans might have been. Joey was also fairly certain that Hamish would have been a bit hurt that he hadn't been included. Although Hamish had always understood the almost telepathic synergy between Joey and Bobby, he did feel that the three of them were pretty close. But he was always a bit of a maverick, and his status within the school was only one of a number of complex contradictions in his life.

Hamish's mum was a cleaner who worked part-time for some of the large house-owners down the expensive end of London Road. His dad was employed within the United Kingdom's impregnable diplomatic service and spent much of his time overseas in exotic places like Tangier, Marrakech and Tripoli. It was always a bit of an event when Hamish's dad was back in town, and both Bobby and Joey had a great liking for Stan May. His eccentricity – and the bizarre stories he told about these strange places – was exhilarating. It was easy to see where Hamish got his independent spirit.

For a working-class Ayrshire family, the May children had unique and unusual names. As well as Hamish, there was Dolly, Glendale, Winston, Elliot, Donovan, Aretha and Tess. Bobby and Joey both loved re-telling the story of the time Hamish's dad came home after six months away in 1978. Hamish had made it known to everyone who would listen that his dad had made a fantastic deal in getting a new car and he'd be driving it back up from Portsmouth. Stan had been decidedly vague about the make, but Hamish reckoned it might have been one of the new MKIII Capris – a highly impractical selection, as there were eleven members of the immediate May family, including a live-in granny.

Eventually, during one long afternoon in early June '78, Stan May drove up to 46 Ellis Avenue in a new-*ish* – but highly distinctive – vehicle to be greeted by around thirty people who had been waiting in the front garden for almost an hour. No-one was sure what type of car it actually was, but a next-door neighbour asked if Stan had bought it from the Ant Hill Mob, drawing a collective 'Aaahhhh …' as if to say '*That's* where I've seen it before.'

It was an El Camino station wagon of sorts, and it was certainly distinctive. The car looked like it should have been taking a barefoot fourteen-year-old Ohio bride and her toothless cousin to the place where their union would be confirmed.

Bobby nudged Joey. 'Jesus fuck, Joey. Look at the state o' that motor.'

The wooden-panelled side door opened and Hamish's dad slid out. He had a triumphant look on his face.

'Never mind the motor, get a swatch at the *threads*! Ah widnae get *cremated* in that!' smirked Joey.

Stan looked as striking as the car, with a beige zoot suit and a massive brown kipper tie complementing the vehicle's earthy colour palette. The entire May family – and one of their dogs – fit easily into the three rows of seats and, with the windows rolled down to allow mass waving, they set off up the hill. Predictably, they didn't get far. Unknown to its passengers, the car's journey from the south of England had been a largely subservient one, having been towed for more than half of its route. Perhaps thirty yards and a bang from the exhaust signalled the end of the adventure, and happy smiling faces turned first to concern and then to dismay as the car's large antiquated wheels rolled backwards.

Joey smiled yet again at the memory of that afternoon as he walked the short distance down Ellis Avenue towards Bobby's house at Almond Avenue. From there, they'd walk to the bus station for the journey to their destiny.

9TH FEBRUARY 1982: 3:21PM

'Dunno why ah bother readin' these fuckin' papers,' said Joey. 'Nae cunt's got a job an' yet the main story's about fuckin' Booga Benson an' Tucker Jenkins.'

'Heatwave's a good name though, intit?' Bobby was distracted and more than a bit nervous.

'There's nae way the Tories are gonnae get back in after this. Nae cunt our age has got any chance of workin'. Everybody's either on the broo, or on wan ae these useless fuckin' YOP schemes.' Joey was aware that Bobby wasn't really listening. He was away in another world; a world of shiny lights and massive glitter balls.

'Ah think we should get off here,' said Bobby. There was no bus stop in sight but Joey got up and followed him to the front of the bus.

'Can ye let us off here, driver? We're goin' tae Crosshands Farm an' ah think it's roon about here.'

The driver pulled over to one side and opened the door, letting in the bitingly cold air.

'Cheers, mate,' said Bobby, as Joey shivered behind him.

Although not entirely certain that it was the correct road, the two friends began the walk up the single-track hill in the hope that a farm would be at the other end of it. It was freezing and a shower had just started to drive into their faces. *This had better be worth it,* thought Joey. He pulled the hood of his fish-tailed parka up as a defence. Bobby hadn't had the same foresight and had to make do with zipping up his beige Harrington as far as the zip would go. As they tramped on, the beige got rapidly darker.

'Remember in *Sons of the Desert,* when the two ae them are strugglin' tae walk up that sand dune? That's whit this is like.' Bobby knew this would lighten Joey's mood. They were both fans of Laurel and Hardy and often compared something they were doing to a scene from one of the old films. In these analogies, Bobby was always Ollie the organiser, and Joey was always the clumsy, child-like Stan.

The rain was coming down in angular sheets and Bobby was extremely relieved to see the sign for Crosshands Farm at a junction in the road, just over the brow of the hill. Less pleasing was the figure '2', written in smaller type next to the words.

'Two fuckin' miles!' shouted Joey. 'We've already walked about *three* in the pishin' rain!'

'*You* were the one that got the directions fae that McGarry boy.'

Joey had to reluctantly concede that 'a big ferm near tae Hurlford' wasn't the most precise of Ordnance Survey coordinates. At least the remainder of the journey was basically downhill. It was endured in silence, though. Bobby's anxiety grew as he rehearsed the negotiations with Hairy Doug, the sound-and-light man. Joey was simply dreaming of getting home and into a hot bath.

They approached the rustic collection of sheds and outhouses that surrounded the original farmhouse. The driving rain had abated slightly.

'Look at ma' fuckin' desi boots!' moaned Joey. In looking down mournfully at his feet, he didn't see the enormous black Alsatian dog moving at speed towards him. Bobby saw it and instinctively pushed Joey away. A rope attached to the dog prevented the animal from reaching them, yanking it back at its extremity in cartoon fashion. Bobby laughed, and the restrained, angry dog vented its fury. When he looked round, Joey was getting up from the shallow swamp into which Bobby had just pushed him. His Levi's were covered in wet, slimy mud; his parka's Mod insignia almost completely obscured. Only the head of an arrow and the letters T and W from the words 'The Who' were still decipherable.

'Aw, fuckin' thanks, man!' grunted Joey, mucky water dripping from his hands.

'Can ah help ye?' A gruff, elderly voice could be heard but – unlike the howling and barking – it wasn't apparent where it was coming from. Bobby rotated 180 degrees and back, but still couldn't see the source.

'Hey you twa! Who ye lookin' fur?' The voice seemed to be coming from a higher level. Bobby looked up towards the farmhouse itself. Joey was leaning against the gate, one foot up, trying to scrape large sods of mud from his distressed suede boots.

'Hullo. Ma name's Bobby Cassidy. Is Doug about? I'm here to buy some disco lights aff him.' Bobby called out towards the source of the voice even though he still couldn't see its owner.

'Yer lookin' fur *Hairy* Doug.' The intonation suggested more than one Doug worked on the farm. The voice paused then continued. 'He's ower ther, in the blue shed. Dunno if he's in though.'

'Cheers … em … mate,' said Bobby, before whispering, 'wherever the fuck y'are!'

Bobby and Joey walked gingerly across the deep ripples of mud towards the shed. For Joey, it was very much a case of the horse having bolted, as everything from his shins down couldn't have got any filthier. Bobby had been more careful and, having worn black Doc Marten lace-up boots, was much more prepared for the conditions.

Hairy Doug's blue corrugated iron shed was the most distant building from the main house. A few old horse troughs had to be navigated before Joey spotted a path that reached a different gate from the one they'd just clambered over. The whole area in front of the building had that bomb-blast appearance of places in the Lebanon, from which that Kate Adie regularly reported. Bits of engines lay rusting next to an oven; piles of dense grey-concrete blocks rested on numerous fragments of broken glass. Isolated bricks were strewn around and – as cliché dictated – an armless, boss-eyed Tiny Tears doll stared up at them, like a miniature Marty Feldman.

The rain intensified. Joey spotted a door. It was clad in the same furrowed material as the rest of the building and was, as a consequence, easy to miss. Beyond it, and almost totally concealed by a clump of overgrown shrubbery, was a small inset pane of dirty, cobwebbed glass. There was no door handle, nor obvious mechanism for alerting anyone inside. As Bobby approached the door, the tinny sound of 'Since You Been Gone' could be heard. This prompted him to push back the heavy bushes and step up on a few bricks to peek through the glass.

'Joey … *Joe!*' he whispered, barely audible. 'Fuckin' hell, Joe. That must be him. He's in there havin' a wank!'

'Honestly? Fuckin' pervert! Is there anybody else wi' him? Joey spoke even more quietly than Bobby, for fear of Hairy Doug coming outside with the 'Biggest Cock in Scotland' still in his hand.

'Naw. He's goin' mental wi' it in there hisself. Tell ye whit though, yer pal Jeff wisnae exaggeratin'. That thing's the length ae a fuckin' javelin. He's got hands like Sepp Maier an' there's still mer cock showin' than covered up. When he shoots, its gauny be like Mount Etna eruptin'.' For the first time since they got off the bus, Joey was struggling to contain his laughter. 'On ye go … *Get in there!*'

'Shift ower an' gies a look then,' whispered Joey.

'Aye. Watch yer feet,' warned Bobby, both of them still speaking in whispered tones. Bobby's extra few inches in height permitted him a view without having to stand on the top level of bricks. He felt they looked a bit unsteady. Joey needed this extra elevation, but before he could see in through the glass, the highest row gave way and he crashed into the adjacent bush. Bobby jumped to attention and positioned himself in front of the door seconds before it opened. The python was back in its basket, but the lid remained off. Hairy Doug's filthy jeans had been pulled up quickly, but, apparently unknown to its handler, the business end was still visible. From his vantage point at the bottom of the makeshift steps, Bobby realised that he was almost exactly at eye-level with the 'Biggest Cock in Scotland'.

It was an average-sized door opening, but it still struggled to contain Doug's massive frame. He was well named; there was little skin on his face that was not covered by unruly, lengthy dark hair. It hung down over his eyebrows and rose up from an almost comedy *ZZ Top* beard to a level above his nose. The figure-of-eight patch of oily skin around his eyes resembled a ski mask. Everything else was stereotypical rocker – armless, ripped leather biker's *waistie* over dirty denim jacket over black, torn Grateful Dead T-shirt. Silver skeleton-head buckle belt holding up oil-stained, faded blue jeans – zip still wide open; python coiled. Biker boots of a size that nursery-rhyme families could've lived in. Fortunately, Bobby detected no hint – or shame – that the Hairy behemoth in front of him was aware he'd been caught masturbating to a soft-rock Rainbow song. So he opened with the only thing he could think of.

'You must be Hairy Doug. Ah'm Bobby. Ah phoned ye earlier?'

'Aye, lad. Come in.' He looked down at Joey, who was pulling himself free of the thorny overgrown bushes. 'Is yer pal all right? Hairy Doug smiled warmly and extended the hand that had only minutes earlier been *wrangling* his own rope. Bobby tentatively and weakly shook the hand. It was warm, and a bit moist. Sweat, Bobby hoped.

Clearly one for the understatement, Doug offered, 'Sorry. Place is a wee bit of a mess.'

Bobby couldn't place the accent. It seemed to be a bizarre mix of many identifiable regional dialects, such as Cockney, Cornish and the Doric. Looking around his war zone, it was apparent that Hairy Doug was no believer in putting down roots. His place – with the Army-style fold-up camp bed in one corner – had a look of an environment that could be evacuated in minutes, if the wrong people came calling. It was cramped with the same sort of debris that was out in the yard, only there was far more of it, and forced into a much smaller area. Shelves of oil cans, car batteries, and paint tins; a small TV set with a coat hanger aerial teetered on a old Edwardian-style coach-built pram. A large woodwork bench sat in the middle of the room, causing Joey to look twice at the door and ponder whether the shell of the structure had been built after the bench had been bolted to the shed's concrete floor.

'Just grab a seat, lads,' said Hairy Doug as he went over to a small stove that was concealed behind a sheet hanging from a line strung across the width. 'Tea?'

'Eh, no for me mate,' said Bobby. Joey had found somewhere to perch, although he jumped back up from the newspaper-covered stool, believing that something living had just moved when he'd sat on it.

'How did you get my name, agin?' said Doug, his previous cheeriness now replaced by a more serious, lets-get-down-to-business tone.

Joey felt that he should take this one. 'Eh … Jeff McGarry gied me your name. Said ye hired out mobile disco gear and lights, an' that.'

'Ah. OK. The boy McGarry. Is he your mate?'

'Naw, no really. Ah've kent his family for a while but …'

'Likes the cows, does that boy. A bit too much, I think,' said Doug, interrupting Joey.

Bobby knew a bit about Jeff's story. It had become part of Ayrshire folklore in recent years. Almost three years before, a *Kilmarnock Standard* report, hidden away on an inside page, had told of rustling at McAdam Farm, near Kilmaurs. Four young men, three of them brothers and the fourth a cousin, had stolen a prize-winning cow from a barn in the middle of the night. Amazingly, they'd managed to walk it about three miles back to a vacant, boarded-up council house in Onthank, with the purpose of killing it and selling the meat. The premise was born in Hollywood. Fifteen-year-old ringleader Jeff had come up with the idea after seeing an eye-wateringly gory scene in *The Texas Chainsaw Massacre*. The gang had managed to get the petrified beast into a ground-floor bathroom, although, by all accounts, squeezing its girth through the two doors to get it there was a major exercise in patience.

Jeff hadn't thought the plan through properly, so when it came time to fire up the electric hedgecutters that were playing the role of chainsaw and look into those big brown eyes, none of the rustlers had the bottle. They also couldn't get it into the bathtub, from where the blood might have been more easily disposed. They spent the night in there, getting drunk in the hope that courage would be plucked up, but the moment had passed. The McGarrys felt the best plan of action was to disappear over the back gardens, leaving the cow in the bathroom for someone else to find.

Someone else *did* find it almost two days later. The smell and the incessant moo-ing had been traced by a neighbouring Columbo to the empty house. He'd had a look around earlier, but had assumed the noises were a practical joke – as opposed to a cow having taken up rent-free residence in the nearby house. The local police caught up with the gang without too much investigation. One of them had left a list of potential carnivorous customers – and their phone numbers – on the top of the cistern. It was entitled 'Jeff's Coo Meat'.

Bobby was staggered to discover that, following his time in a Young Offenders' Institute, Jeff had been offered a chance at rehabilitation with a job. On this farm. And surrounded by cows.

There was a pause as Doug sipped his tea from a metal cup. Bobby broke the short silence.

'So whit is it that *you* dae on the farm?'

'Oh, not much really. Mr and Mrs Wallace let me stay here and work from the shed if I fix the tractor engines for them. I'm away a lot of the time … roadying for bands mostly. Black Sabbath, AC/DC, The Clash y'know.' This last entry seemed a bit out of kilter, but Doug went on to explain that you didn't have to like their music to take their money. Joey had a feeling that Heatwave Disco's motto might ultimately be the same as Hairy Doug's.

'So what do you need then?' asked Doug.

'Well, we're just startin' out so … basically everythin',' replied Bobby, sensing that Doug might be a man who could be trusted not to take advantage of a couple of virgins. 'We've got a few bookings,' Bobby lied. 'Mobile disco pairties … so decks, speakers and a few lights tae start wi', ah'd have thought.'

'Come on through here.' Hairy Doug flicked a switch and three industrial fluorescent strip lights came on. They helped illuminate a cluttered path to a previously unseen second door in the far corner of the room.

Walking through the door was like entering Narnia. The contrast between the chaos of Doug's 'front room' and his private store was breathtaking. Rows of Marshall PA columns were stacked neatly in one corner. Four double-decked turntable units were laid out in an immaculate row on the central table, alongside a large group of sound mixers. Hundreds of feet of cables were hanging on hooks with labels reading '5ft', '10ft', '15ft' and '20ft and over' stuck to the white-painted block wall about them.

At the far end of the room were boxes of lights. Many purloined from Hairy Doug's time on the road. There were spots on bars, long, twisting rope lights, cabinets of various shapes and sizes, major Super-Trouper field lights, disco balls, strobe lights, and blacklights and smoke machines; all stacked so neatly it was as if Hairy Doug had just divorced Mary Poppins and she'd been granted custody of the sound and light store.

'So, I can hire you the basic package. Deck, sound-to-light mixer, base cabinets and speakers. How does that sound? If you want to make a real go of it, you bring them back and we talk price for buying.' Even before asking, Bobby knew this first gig wasn't going to make them rich.

'Yeah. OK,' said Bobby. 'How much for aw that?'

'Forty quid, lads – 24-hour hire,' replied Hairy Doug. 'When d'you want the gear for?'

'The gig's on the seventeenth. Tail end of next week,' said Bobby.

'No problem. Fifty per cent deposit up front, OK?' Hairy Doug moved over to a desk and picked up a small diary. He opened it up and Joey was able to glimpse that there were no other names or bookings in the few pages flicked over to get to the seventeenth of February.

They left shortly afterwards, way down in profit, but childishly excited and contented. A couple of clowns celebrating their deal with Hairy Doug – hefty of frame *and* of price, and accepted as the owner of *one* of the 'Biggest Cocks in Scotland'. Jeff McGarry couldn't possibly have seen them *all*.

A WALK ON THE BEACH WITH A SOLDIER

Hettie – only her birth certificate and the odd doctor's letter used her given name of Heather – was undeniably impressed by her brother's stamina. He'd left home almost two years earlier and she couldn't recall him being particularly energetic before. She did remember his idleness being the stimulus for many of the arguments between Gary and their dad, though, leading to his leaving. When he'd initially come back, Hettie had barely recognised him. He appeared much taller, definitely leaner and – with his hair buzzcut short – infinitely more attractive than the emaciated slob of old.

He'd been carrying her on his back for almost twenty-five minutes. For the first ten of those, Gary had been jogging; bare feet tracking deep footprints in the wet sand of Troon beach. Hettie told him about the scene in *Chariots of Fire* she'd seen at the cinema two weeks ago. Gary didn't know what she was talking about. He'd only stopped jogging because the bouncing motion had caused Hettie to drop the best part of a '99 down the back of his neck. The whole routine had resulted from Hettie enquiring about the weight of the pack Gary might be expected to have to haul if he was ever involved in a conflict.

'About the same weight as you, Hets,' said Gary exaggerating, before insisting he prove his recently acquired strength.

They had started off at the upper esplanade near the ferry terminal, having caught the No. 10 bus from Kilmarnock. The walk from the centre of Troon took Gary and Hettie along Templehill, past the Anchorage pub to the tip of the small penis-shaped promontory, where the boats went back and forth to Larne. It had been raining heavily when they left home, but the wind had swept up nearer the coast and it seemed to be keeping the worst of the precipitation at bay.

It had been Hettie's idea to come down to Troon on this last Sunday before Gary went back to Wellington Barracks in London. She hadn't seen all that much of him and certainly not on her own. Bobby's birthday and catching up with the few remaining mates he had wanted to see had meant Gary's time had been almost fully occupied. Hettie had always felt a special bond with Gary. It wasn't that either of them disliked Bobby; far from it, they were a trio who had always got on well, and, perhaps unusually, there had never been any major sibling conflicts for Harry and Ethel to referee and arbitrate. It was just that daughter and eldest son shared something intuitive that was difficult to explain. They weren't especially alike. They certainly didn't look like each other. Hettie shared the remainder of her family's stocky *plumpishness* and slightly sallow skin. She wore clothes from Oxfam but in a way that marked her as quirky or bohemian.

Hettie was creative; artistic and musical. She was clever. She read constantly, quoting lines from Shelagh Delaney or J.D. Salinger, which gave her an air of being from an earlier era. Gary was none of these things. He was as stereotypical a product of his '70s working-class, west-of-Scotland upbringing as it was possible to get: repressed, angry, defiant, sullen and a magnet for trouble and chaos. None of this was evident in his relationship with Hettie.

Since his basic training had ended, Gary's battalion had been performing domestic duties. He hadn't been permitted leave to come home – or so he had informed Hettie in his letters, which were, in themselves, a major indication of his change in attitude. Although he had jokingly hinted at being permanently confined to barracks, Hettie had suspected Gary was simply avoiding his father. In truth, the first six months had been somewhat underwhelming for Gary and there hadn't been much to write home about. It might make Ethel feel happier that her son wasn't a constant target for various terrorist groups, but guarding St James's Palace wearing a full-dress uniform of red tunic and bearskin wasn't what Gary anticipated when the recruitment office in London talked about 'life-changing experiences'. Gary hoped for a more exciting challenge in the six months that lay ahead. Hettie simply wanted him to be happy. And although she'd rather he'd found happiness in a career less potentially hazardous, she also saw the positive attributes it had fostered in him.

She knew Gary loved this beach. Her family hadn't gone on many holidays when she was growing up – a couple of times to Butlin's at the Heads of Ayr and once all the way by train to a miserably windswept caravan site in Arbroath, where they were regularly soaked by the violent waves coming over the sea wall. But they did travel the short journey to Troon regularly in the summer, and Gary had often been the one nagging his parents to take them.

The Ailsa Craig had always fascinated Gary, and he found it the most bizarre thing to contemplate: a volcanic plug, perfectly framed between the Heads of Ayr and the slopes of Arran's southernmost edge, which didn't seem to correspond to the local geography. It seemed to him that it should be up near Mull or Skye, with violent waves making it almost impossible to access. Instead it just sat there, in relative isolation, in generally calm waters, easy to get to … but why would anyone bother? When relations with Harry were at their most strained, Gary would come here and clear his overheated brain by imagining himself living there. Alone, except for the gannets and gulls. He figured that an enforced isolation was a far more attractive option than living in a pressurised environment alongside a disinterested father with whom he could no longer make any connections. He loved that view; imagining it to look wildly different from the side that faced the northern tip of Ulster.

Harry had sometimes brought his three children around to the harbour, where a large brown van sold fish suppers 'straight off the boats'. He'd carry the steaming hot food wrapped in newsprint across to the small rectangular parking area where Gary, Bobby and Hettie were waiting expectantly. Together they'd sit in contented silence, watching this lonely piece of rock until the streetlights around the island's only perimeter road gradually illuminated its base and it was time to head home. The only movement was the stocky, lugubrious, black-and-white ferries that traversed the normally calm water between Ardrossan in the distance, and Brodick on the Isle of Arran. They moved so slowly and directly it was as if they were being operated by a pulley system. It was entirely appropriate that Hettie and Gary should spend this last day of his R 'n' R here.

They were way beyond the starter's hut on the Royal Troon Golf Course when Gary eventually stopped and set Hettie back on her feet. He'd spotted a sheltered section of the dunes and motioned for her to follow him over. The rain was still relatively light, but the sand was dry within the protective structure of the banking and the westerly wind that had been blowing into their faces as they had progressed down the beach towards Prestwick was now billowing far above their heads. They both sat down on Gary's jacket. He pulled black sandshoes from its inside pockets and arched his long, bony feet into them.

'Mum'll have been pleased wi' yer prelim results then,' said Gary before lighting a cigarette.

'Yeah, but Dad's a bit annoyed that ah've dropped the biology. Ah was doing OK, but ah couldn't do that and art *and* music.'

'You need to do the subjects that *you* want tae do. It's got fu … It's nuthin' tae do wi' him.' Gary worked hard to avoid swearing in Hettie's presence. She had never asked him not to; it was just a self-imposed boundary he had always felt that he shouldn't cross.

'He doesn't mean to be negative,' said Hettie. 'He just can't see how a good job can come out of goin' tae art school. He's obsessed wi' me doin' medicine or law or something …'

Gary cut across her. ' … Aye but just so he can brag about it tae auld bags like Sadie Flanagan! Trust me, you dae exactly whit fires ye. Yer cleverer than any ae' us an' when ah come back up after the summer, ah'm no wantin' tae hear that you've dropped these subjects cos' a *school jannie* made ye.'

'What do ye mean … after the summer?' asked Hettie, a little aggressively.

'Ach … we're maybe gettin' a postin' in the next few weeks.' Gary said this quietly and then paused before adding, ' … an' there's a lassie … doon in London, ken? Anyway auld Harry'll be glad ae' the peace after this wee trip.'

'He's really proud ae you tae, Gary. Ah ken it. Ah've heard him talkin' to Mum about ye. About how ye've done somethin' he dreamed about himself. Somethin' he'd always wanted tae dae, but never got the chance.'

'Ah didnae ken he'd wanted tae join the Army!' said Gary.

'Naw, go an' get a *tattoo*,' laughed Hettie. This made the proud Scots Guardsman laugh as well, before pushing his sister over onto her side then leaning over and gently and repeatedly dummy-punching her left upper arm.

'Gary, stop it. *Stop!* Ah'll pee myself,' she giggled. Gary eventually let her up and they sat side-by-side on his black donkey jacket, gazing out over the Firth of Clyde, neither of them speaking until Hettie eventually broke the silence.

'So, a lassie, then? Ye kept *this* quiet. C'mon, spill. Whit's her name? Whit's she like?'

Gary blushed a bit. He'd been partly hoping she hadn't fully heard him.

'Ah dunno if anythin'll come ae it. She works in a hotel near the barracks. Ah saw her a couple of times when the platoon was out runnin'. Then, later, we got talkin'.' Gary turned away. He was beginning to wish he'd kept this part of his life a secret.

'Has she actually *got* a name?' asked Hettie, prodding her brother in the ribs.

'Eh … aye, it's Debbie.'

'Anything else? Any distinguishin' marks? Facial ticks? Whit does her dad do?'

'Jesus Christ, Hets. It's probably nuthin'. I like her but we've only been out the once.'

'Ye've been out wi' her … and that's me just finding out about it? Aw those bloody borin' letters about marchin' and funny chinstraps an' ye miss *this* out!' Hettie was enjoying tormenting her brother and she could see he was also trying hard to suppress a smile. She beamed as she began to realise that, for the first time in ages, he was genuinely happy.

'We went for a walk through St James's Park a coupla' weeks ago. It was freezin', but really great, ken? Had a coffee an' that, an' talked for ages.' He could sense Hettie was desperate for more information. He decided she deserved to hear it.

'You'd like her Het. She reminds me a lot ae' you. Her mam's an artist. She was born in India. No sure whit 'er dad does but ah think it's somethin' along the same lines as Stan May. She's lived in aw these bizarre places like Cairo an' Marrakech an' that. Loads more ah huvnae even heard ae.' Gary was aware that Hettie was enthralled by this and that she would already be thinking about when they could meet and visit an art gallery together. Gary kept going.

'Her dad was really sick, so they came back tae Wakefield when she was fifteen. But they didnae settle. *Nomads,* she calls them. So they're aw doon in London now an' she's working for a wee while before college after the summer. That's about it.' Gary sat back as if in need of respite after an emotional confession.

'Age?' asked Hettie.

'Twenty-two … naw -three, ah think.'

'Ye huvnae asked? Whit if her birthday's next week when ye go back? When are ye seein' her again?' Hettie was becoming a touch impatient at her brother's apparent lack of direct action.

'Ah'm no sure. Nothing really planned.' Hettie found this too much.

'Nothin' planned? Jesus, Gary, how many girlfriends have you actually had?'

Gary formed the words to answer without appreciating the rhetorical nature of the question.

'No that many that ye can afford tae play the *hard-tae-get,* ah'd have thought!' continued Hettie. 'When ye were talking about her there, yer face was glowin'. Whit's the matter wi' ye? *Get in there!*'

This last phrase was designed to make him laugh. When talking to Joey Miller, Bobby used it as a catchphrase so often that Gary and Hettie had made a pact that they would have it inscribed on his gravestone. Unusually, though, Gary didn't laugh this time.

'Ah'm no really wantin' it tae get too serious just now,' said Gary. Hettie suspected something important was coming so she let the resultant pause play itself out.

'It looks like ah'm goin' tae Belfast in a few weeks.' Gary stared more intently as if he could now visualise himself on a patrol away over on the other side of this black stretch of freezing water.

'A few ae the boys have been talkin' about it doon in London. They've said it's no actually that bad. We might be goin' tae the Bogside, just mainly doin' foot patrols an' helpin' the polis wi' searches an' that.' It was clear that this wasn't going to be a two-way conversation, but Gary pressed on in his well-intentioned attempts to inform and placate his sister. He was now nervous and he sensed that Hettie knew it.

'We're a deterrent tae the bampots. The foot patrols can maintain contact wi' local folk an' it makes us seem more human an' no whit aw the Republican propaganda would want them tae think.'

Hettie had never heard her brother talk like this before. It seemed like he was using words he had learned from an Army training manual; repeated so often that he had brainwashed himself with them. Gary had never been a respecter of Queen and country before, and Hettie couldn't understand why he was now.

'Ye ken, Hets, after ah went doon tae London … once ah'd been there for about six months, ah just wanted tae have somethin' tae belong tae. There wisnae any work, an' ah'd been caught sleepin' rough in the park twice. There's loadsa guys ah kent for a wee while; aw ended up on the rent at Euston. Ah could see maself goin' the same way. Last time ah got picked up, it was the polis guy that told me tae go tae the Army recruitment station. Even gave me a few quid tae get cleaned up an' that. Came back two days later wi' a shirt and a tie as well. Best thing that coulda happened tae be honest.'

Hettie was still sitting with her knees pulled up, hiding her face – and the fact that she was now gently sobbing – from Gary.

'The Army's been really good for me. Ye said so yerself. The barracks are a'right an' ah've got good mates now. Everythin's goin' well for me.' He stood up. 'Don't you worry about me. Belfast'll be a breeze, man.'

Gary wasn't sure what else to say. He didn't want his last day for six months to be remembered as one when he had upset Hettie. But he needed to tell her that a tour of duty in Belfast was looking likely. It was one of the main reasons for suggesting they spend the day together. This couldn't be something that he'd write in a letter from the comparative safety of his cramped London barracks.

'Come on, H. Ah'll race ye back tae the Forum Café. The fish suppers are on me, eh?' He suspected she was crying, but didn't want to see it. So he burst away up the hill and over the rolling dunes, only looking back when he knew he wouldn't be able to witness the hurt he'd caused her. *Yer a fuckin' coward, Cassidy*, he thought to himself. The bombs and bullets of County Fermanagh would surely be easier to cope with than the tears on his sister's face, but this had just been the rehearsal before the main act. Gary still had Ethel, his hypertensive mum, to face.

PART II

INITIAL EXCHANGES

Llew Gardner, journalist for Thames TV
'Prime Minister, how long do you wish to go on being Prime Minister?'
Mrs Margaret Thatcher, the Prime Minister
'Until I'm tired of it.'
Llew Gardner
'How long will that be?'
Mrs Margaret Thatcher
'Oh, I don't get tired very easily.'

18th February 1982
Interview for Thames Television's *TV Eye*

5

THERE'S AN OLD PIANO ...

'Well, whit dae ye think? Ah thought that went a'right.'

'Ah *think* you're fuckin' mental if ye think ah'm doin' that again.'

Two friends sat on a Kilmarnock pavement after their first mobile DJ experience, reflecting on an evening of unexpected surrealism. Two halves of the same coin: Bobby Cassidy – optimistic entrepreneur – relentlessly *heads* up; Joey Miller – pragmatic fixer – obstinately *tails* down.

'We're out here stood on the fuckin' pavement ... it's half-past two in the mornin' ... the gear's gettin' soaked fae aw this fuckin' rain ... we didnae get paid ... an' there's nae van here to pick us up!' Joey stood up for greater effect. 'Ah'm really not sure how that fits intae the definition ae *a'right*.'

'But ...'

'An' another thing. If ah hear that fuckin' Shakin' Stevens record one more time, I'm gonnae fuckin' kill somebody ... probably you!' Joey sat back down on the big black speaker and folded his arms. He was breathing hard and had turned away from Bobby to look down the length of John Finnie Street.

Bobby decided not to push it further for the moment. He reckoned that Joey's frustration was borne of crushing disappointment. In the week running up to the gig – even though there only was one, Bobby had continually referred to it as a 'gig' to seduce Joey into believing that they were a part of the live music industry – Joey's demeanour had changed to one in which his nervous anticipation was palpable. There remained a lingering concern about the number of records required for a night of mobile DJ-ing and it was clear from the outset that neither man would be making any money from this inaugural activity. But both had recognised the excitement of this do-it-yourself venture when rehearsing with the decks in Bobby's bedroom. They had become comfortable with the equipment since picking it up from Hairy Doug's at the beginning of a week-long hire. He'd turned out to be a decent – if unapologetically squalid – *geezer*, patiently demonstrating how the spaghetti of cables all found their various input and output points to provide life for the machine.

'It's all pretty easy, boys. And if that fat cunt Duncan can do it, well that should tell ya … any fooker can.' And with that send-off, Hairy Doug truly endeared himself to Joey Miller.

The only thing the hirsute rocker couldn't give them was a working microphone; but Bobby called in a favour and borrowed an old one from Dale Wishart – singer with local Mod band, The Vespas. But they didn't rehearse with the microphone. They didn't decide on who would speak, preferring to leave it until they got to the venue. The logic for this was similar to that of the football team awarded a penalty, but electing to let the taker be the player who most felt up to it on the night. It was often heard from professional football players that they couldn't really practise for a vital penalty because the pressured context of a real match was impossible to create. And so Bobby Cassidy assuaged his embarrassment and prevaricated on the one key skill that a DJ needed. It would be a wrong call that would be regretted by more than just the two budding disc jockeys.

'Whaur's ma new rid lippy, ya wee gadgie!' Audrey King knew what was coming, but wasn't quick enough to avoid it.

'*Maaaaammmmm!*' she howled as her elder sister yanked her back into the room they both shared by her long bleached hair. 'Ah … *sob* huvnae … *sob* even seen it … *sob* … ya big *fat cow!*'

Lizzie King instinctively let go just as their step-mother strode in.

'Whit? Ah ne'er even touched 'er,' exclaimed Lizzie, arms outstretched. 'She's ay fuckin' whinin' aboot suhin', her.'

Lizzie was the second eldest of five children, all living in a three-bedroomed, mid-block council flat in Shortlees, with their Dad, Frank King – an Elvis Presley fanatic – and his third wife, Anne. The Kings' was the only flat in a block of six that didn't have its windows boarded up.

Back in the small, square bedroom, Tony Hadley gazed down impassively from the wall at the familiar scene.

'Hey you. Language. Audrey, huv you been at her stuff again?' Anne had her hands on her hips like a contemporary *Maw Broon*.

'Niver touched it,' bubbled Audrey, feeling her scalp and repeatedly investigating her hand for incriminating evidence of her own blood.

'*Liar!*' Lizzie screeched. She made a grab for Audrey again, but Anne had positioned herself between the girls.

'You, awa' intae the livin' room.' Audrey didn't need a second invitation. Anne turned to Lizzie, pushing the door closed behind her. 'Whit's up wi' ye? It's yer party tonight an' ye look bloody miserable. Everybody's been on flamin' eggshells wi' ye aw week. Whit's goin' on?'

'It's nothin' a'right. Just leave it, Mam,' said Lizzie.

Anne smiled.

'Whit?' asked Lizzie.

'Ah just like it when ye call me *Mam*.' It hadn't always been like this, but after a difficult couple of years, this last twelve months had seen them become more familiar with each other.

'Ye've earnt *that*, ah suppose.' Lizzie smiled briefly, then turned away to conceal it. She was still angry with Audrey.

'Thanks ... ah think,' said Anne.

'Well, it's no like ye've had tae compete wi' the auld yin,' said Lizzie.

Frank's previous wife, Isa, had up and left. If she had died, Anne might have had some memory to contend with. As it was, while Lizzie and her siblings hadn't exactly made life easy for her at the beginning, it was obvious their father couldn't look after them all by himself. As Lizzie saw it, without Anne, they'd have been on the phone to Esther Rantzen every week.

For her part, Anne had known taking on a man like Frank – set in his ways and with four headstrong kids – wasn't going to be a walk in the park. She smiled at Lizzie. 'It would've been a lot harder if you . . . well, ye ken whit ah mean.'

'Just keep him oot the bookies an' we'll aw be happy,' said Lizzie.

'He's just goin' through a bad patch. He's got too much time on his hands, an' nothin' tae dae. Ken, he says tae me the other night, aw serious tae ... "Whit age dae ye have to be tae get oan a Youth Opportunities Scheme?" Ye shouldnae laugh, but Christ, he's nearly forty!'

'Naw, yer right, Mam ... ye *shouldnae* laugh. He's fritterin' away and jist dyin' ae apathy. Three million folk ... Jesus, whit a waste of life. If only they aw realised that ye could start a revolution wi' they numbers. But then, the three-thirty at Cheltenham always gets in the way an' diverts their attention.' Lizzie looked she was going to cry. Anne moved closer and touched Lizzie's arm. 'Ah'm fine,' said Lizzie.

'Listen, Lizzie, there was somethin' ah wanted tae tell ...'

'*Shit*!' Lizzie interrupted.

'Whit ...? Whit've ye done?'

'Ach, ah've just broken a bloody nail. Been ages paintin' them anaw. Shit!' Lizzie was annoyed again.

'Ye sure you're a'right? Time ae the month?' enquired Anne.

'Aye, but it's no that. It's just gettin' a bit claustrophobic in here

… sharin' a room wi' *her* an' Linda,' sighed Lizzie.

Anne gulped. 'Are ye worried it's no' gonnae go well tonight? You've got loadsa folk comin'. This'll just be nerves, eh?' Anne had her arm around Lizzie.

'Aye, probably right. Ah'll snap oot of it once ah've hud a wee voddy,' said Lizzie.

'Yer first legal drink, eh! Ye excited?'

There was a pause after Anne said this, and then both women laughed loudly. They would need to leave soon and, although Lizzie had selfishly insisted that none of her brothers and sisters be allowed to attend – especially the hated Audrey – Anne was looking forward to a night out with Frank. It was important that Lizzie was in a good mood or they would be on edge all evening.

'Are ye still upset about Theresa?' enquired Anne softly.

Lizzie sighed. 'Naw. It was aw her fault. She shouldnae have said that stuff about me. She said it was a joke, but it wisnae. It was vindictive.' Lizzie had now regained her cocksure composure. 'An' anyway, the baw was on the slates when ah gave the DJ job tae that Cassidy boy. Efter whit she said but, there was nae way that fat man ae' hers was gettin' it. Ah'm fine. C'mon, let's go. Is Dad ready?'

'Whit about yer lipstick?'

'Ah had it in ma handbag all along.'

'Awa' an apologise tae yer sister, then.' But both women knew there was more chance of Tony Hadley climbing down off the wall and coming to the party with them, than of *that* happening.

'Whit was it ye wanted to tell me?' asked Lizzie.

Anne breathed deeply. 'Ach … it'll keep.'

17TH FEBRUARY 1982: 7:11PM

About five miles across Kilmarnock – in a similarly sized bedroom – a young man nervously stared at his reflection in a full-length mirror.

'Are you lookin' at me? Are *you* lookin' at … cos ah'm the only wan here. Well, who are ye lookin' at then … if no me?' Bobby leaned over and kissed his reflection.

'It's you … you … ah' jist want you … ma coo-gah-choo … ma-coo-gah-CHOOOO.' Bobby turned to the left. He was now side-on to the mirror. He adopted a cod-American accent, as he interviewed himself.

'Alvin, what's been the secret of your incredible success?' Bobby now turned to the right and looked straight into the mirror.

'Well, Kid, I'd have to put it down to the size of my enormous knob!' Bobby looked down. He picked up a folded pair of socks and shoved them down the front of his pants.

'Ah … I can certainly see what you mean, Alvin.' Bobby picked out a record and put it on the turntable. He began prancing around and singing to 'Da Ya Think I'm Sexy' by Rod Stewart.

'Hoi, Rodney.' Bobby looked round, startled.

It was Joey. 'You're a fanny.'

'For fuck's sake, Joe. Ye nearly gied me a heart attack there.'

'Whit are you oan, Boab?'

'Well, obviously ah' didnae ken ye were there. Jesus Christ, ah' don't make a habit ae jigglin' aboot in ma pants in front ae folk.'

'Whit … even though you've got an enormous knob?' asked Joey.

'Christ … how long had ye been stood there?' Bobby sheepishly extracted the socks from inside his Y-fronts

'Well, ah watched *Taxi Driver* … then ah saw ye snoggin' yersel', ya bender … then ye were Alvin Stardust, and Kid Jensen, oan *Top ae the Pops* … an' then finally …'

'Aye, aye … ah get it, ya prick,' said Bobby, slightly annoyed.

'Whit's the score, then?' asked Joey, rubbing his cold hands together.

'Ah'm jist gauny get ready … splash a wee bit ae the auld Brut 55 oan, then we're ready for the off, eh? Ah'm a bit nervous, but cannae fuckin' wait, man.' Bobby was extremely apprehensive, but he didn't want it to show too much. This was a dream in the making and he wished he could enjoy it a bit more than the tension was allowing.

'Ye sure we've got enough records, Boab? An' did ye get a mic? Cos' ah don't think ye'll get much sound oota that hairbrush.'

'Ah got an auld yin earlier fae Dale, the singer oot the Vespas. Huvnae tried it oot yet. We'll wait til' we get there, eh? An' ah'm sure we've got enough records. Christ, these kinda pairties don't get goin' until aboot half-nine anyway. We'll only need aboot an hour and a half's worth for the bits that folk'll actually be listenin' tae.' Bobby looked out of his bedroom window again.

'Where the fuck is he?' asked Bobby. Even though he had still to conclude his own final preparations, his mounting anxiety was now being directed towards the driver of the van hired to pick up the gear.

'He'll be here. McGarry promised me.' Joey was equally annoyed, but began to suspect the blame for the van driver's no-show would be directed at him. And it would be difficult to avoid since it had been his job to ask Jeff McGarry if he could sort out the transport. But still …

'Ye did tell him half-six?' said Bobby, now staring intently out to the street, his head moving from side to side as if he was watching Connors and McEnroe on centre court.

'Aye, ah did. Told him we had to be there for seven. Even fuckin' paid him the twenty quid up front.'

'Haud on,' said Bobby. 'That might be him there.'

A large white transit van had pulled up on the grass verge outside. It was another cold, wet, late-winter night and still dark outside, but the stocky figure who clambered out of the driver's side, looked at a bit of paper and then peered over at the house could only be Heatwave's new driver and roadie. Bobby bounded down the stairs to meet him, leaving Joey to start struggling with the gear. A couple of minutes later Bobby was on his way back up the stairs. He wasn't as jaunty as when he'd descended them.

'Whit's up, is it no him?' said Joey putting down a Marshall Speaker column.

'Naw … ah mean, aye, it's him, but …' Bobby looked round to

ensure no-one was behind him. 'It's Barry fuckin' Baird!'

Joey stood bolt upright. Bobby sensed the immediate trepidation at even the mention of the name.

Barry Baird was a renowned local headcase. A few weeks ago – just before Christmas – he was standing at a street corner with three others, when Joey approached on his own. Joey was aware of him watching as he got closer, but he didn't want to cross to the other side of the road for fear that Barry Baird would sense his anxiety. So Joey aimed at walking straight past, his pace quickening as he came within kicking distance.

'Hey you, fuckface! Dae ah ken you?' said Barry Baird, in a calm, quiet tone

'Eh, naw … ah don't think so,' replied Joey, his own tone as calm as his churning stomach would allow.

'Dae you ken *me*, then?' As Joey recounted this story to a laughing Bobby later, he said he knew this was a trick question.

'No sure!'

Wrong answer. A right arm shot out from its rigid frame as if it belonged to one of the mechanical pugilists from the Raving Bonkers boxing game. It thumped Joey on the side of the jaw causing him to double over both in pain and in anticipation of further blows and kicks. They didn't come, though. Joey looked up and saw that Barry Baird's focus had moved away from him. Something had happened over Joey's shoulder that now held his attention. Joey didn't know what it was, but it had Barry Baird as rapt as a little dog, mesmerised by the movements of a stick about to be thrown. Joey sloped away, thanking his good fortune that psychos like Barry Baird had such limited multi-tasking abilities. And no memory, apparently.

For here he was now, standing in Bobby's hall, looking straight up at Joey and saying, 'Right, mate. Aw the fuckin' gear up the stairs, is it?'

'Eh, aye. Just come up …' said Bobby.

'Ye a'right, mate?' enquired Barry Baird, as he passed Joey on the stairs.

'Aye ...' and under his breath, '... Ah will be in a fuckin' minute, once this heart attack's by!'

'The room's too wee! The room's too dark! The cake's no big enough! The bar's got nae Pernod. The disco husnae turned up!'

For fuck's sake, none of these things were his fault. Frank King was getting increasingly annoyed. He didn't even want to be here, far less to have to deal with his daughter's high-pitched carping. Anne had even made him wear a suit and tie. He felt as if he was going to court. The main condition of his agreeing to this party in the first place was that it would be for Lizzie and her pals. He would pay, but he didn't need to be there in person. Had everyone forgotten this clause?

'Cheer up, Frank, eh?' said Anne. She was irritated by his attitude on their first night out for months. He hadn't actually made it clear that he didn't want to come, or at least not to her, but Anne suspected her revelation earlier in the week was the root cause. 'Look, this is Lizzie's big night. Ye've no even had to buy a round yet. And whit else would ye have been doin'?'

Frank lit a cigarette. '*Shine on Harvey Moon* was oan,' he proclaimed.

'Typical,' sighed Anne.

'Have ye tried phonin' his house?' Frank offered to Lizzie, in an attempt to change the subject.

'Aye. The lassie behind the bar's been ringin' it for about half an hour. Ah'm away outside. Ah need another smoke. Everybody's here an' there's nae disco. Ah'm black affronted!' Lizzie stormed through the glass swing doors of the Sandriane pub, already plotting a revenge on Bobby Cassidy and anyone related to him. Just as she lit up her sixth cigarette in less than an hour, Barry Baird's ramshackle transit van pulled up at the kerb.

'Fuck ae you been?' shouted Lizzie, almost nose to nose with a bemused Barry Baird.

'No me, hen. Ah'm just the driver,' said Barry calmly, despite thinking that in different circumstances, he'd have decked someone for that tone, *lassie or no*.

'Eh, ah'm really sorry. The van broke doon,' said Bobby, offering a handshake, which was totally ignored, and shooting a nervous look over at Barry Baird for fear the psycho would expose the lie.

Lizzie looked at the van and, in particular, at Joey, who'd had to stand in the back holding the broken sliding door shut to stop the contents falling out as the van cornered. She conceded that *breakdown* was a distinct possibility.

'Fuckin' hurry up and get started then … an' ah'm still dockin' ye for being late.'

She stubbed out her cigarette *Olivia Newton John* style, turned and sashayed back into the pub, fully aware that the three lads would have been staring at her arse in her ridiculously tight, pinstriped jeans.

'No quite whit ah pictured,' said Bobby with a big grin. 'Ah thought she'd be about twenty stone …'

'Easy tae see where she hides aw the snakes in aw that hair,' observed Joey. He was the only one actually unloading anything onto the wet pavement.

'Ah thought she looked fuckin' lovely,' Bobby enthused. He was already imagining that going home with the hostess might be a regular perk of these nights. After all, somebody always went home with Mick Jagger when *he* played a gig.

'That'll be twenty quid, boys,' said Barry.

Joey dropped a box of records, shaking Bobby out of his brief daydream.

'Eh!' exclaimed Joey, with a bit more vigour than he'd intended. 'Ah've already paid Jeff the twenty!'

'Naw, mate. That was *his* twenty. This is mine.' Barry Baird was not going to be talked down. 'Any problems wi' that?'

'Aw, naw. No!' said Bobby reaching for his wallet. 'It's just that we assumed the twenty was all in.'

'Don't assume, pal. It makes an ASS of U an' ME.' Barry Baird had listened to this statement aimed in his direction by numerous teachers in his short-lived academic life. It was ingrained in him like the writing running through a stick of Blackpool rock. Now it was his turn. With the gear on the pavement and Bobby's twenty-pound note in his pocket, Barry Baird jumped back in the van.

'Pick us up at half one?' shouted Bobby, as the van pulled away. A right hand emerged from the driver's side window. It simply waved, as if the Queen was on the other end of it.

Bobby and Joey had never been so pleased to see Hamish May. Having decided to come down unannounced and lend some moral support, he'd been inside the pub for the past twenty minutes. Lizzie had presumed him to be a bouncer, knowing that he wasn't one of her guests.

'Fuck me, it's the Hamster. Whit ae *you* doin' here?' said Bobby, and then, before Hamish could answer, 'Fuck it, never mind. Gies a hand wi' aw this will ye?'

'Ah'm ah gettin' paid?' said Hamish, half-jokingly.

'Ye'll get rewarded in Heaven,' said Bobby.

'Jist like the rest ae us,' added Joey.

'... now let's go afore the fuckin' pub shuts,' instructed the Heatwave Disco CEO.

'Is there any grub, at least?' If he couldn't get paid in hard cash, Hamish May figured food was the next best currency.

'Spotted a decent spread through the back. Continental stuff an' a buffett, an' that,' said Bobby.

'It's a boo-fay, ya fanny. Christ, ah'm fae Onthank an' *ah'm* mair cultured than you!' exclaimed Joey.

'Magic. Ah'm sweatin' like a cunt in this coat, but ah' thought the big pockets would come in handy for collectin' scran. Want a pint?'

Joey and Bobby both nodded and laughed at Hamish's pre-planning. Hamish headed towards the bar.

The first hour passed without real incident. It had taken the three of them almost half an hour to put the complicated tangle of cables together but, once achieved, the sound and light worked first time – and to a highly impressive volume. It had somewhat concerned Joey that four plugs were all going into one basic little adaptor, but since everything seemed to be operational, he put that concern to the back of his mind.

Most of the parties that Bobby had been to started slowly. People progressively drifted in up to about half-past nine, and the pattern held true for Lizzie King's eighteenth-birthday party. It allowed the novice DJs time to get to grips with the fading of one record into another; to master the co-ordination of the music's syncopation with the rope light and – although there were a few false starts – to get the cueing of each record lined up with the help of the headphones. Musically, Heatwave Disco's inaugural night on the wheels of steel was fairly mid tempo. Some middle-of-the-road soul via Luther Vandross, George Benson, Shalamar and the like, mixed with a few older records from Rod Stewart and Elton John. Nothing too challenging; simply background music to allow people to come in, say hello to the family, find a seat, get a drink and have a chat. No dancing. Not yet. Not usually until the cake's been cut and the vol-au-vents distributed.

The plan to wait until the night of the disco to establish *who* was best suited to be the vocalist for Lizzie King's party hadn't been a good one. Cometh the hour, *goeth* the man. Both Bobby and Joey passed the microphone to each other as if it was possessed.

'Scuse' me mate! Ye got anythin' fae the charts?' It was almost ten o'clock and Heatwave Disco had received it's first-ever request.

'Aye, mate. Nae bother,' said Joey, as Bobby bent down to look through the small black box of seven-inch singles that held the most up-to-date material. He picked up a black vinyl disc and put it straight onto the deck, lifting the needle over and cueing it up for its beginning. As the previous record faded, he pressed the button and faded up the volume control. Immediately Joey turned round and shot him a glance.

'Well … it's in the fuckin' charts, intit?' proclaimed Bobby.

'Aye, but fuckin' *Shakin Stevens*!' Joey was about to remind Bobby of the rules they'd made about playing rubbish, when Bobby grabbed his hand and turned him round to see the majority of the guests bouncing towards the wooden dancefloor.

'Nae accountin' for taste, eh Joey?' said Hamish, before draining another pint.

Over at the hostess's table on the other side of the dancefloor, Frank King's aggravation was escalating.

'Ah can take so much, but this …' Frank was complaining, but no-one seated around him was quite sure about what.

'Whit's he moanin' aboot noo, Mam?' groaned Lizzie.

'Ach … never mind him, Lizzie. He's had the jaggy bunnett since he got here. It's nice tae see auld Betty here, intit? Ah never thought she'd get oot wi' her legs,' said Anne. Deflecting attention away from the aggravating Frank was feeling like her sole function of the evening.

'Aye. She's milkin' it fur aw it's worth though. *"Get us a wee brandy, love … yer Aunty Betty's no as mobile as she used tae be."* The only thing mair static than her is her purse.'

Anne laughed. She was desperate for Lizzie to enjoy her night, but Anne had other news she needed to break to Lizzie, before she heard it from a less-sensitive source. Anne was now angry at herself for not getting it over with before they left the house.

'Ah'm gauny have tae get up. Go an' say somethin'.' Frank still seemed to be talking to himself.

'Dad, whit are ye talkin' aboot?' Lizzie's irritation at her father was becoming substantial.

Frank stood up. 'He's only been deid five year. Aw these bloody charlatans … it's a disgrace, so it is.' With that, Frank strode away in the direction of the Heatwave decks. Anne looked at Lizzie and both shrugged their shoulders.

'So, ye havin' a good time? Ye've got some decent presents here.' Anne picked up a bumper sachet of hair dye. '… And some pretty shite yins.'

'Ah'm a bit mair settled noo the DJ's turned up. Ah'm no gie'in him the full money though.' Lizzie folded her arms.

'No bad-lookin' though … the wan wi' the tie, ah mean,' said Anne.

'If ye like that type … then, ah suppose … mibbe.' Lizzie looked over. 'The other yin looks like a moron, though.' Lizzie paused. 'Whit's ma dad sayin' tae him?'

'Christ, who kens. He's got a bee up his arse aboot somethin' the night.' Anne breathed in deeply. She needed to tell Lizzie. On balance it was better coming from her now than from her erratic father. Anne looked down at the table. 'Mibbe ah shouldnae have telt him ah'm pregnant …' Anne couldn't look at Lizzie.

It seemed to take a while for the news to sink in, but Lizzie responded in typically feisty fashion.

'Holy fuck, Anne!' This was definitely not a 'Mam' moment for Lizzie. 'It's like Noah's Ark in that flat as it is.' Lizzie glared at her father as he remonstrated with the DJs across the hall.

'If only he was as good at job creation as he is at *pro*-creation …' Lizzie stood up.

'Jesus … ah think ah'm gauny be sick,' she declared, as she headed off in the direction of the toilets.

'Lizzie!' But Lizzie wasn't listening. 'Shite.' Anne put her head in her hands.

Aneka's 'Japanese Boy' segued awkwardly into the end of The Piranhas' 'Tom Hark' single. The dancing queens went mental again, and the fledgling DJs debated Frank King's earlier outburst. It allowed them to avoid dealing with the impending microphone conundrum.

'Thank fuck ye got rid ae Eddie fuckin' Cochran there. Whit a prick!' said Joey.

'Whit wis he sayin' tae ye at the beginning? Ah wisnae listenin'.' Bobby admitted.

'Some bollocks aboot Shakin' Stevens bein' total shite,' said Joey. 'Ah'm fuckin' *agreein'* wi' him an' he calls me "a cheeky wee cunt".'

'Ach, he's away noo. He'll no be back. It'll be fine.' Bobby turned to face Joey. Joey knew why.

'Ah canny dae it. Ah'm fuckin' shitin' it,' said Bobby

'Fuckin' hell, Boab. This was aw your idea. An' it's fuckin' mobbed in here. Ah canny dae it either.'

This to-and-fro went on for a while before Bobby, and then Joey looked at Hamish.

'Naw,' he laughed, and then stopped when he realised they were serious. '*Naw*! Nae fuckin' way, man. Are you two radio rental?'

'C'mon Hammy ... there's another pint in it for ye!' Bobby knew the time was coming when somebody would *have* to speak – if for no other reason than to call for order while the cake was cut.

'Yer havin' a fuckin' laugh, the two ae ye'se,' protested Hamish.

Lizzie King came over. Her mood clearly hadn't improved.

'Can ye play a dedication for ma Mam? Squeeze. 'Up The Junction'? Have ye got it?'

'Eh, aye. I'll put it on next, eh?' said Bobby. He looked at this stern faced vision of loveliness, with her blonde hair all backcombed and *Silvikrinned* in place. *Like Farah Fawcett-Majors, but with darker roots*, he thought to himself. Deep-red lipstick, smudged from kissing people and being kissed. Dark, vibrant eye-shadow and thick eyeliner. Heavy blusher. Bobby had had a few pints, it was true, but he definitely fancied her.

'Make sure ye say that it's fae me?' With that, she turned sharply and walked back, impressive arse in those taut jeans, legwarmers down to her white high heels, green string vest-top over tight white T-shirt. Bobby was mesmerised.

'Fuck, Boab. Fuckin' wake up!' said Joey. 'Somebody needs tae fuckin' speak over this next record. Hammy, you'll need tae dae it. You've had more tae drink than us.'

Hamish drew several deep breaths between gritted teeth. 'Aw for fuck's sake. Ah'm only sayin' one line. This is gonnae cost ye more than a pint, ya pair ae fuckin' bampots. Gies it!' Hamish moved to the side of the lighting cabinet and took the microphone from Joey.

'Whit's her name again?' Hamish groaned.

'It's Lizzie. Right, ye ready? Ah'm fading it down.' Joey nodded to Hamish and for a brief time – although it seemed like an age – there was comparative silence. Only Hamish's hasty, anxious words – but expressed without the required amplification. Joey pushed the fader up and the familiar drum-pattern start of 'Up The Junction' had the momentarily bemused dancers going again. Lizzie King looked over expectantly.

'Ye need tae fuckin' switch it on,' said Bobby. 'Right. Ye ready *this* time?'

Hamish looked at the mic. There was a small switch halfway up its length. He pressed it. A bang. A blue flash. A high-pitched shriek.

And then the still unamplified but now perfectly audible, 'Ah! *Ya fuckin' bastart hoor, ye!*'

The flash had thrown Hamish backwards and he'd fallen against a table, knocking it – and the drinks it was supporting – onto the dancefloor. The mic itself had been projected high into the air and had come down on top of a speaker, knocking over Hamish's pint of lager, spraying the contents into the larger of the two record boxes. Amazingly, Squeeze played on, even if the dancers were now motionless. Bobby quickly pulled another record randomly from the small box and stuck it on just in time.

'*There's an old piano and they play it hot behind the green door …*'

18TH FEBRUARY 1982: 2:36AM

In the hour since Bobby had called his dad, there had been no vehicles travelling up the one-way street towards the end where the Sandriane was located. It was now pretty clear that Barry Baird wouldn't be returning, and, in the final act before locking up, Bobby had been granted access to the office phone. They were helpless.

There was too much stuff to carry and they were miles away from anywhere they could've carried it to. Bobby had regretted not asking if they could've left the gear and returned for it the next day. But, in the mêlée of the party's culmination, he hadn't been thinking straight.

It had been an expensive night: the unforeseen costs of the Barry Baird twenty quid, added to a fiver to Hamish May for a taxi to A&E, on top of Lizzie's deductions.

'If ye think ah'm payin' ye full whack for *that*! Ye were late! Ye only had about three fuckin' records ... an' ah had tae fuckin' sing "Happy Birthday" tae maself cos' ye'd nae bastardin' microphone!'

Bobby had to concede that all of the above was true, although there were slightly more than three records. Hamish May's pint spill had rendered many of the better ones unusable and – since Shaky had gone down so well earlier – Bobby had elected to rotate a few of the more popular ones from the same genre.

'Jesus Christ, Boab. Darts, Showaddywaddy and that hopeless Welsh cunt! It was like a fuckin' rockabilly convention at one point.' Joey's moaning had eventually made both of them laugh, as they sat out in the street, minding the junk, like Steptoe & Son waiting for their horse and cart.

'Ah didnae want tae laugh at the time, but did ye see that sausage roll hittin' Hammy right in the coupon when ah wis helpin' him out tae the taxi?'

'Naw,' replied Joey, trying to conceal his laughter. 'Ah wis gettin' hassled by that lassie's faither. Tellin' me tae stop playin' Shakin' Stevens because it's an affront tae Elvis.' Bobby was now bent over, convulsing with laughter. '"*Elvis is deid*" ah says tae him. "Right. Fuckin' outside ... *now*!" he shouts at me!'

Tears are rolling down Bobby Cassidy's face. 'Fuck sake. Whit a night! Whit was the damage then?'

'Ah reckon a hundred and ten,' said Bobby wiping his face. 'Possibly more if ah have tae gie this new driver guy cash tonight.'

'Fuckin' hell, Boab. No really worth it, is it?' Joey had already resigned himself to this being Heatwave's one and only outing.

'Ye jokin'? Ah thought it was brilliant!'

Joey turned round to face his friend, with a look of astonishment on his face.

'See that bit where they were aw' up dancin' and singin' tae "One Step Beyond"?' Bobby paused. ' … Or "Do The Hucklebuck"?' He could see the look on Joey's face slowly changing. ' … Or even the slow dances?'

Joey had to concede that these few moments were actually quite good. He'd felt the power a DJ has over a crowd at those times. He'd sensed the anticipation people had about what record might come next – and the fleeting feeling of the music building an atmosphere. He'd also seen the effect of the slow songs at the end and, in particular, the reaction to 'Tracks of My Tears', which he had picked out to be the last song before they had even left Bobby's house. It must have had a calming effect on Lizzie King, too, as there she was, on her eighteenth birthday, conciliatory tongue down Bobby Cassidy's throat as part of a deal struck whereby she'd pay him only £10. All those other *Brylcreemed* heads resting drunkenly on shoulder pads – wide enough to support a team of abseilers. The music had them entranced. They were like the ponderous and desperate participants in *They Shoot Horses, Don't They?*, but due to the classic soundtrack, it was the evening's undisputed highlight.

Maybe Bobby was right. Maybe this would be a good laugh … eventually. And just as Joey Miller and Bobby Cassidy talked themselves into giving it another go, headlights illuminated the bottom of John Finnie Street. Salvation had arrived in the distinctive form of Jimmy Stevenson: newly out of prison and one of the more than three million unemployed, but, tonight, riding to the rescue in a beige 1972 Volkswagen Campervan.

Llew Gardner, journalist for Thames TV

'Prime Minister, can I ask you something? Will we ever return to full employment, Prime Minister? What was known as full employment?'

Mrs Margaret Thatcher, the Prime Minister

'I don't know. It depends on your definition of full employment.'

6

THE THREE BEFORE EIGHT

TEN MONTHS EARLIER ...

Jimmy Stevenson was there on the night Bobby Cassidy's dreams of being a DJ were born.

Having had his musical interest ignited by punk, Bobby found a true home in the Mod revival of the late '70s. For Bobby – who also harboured a secret desire to be Rod Stewart – punk rock had always had that short-burning fuse feel about it. A clearing of the old, safe, boring prog-rock decks for something new, fresh and accessible. Bobby eventually discovered the latter of these attributes in The Jam. He developed an interest in the clothes, in the Mod iconography, in Quadrophenia; and in that whole sense of belonging – which he shared with Joey Miller and thousands of others across Britain. It all began with *All Mod Cons*, Bobby's favourite LP. Bobby and Joey knew of many other friends who were similarly affected. A small local scene was developing. It was at odds with the pub-rock culture populated by Ayrshire groups like Penetration and the biker fans that followed them. They were generally older, definitely smellier and wouldn't be featuring as a target demographic for any aspiring hairdressers.

Bobby recalled his dad once telling Gary – who preferred bands like Focus and Black Sabbath – that to become part of a biker gang you had to shit in your pants and not change them for a week. He delivered this assertion with an authority that persuaded Bobby his dad had once tried, but probably given up around day five. It wasn't for Bobby, though, and the Kilmarnock Mods with their scooter club became his spiritual home. The re-emergence of scooters, parkas and target T-shirts began with Paul Weller and his obsession with the look and sound of the Small Faces – and the power and energy of older records like The Who's 'My Generation'. It made everyone want to be in a gang, and to go to the weekly all-nighter at Wigan Casino.

Wigan Casino was a *Mecca* for young fledgling Mods intent on gorging themselves on influences from before they were born. Although the Kilmarnock Mods had heard of other venues, like the Blackpool Highland Rooms, the Casino was where they all wanted to be. By 1981, its peak years were well behind it, but it was still accepted as the primary venue for Northern Soul music. It was open all night – closing just after eight a.m. – and, most importantly for kids like Bobby and Joey, sixteen-year-olds could get in, as the club was alcohol-free.

When the plans to go were finally put in place and a date set, Joey pulled out. He'd been having a tough time at home and his parents were on the verge of splitting up. Bobby went with around twelve other friends.

Bobby's preconceptions of Wigan were from George Orwell's book *The Road to Wigan Pier*, which was a set text for his English O-level class. Wigan itself was nothing like the Wigan Bobby had anticipated from Orwell's text. It was very similar to the Kilmarnock of the early '80s that they'd left behind. Dull, grey concrete and monotonous low-rise red brick dominated and intimidated more expressive buildings from an earlier age. The small Northern towns that they stopped at or passed by on the road to Wigan seemed to share these features. They had a *grime* that seemed somehow intoxicating to Bobby. Not in a glamorous way, certainly, but this journey gave birth to his passion for the North of England and its back catalogue of literary and artistic achievements.

The journey down was pretty uneventful. Thirteen people in a *hippyish* van, owned and driven by Jimmy Stevenson, an old friend of his dad, Harry. Jimmy was five foot four; in his mid-fifties, he looked a decade older. He appeared to be in some degree of proportion from the rear, but from side and front he looked pregnant. A mass of belly cantilevered precariously over the belt of his flared Farah slacks. The flares themselves partially concealed brown shoes that resembled the meat pasties sold in Greggs bakery. He had a penchant for sleeveless cardigans, and the green one he was wearing was fighting a technicolor battle with a blue-and-purple checked shirt at which countless Scotsport presenters would've turned up their noses. His most defining characteristic was his hair – part Charlton sweep-over, part Oliver Cromwell bell-shaped bob. A rusty, ginger-coloured moustache sat below beady eyes and above a large mouth from which the coarsest Ayrshire dialect emanated.

Jimmy's cramped van left Kilmarnock just after seven at night, aiming to get to the casino before midnight. Jimmy acceded to the demands of his short-term employers and permitted the tapes of Mod classics to soundtrack the journey. In the back, Tennent's lager, Bacardi and speed were concealed in various bags, and their consumption was slow to begin with, gradually increasing towards the border and becoming voracious as they approached Wigan. Consequently, Bobby was absolutely buzzing when the group reached the old Empress Ballroom building. Jimmy parked the van in an open yard next to the entrance to a multi-storey concrete monstrosity. He planned to sleep while the Kilmarnock Mods were in the casino, driving back the next morning. The group approached the queues stretching around the corner of Compton Street, and it was around forty-five minutes before Bobby actually got into the building. The bouncers at the door were operating a confusing policy of letting three in and turning the fourth away.

Bobby couldn't determine any rhyme or reason for this quota, and there was certainly no explanation being offered to the vanquished. The Ayrshire contingent faired reasonably well out of this lottery, and only two were refused. Bobby saw them inside later and assumed they had gone back to the end of the queue, praying that the random sequencing would be kind to them. Once in, most of the herd around Bobby climbed the two flights of stairs to enter at the balcony level. From here, Bobby got his first glimpse of the sheer scale of the hall. As a structure, the casino was clearly on its last legs, but the free-spanning curved roof over the old ballroom, containing the biggest and bounciest dancefloor he'd ever seen, was incredible.

At the beginning of the night, the vibe was relatively loose, and the musical choices of legendary DJ Russ Winstanley created large open spaces in the main dancefloor. The lights were generally non-existent and the interior could only really be described as seedy. Bobby briefly wondered whether all that anticipatory excitement had been worth it. But, following the first hour, the atmosphere ramped up dramatically. The music got louder and faster. The energy palpably increased. It was dark – and getting darker. The very few lights were dimmed. The condensation level was astounding, but it was the music and the dancing that marked Bobby in a way he'd never, ever forget. This was the origin of the dream. Once it got going, Winstanley had complete control of the dancers via the music he was playing. He was like a puppeteer high up on the stage, operating everybody by strings.

Bobby watched rapt, as skinny guys in vests and thirty-inch flares danced alone, constantly spinning and kicking Bruce Lee's kung fu moves to music rich in soulful grooves. Bobby had taken a few pills in the van on the way down but he began to feel that he didn't need them. It was euphoric. The music seemed to ferment during the evening, becoming richer, stronger and louder as night became morning. There was so much great stuff, Bobby later told Joey, that only a few songs really stood out. Mary Love's 'You Turned My Bitter into Sweet' had Bobby up dancing with a pleat-skirted girl from Bolton called Norma. Dobie Gray's 'Out on the Floor' had him spiralling away on his own, but inconspicuously, for fear of drawing too much attention. He heard the original Gloria Jones recording of 'Tainted Love' (which would become one of the first records bought by Bobby as a DJ, the following year, when re-recorded by Soft Cell). The famous '3 before 8' were brilliant, simply because devotees knew they were coming.

When Bobby left the old, red-brick cinema as the sunlight was beginning to generate some heat, his white Fred Perry shirt was soaked in sweat, and his Levi's seemed to be a much deeper blue than when he had gone in. He was surrounded in a fog of his own steam. He felt exhilarated. The amphetamines would still be having their effect, but the spirit of the music was the main reason for his exaltation. The group had fragmented just after they had all got in and he had left on his own. Without the pressure of buying rounds of drinks, everyone just split to get off on the vibe.

Heading back to the car park, Bobby felt like there was a glow around him – like the people in the *Ready Brek* advert. He was smiling incessantly – like the Joker. As he approached the rustic-toned van, Bobby caught sight of two young coppers taking interest in what had apparently been a bit of bother. The van's side door was slid open and a clearly dazed Jimmy Stevenson sat on its second step. One copper circled the vehicle tentatively, as if it contained a suspect device that might go off any minute. The other stood stock-still in front of Jimmy, attempting to take notes in his small black book.

'Whit's goin' on, Jim?' enquired Bobby; a logical question given that the driver had clearly been in a fight of some sort. It was also equally clear that he'd lost.

'Git tha'sen lost, son,' offered the policeman with the notebook. Bobby wasn't sure what had just been said to him. It sounded like a foreign language but he understood he was being directed towards a café where two of his group had already been sent. He found them in there.

'Where's everybody else?' he asked.

'Fuck knows. Probably still in there,' offered Tam Wood.

'Whit's goin' on wi' oor driver?' Bobby asked.

'Nae idea, bud,' said Tam. 'We came oot an' saw wan polis batterin' him wi' a truncheon. The other yin was kickin' him up the arse.'

Bobby bought himself a Coke and an egg roll. He finished his breakfast quickly and they all went back to the van. The scene was generally as they'd left it, but Jimmy was now on his feet and being asked to accompany the policemen to the local station. The rest of their group still hadn't returned, but the three young Mods were asked to wait in the van, having been informed that their driver would be brought back later.

'Art-or-reet?' said the note-taking policeman, as the distressed Jimmy cracked his head off the edge of the Vauxhall Astra with its jam-sandwich markings. Bobby watched in open-mouthed shock as Jimmy started crying.

'If tha dunt ztop cryin' thall ger another crak in a minit!' said the other policeman, admitting to those listening that *they* had indeed been responsible for an earlier 'crack'.

Four hours later, Jimmy was returned to his van and the reassembled tour party made their way home.

When Bobby recounted the tale to Joey, he couldn't be sure anyone who travelled to Wigan that weekend knew exactly what happened in the yard next to the multi-storey during the night. But Jimmy returned to Lancashire four months later, and stayed on for a further four as a reluctant guest of Her Majesty. He'd been sentenced to a year, reduced to six months and released two months early for good behaviour.

And now here he was, ten months after first meeting Bobby Cassidy, off the dole and in a new job as Heatwave Disco's regular driver. Things were looking up, and not just for Jimmy.

7

THE ROLLED-UP TROUSER-LEG PRESERVATION SOCIETY

20TH FEBRUARY 1982: 1:15PM

'The food was fuckin' magic.'

'Aye. He's no wrong, boss! Wee cheesy baws, an' white breid sang-windgies … wi' the crusts cut off! Real posh, man,' enthused Des Brick, backing up the more general summary from his smaller colleague, Wullie the Painter.

'Soft … nothin' burnt. Ah had loadsae it,' added Wullie.

'Flaky pastry on the sausage rolls tae. Magic.' Des Brick gazed into space momentarily, before catching Fat Franny's frustrated expression. He turned to face Wullie. 'Did ye see the way the pastry exploded when it hit that cunt on the face?'

'Aye. Nearly pished maself laughin,' said the painter. 'Great fuckin' throw, Des. Brilliant aimin,' he added, clapping his hands together. 'Shame aboot the sausage roll though. That was the last yin.'

'Ah don't gie a flyin' fuck about the grub! Ah'm no the Gallopin' fuckin' Gourmet!'

Fat Franny stood up suddenly, knocking over the bar stool that had been holding him. Des and Wullie snapped to attention.

'Ah want tae ken whit happened! Should ah be worried?'

'Naw boss,' said Des. 'They were fuckin' hopeless. Nane ae the

97

pricks spoke a word aw night, an' wan ae them fuckin' electrocuted hisself. It was the best laugh ah've had since *Jim Davidson* at the Gaiety last year.'

'Nae need to bother about they clowns again, boss,' offered Wullie.

'Aye. We'll see,' said Fat Franny, walking behind the bar and through to the office. *His* office.

'Don't think he's pleased,' said Wullie.

'Ah ken ... though ah don't fuckin' ken why.' Des's tone was one of resigned annoyance. He and Wullie had done what they were told, yet still the Fatman was irritated. And as for any gratitude, forget it.

Des and Wullie walked through to the front of the Portman Hotel. It was their regular haunt and had become the base for Fat Franny's operations. He often had his entourage travel up to the 'Ponderosie' – his Onthank home, named after Rose, his mum – but since she had become a bit forgetful and embarrassing of late, he'd started spending more time in the Portman. In his eyes he part-owned this establishment with Mickey Martin, who was known as 'Doc' to virtually everyone apart from his wife, Ella. Fat Franny had won a poker game against Mickey Martin, who had put up sizeable IOUs and had since avoiding paying them. Normally that would have resulted in a few good kickings, but Mickey Martin was the bigger fish.

Fat Franny was local; Mickey Martin was *regional*. Fat Franny was outranked, so the perception of ownership of this rundown pub on the outskirts of the town would have to do for now. He'd taken over the small cupboard and turned it into his office. He'd also changed its name by adding the word 'Hotel', even though there were no bedrooms. Mickey Martin picked up his cut once a month, but otherwise had nothing to do with this loss leader. It was an arrangement that seemed to suit both men just fine.

In the room with the pool table, Wullie the Painter sat at the round table near the door. Des went behind the bar and poured both of them a pint of lager. When he brought them back, Wullie was shaking his head at a newspaper headline.

'Fuckin' unemployment numbers, Jesus Christ,' he sighed.

'Difference does it make tae you, anyway?' Des challenged his colleague. 'It's no as if yer National Insurance subs are oan the line, is it? Plus, skint gadgies are good for business. If naebody's goat a job, it'll no stop them fae smokin' or drinkin' or buyin' their weans shit they cannae afford. That's where we come in. We're providin' a public service here. Don't fuckin' knock it, mate.'

'Jeezo, you sound like him!' Wullie gestured over his shoulder then immediately wished he hadn't said it – Hobnail had just walked into the lounge.

'Dinnae be growin' a conscience noo, William. There's nae room for it in oor line ae work,' said Des.

'It's just that everythin's that fuckin' depressin'. That's why ...' Wullie squinted at the newsprint, '... wee Sophie fae Essex should be oan the front page an' no the third, eh H?' Wullie winked at Hobnail, who remained stoney-faced. Wullie tutted.

'Sticking the news three-quarters ae the way through the paper ... efter the telly an' fuckin' Darlinda, would pit smiles oan punters faces again. Page three oan page wan, an' then eight pages ae fitba. That should be the new order tae keep bampots fae gettin' oot their pram an' rioting aboot the auld milk snatcher ...'

Wullie's theory was well thought through, and Des signalled his approval with a nod of his head.

'Ah should be her special advisor,' continued the Painter. 'I'd start by advisin' her tae dump the blue, an' wear green an' white hoops, mind ...'

Des and Wullie both laughed at this. Hobnail predictably didn't. He walked away from both of them and stared blankly through the vertical blinds to the open fields beyond.

Wullie leaned in and whispered, 'Whit's his problem? Miserable bastart. Ah' ken ah'm new tae the *inner* circle but ah' cannae understand why he's the number two, an' no you.'

'*He* didnae go tae Our Lady of Mount Carmel Primary ... 'nuff said ...' said Des, as Wullie shook his head. 'Haud up ...' warned Des, as Fat Franny wandered back into the room. 'Rack 'em up, Painterman,' cried Des, as he headed off to the Gents.

Wullie organised the spots and stripes inside the wooden triangle and then selected his cue.

Wullie the Painter – so-called not because of his trade, but because he had once painted an ex-girlfriend's house bright red in the middle of the night, while she and one of Wullie's former friends slept inside – and Des had been mates for a long time. They performed 'security' roles for Fat Franny and worked as bouncers at a number of diverse local establishments with which the Fatman had connections. They had originally been recruited by Des's brother-in-law, Bob 'Hobnail' Dale. The house-painting had actually been Hobnail's idea, and at six-foot-five to Wullie's five-foot-eight, he was useful in getting to those difficult-to-reach bits under the eaves. Wullie had recently been promoted by the Fatman and, although Hobnail was furious about it, he had typically kept his emotions hidden.

Senga – Des's viperish sister and Hobnail's wife – had once gone out with Wullie Blair, before he was 'the Painter'. It still made for uncomfortable encounters when they were together, so Hobnail was under very strict instructions – danger of death, in fact – to keep work and private life totally separate. As a consequence, Des and Senga rarely saw each other nowadays, and had long since given up on the exchange of birthday greetings or Christmas presents. For as long as anyone could remember, Hobnail always had the resigned look of a dead man walking. That his unfortunate vocals sounded as upbeat as the doleful sounding of the Lutine Bell only reinforced the sense of foreboding for anyone in his presence. He wasn't especially good company as a result, and therefore it wasn't difficult to keep Senga away from the Fat Franny side of his life. No-one wanted to spend any time with them.

From Senga's perspective, the principal beneficiary of this stand-off was Grant, their seventeen-year-old son. She partly understood the pressures her husband would have been under to take Grant into Fat Franny's empire. With no children of his own, and a paranoia about the involvement – regardless of how peripheral – of 'outsiders', Grant would have been an obvious candidate for succession planning for the *strong-arm* wing of the business. The boy was tall, muscular and – even at seventeen – possessed of a self-confidence that Fat Franny could have utilised very effectively. But he knew of the underlying tension between Wullie the Painter and Hobnail, and had always previously backed away from any suggestion of a 'bring-your-child-to-work-day' for his *consiglieri*.

Grant was a good-looking boy. He was a fan of the burgeoning New Romantic scene and, although his current fad of wearing eyeliner was a frequent source of conflict with his traditionalist father – 'Realth men don'th wear mek-ūp, ya poofty wee cunth!' – no-one could deny his attractiveness. Senga was suitably proud of her eldest child. Hobnail looked like Frankenstein, and she knew she was no oil painting herself. She hoped his looks might lead Grant somewhere different; towards a different type of future than the one she and her husband – and virtually everyone else she knew – had settled for. None of the people with whom she was friends at school had lives that had turned out the way that they'd dreamed, or even hoped, back then. Almost all of her school friends still lived within a two-mile radius of where they were born. Senga considered herself to be a strong, independent woman, but she hadn't been able to escape the shackles of a stereotypical working-class, Ayrshire environment, with all its small-town mentalities, and actually see something of the world.

Senga was a lover of classical music and yearned to visit Austria and see the New Year's Day concert by the Vienna Philharmonic Orchestra. Hobnail knew nothing of this. In fact, she had admitted it to no-one, for fear of ridicule. It was her own private secret, and had been ever since, late one night, almost ten years ago, she had heard this wondrous sound drifting through the vaulted structures of the Dick Institute, where she worked as a cleaner. Since that time she had booked out almost all of the classical music cassettes in the library, listening to them with headphones during her breaks. It was her dream. Kilmarnock wouldn't take it from her, and she was determined its restrictive boundaries wouldn't kill Grant's future, either.

'It's from Gary,' shouted Hettie excitedly.

'Whit does it say, hen? Is he fine? Is he a'right?' Ethel had called Hettie to come and open a letter she had *hoped* would be from her son, because she couldn't find her glasses.

'Mum, they're hangin' around your neck!' said a frustrated Hettie, before ripping the envelope open. Bobby had bought Ethel the string device with its loops for the legs of the frame. His mum's absent-mindedness was becoming more and more of a concern to all of them, although they all demonstrated that concern in different ways.

'C'mon, hen. Whit's he sayin'?' said Ethel, treating the discovery of the glasses like evidence planted at the scene of a crime – designed to demonstrate her guilt beyond a shadow of a doubt.

'He's fine mum. There's no much here, though. Remember he said the letters would be brief cos' they might get censored?' Hettie quickly scanned the brief lines to the bottom of the second page. She figured her *own* censorship might have to be utilised. Happily, there was good news. 'Gary's not goin' tae Belfast, Mum. He thinks they might have to go to Wales.'

'Wales?' exclaimed Ethel. 'Who are *they* at war wi'?'

'No, mum … it's a trainin' exercise. But he'll be there for a while, he thinks. He's no very pleased aboot that.'

'Well *ah'm* happy,' said Ethel, smiling. 'Ah'd never have slept if he'd ended up at Belfast wi' aw they bombs goin' off.' Truth was, she barely slept anyway. Her dependence on prescription drugs –

required to help her function *at all* – had sharply increased when Gary initially left home heading south.

'He says *hello* tae everybody, and passes on his love tae.' Ethel could see Hettie's eyes light up as she read on. ' ... An' he's wi' a lassie. He told me about her last time he was up. Debbie's her name. She seems really nice.' Hettie looked up, as Ethel dabbed a tear away with her hankie. 'Hey, c'mon Mum ... he seems happy. Probably for the first time in a while, tae.' Hettie went over and gave her mother a cuddle. 'Would ye rather he was here, coming in drunk every night an' fightin' wi Dad aw the time?'

Ethel murmured, but didn't really answer. She simply got up from her seat, kissed her daughter on the cheek and went upstairs to lie down.

Hettie listened to her mother climb the stairs. The slow, ponderous creaking made her sad. Hettie's mum wasn't an old woman, but she seemed to move as if carrying a massive weight on her back.

Ethel sat on the edge of her bed. She looked mournfully at the three photographs on the dressing table and then at her own face reflected in the three-panelled mirror above them. She had changed so much in the last decade. She seemed to be ageing at a rate twice that of the other members of her family. Ethel was the only Catholic in the house but, unlike many who draw strength from their faith in difficult and troubled times, Ethel knew it was her unassailable guilt over sins past that had turned her into the shell that now looked back at her. She picked up her rosary beads and lay down, as yet more tears formed.

10TH MARCH 1982: 9:15PM.

It had been almost three weeks since the Sandriane. Bobby had seen Lizzie King three times since then, and, despite her initial impressions, they were now getting on well. Twice he'd met her coming out of the Johnnie Walker bottling plant gates where she had recently started working. In Thatcher's Britain, despite the mind-numbing boredom of this lowly paid job, it was already depressingly apparent to Lizzie that she was one of the lucky ones.

Hamish May still had the grubby bandage on his blackened and burnt hand. He didn't really need it now, but had enjoyed telling the story; and elaborating on its re-telling.

Joey had actually spent a lot of the time practising with the decks on his own in Bobby's room. He wasn't going to look like an idiot again and had uncharacteristically taken the bull by the horns regarding the microphone responsibility. That was going to be Bobby's job, Joey had decided. After all, it was Bobby's idea and Harry's money that was funding it. Joey had decided he would be happy just getting paid enough cash to buy records and a few pints each night they were out. That was enough for him.

Amazingly, Heatwave Disco had secured four new bookings. They'd also successfully navigated another gig. At the beginning of February, Heatwave was hired by one of the leading lights of the local Mod scene, Stevie Devlin. The circumstances were unusual, but the purpose of the party was a joint celebration of Stevie's twentieth birthday and him leaving his job. Although he didn't so much *leave it* as have it taken away from him.

A new single from The Jam was an event for the Kilmarnock Mods. Bobby, Joey and Stevie were waiting outside a shop in Kilmarnock to buy the record on the last day of January, with around 200 fellow loyalists. On the same day the tickets were released for a gig just up the road at Irvine's Magnum Centre. They had all been queueing since before five a.m. on that particular late-winter's morning and they weren't anywhere near the front of the line. Joey knew Stevie, not especially well, but enough to strike up a conversation. Stevie was going straight to work, which explained his smart suit. Bobby – having been introduced to a potential new customer – talked about his developing plans for a mobile disco unit. Stevie noted his name and phone number and said he'd think about it for a party he was considering.

As the snaking line for the tickets and the new 'Town Called Malice' record began to grow down past the Cross, someone near the front noticed large plumes of acrid, dark-grey smoke coming from behind the roofs of the buildings opposite. Bambers, the retail establishment where Joey – and most of the other Mods – purchased Fred Perrys, Harrington jackets and sta-press trousers, was on fire. Stevie Devlin was faced with the terrible dilemma of staying put and holding his place midway up the line, or leaving and running down to the public telephones at the Cross to alert the Fire Brigade in the hope that they might save his new place of employment. Understandably – to Joey at least – he stayed and held. Bambers perished. For Stevie, the decision was validated by the flawed logic that there would always be other jobs. Two days before the Sandriane, Stevie Devlin stayed true to his word and called Bobby Cassidy's number, leaving a message with his dad. It took four days for Bobby to call him back; the financial pain of the Sandriane gig meant lessons had to be learned, but it was actually Lizzie who persuaded him to call back and accept – just a few nights after her party.

Lizzie had been invited to a house party not far from where she lived. She had phoned the morning after her party to make sure Bobby had made it home, having suffered a pang of guilt at seeing him and Joey out in the street. The phone call lasted an hour, due in the main to Lizzie's lamenting over her father's latest error of judgement. But Lizzie's domestic chaos hadn't put Bobby off and arrangements had been made to meet later in the week. When they arrived, sixty or so teenage kids were crammed into Lorraine Wales's mum's semi-detached, three-bedroom council house, where music was blaring to a level that could've been heard on the moon. Records were strewn around an impressive hi-fi system, but Bobby immediately noted that no-one was *piloting* the equipment. He assumed control.

Most of the people were either drunk or stoned, and Lorraine was nowhere to be seen. Bobby was downstairs and it didn't take long for him to appreciate that parties might just be the perfect occasion to nick other people's records. During the course of the evening, he slowly but carefully stashed a clutch of 45s under a rhododendron bush in the back garden. He covered this by telling Lizzie that he had an embarrassing urine infection; since the upstairs toilet seemed to be permanently occupied, he figured it would be understandable to go out and regularly utilise the cover of the bushes. He walked Lizzie home before midnight, and then returned to recover the stash. Rare Joy Division singles, Lambrettas picture discs, Wire's *154* LP, a signed Secret Affair 'My World' single and 'Maybe Tomorrow' by The Chords were notables in an impressive haul.

These records were highlights of the Stevie Devlin evening. Heatwave was, to a large extent, preaching to the converted that night, and it was much more in line with what Joey believed they should be doing. A few of Stevie's mates had brought their own Stax and Northern Soul singles and the Foxbar Hotel's acoustics made them sound fantastic. The vibe had even prompted Bobby to pick up the microphone for the first time, and, although his pronouncements weren't revolutionary or profound – or even especially regular – he was at least making them.

Of the new bookings, one stood out; mainly for the fact that Bobby and Joey wouldn't be getting paid for it. It was to be a favour to Harry. The venue was the Masonic Club where Harry was a member, and the function was for one of his friends – to celebrate his retirement from his job as a hospital porter.

'Yer aye bloody askin' me about the Masons an' whit goes on … here's yer chance tae find out,' said Harry, noting Bobby's less-than-en-thusiastic reaction. 'Plus, ye owe me here after the cash ah've gied ye.'

Bobby couldn't argue with that point. Harry had used some of his compensation money from the accident to buy the decks from Hairy Doug. He'd also funded the purchase of speakers from a local Mod band, The Vespas. There was also money for lights. Following a second trip to Hairy Doug's store, Bobby had returned with some coils of what could only be described as coloured strips of spaghetti. The spaghetti worked like a 'blacklight'. When strobing effects were applied to them, they supposedly shone like the Northern Lights. In truth, they were completely ineffectual, but Bobby's open-mouthed gaping when he informed him for the umpteenth time, 'Now this *really* is the latest thing from the States', must've convinced Hairy Doug that Bobby was well and truly on the hook. For lighting, the Hairy One's prices were as hefty as him.

'Sixty quid for *this*,' said Harry. 'I gave you that money for lights. Whit bloody use is *this* tae man or beast? Where did you go? Tam Shepherd's?'

Harry's assessment of the cost of ten feet of the absolutely latest thing from the States might have been predicted. Equally so was the return journey to the farm with more of the janitor's wages, in order to purchase some *real* lights. Hairy Doug had a strict 'no-returns' policy so Bobby was stuck with the fluorescent pasta. Joey felt the only thing to do with it was cut it into small bits and staple them to a black backboard to spell out the new name of the enterprise. Given this backdrop – and appreciating the grief Ethel gave Harry for having spent the *double-glazing* money on a 'big bloody record-player' – Bobby felt there was no way he could really say no to his dad. He told Joey they'd just have to roll up their trouser-legs and get on with it.

'A group of Argentines have landed at the British colony of the Falkland Islands in the south Atlantic and planted their nation's flag.'
19th March 1982, BBC Six O'Clock News

22ND MARCH 1982: 3:23PM

Don McAllister was a Mason. It was pretty much taken for granted that being in the police force in Scotland was synonymous with membership of the Fraternity. And, to have reached Don McAllister's exalted level at only forty-nine years of age could only have been possible with the Society's help. He didn't owe it *everything* though; after all, he was a Master of the Universe. So, as Detective Chief Superintendent Don McAllister looked out from his prime vantage point on the top floor of the new police station, over Kilmarnock's High Street and up John Finnie Street – the Procurator's Office to the right; the Sheriff Court to the left of him – he felt like Solomon and Pontius Pilate combined. He looked back around his enormous corner room; at the certificates and commendations on the wall, and at the numerous framed photographs of himself with various local and national dignitaries. And he smiled at the largest one in the middle; the one with the gilt frame on his desk featuring him – six foot five and pale freckled skin – and Mary, his wife of fifteen years.

Don loved the fact that almost everybody knew who he was. A senior policeman should have status in a town like Kilmarnock. He had cultivated that status like a Mafia boss in a Sicilian village. People who walked past the station looked up and waved in respect. Shopkeepers dropped produce off at his expansive house, built on a hillside near Dundonald. He never paid for drinks in bars and rarely paid for meals at the best Ayrshire restaurants. If there was an interview about local affairs to be given, the *Kilmarnock Standard* phoned Don before the Chief Executive of the Council. In return, Don kept the criminal element unseen and underground. This – according to Don – was exactly as it should be. After all, everybody has to make a living, even the bampots.

Mickey 'Doc' Martin was Don's *bampot-world* equivalent. They were a similar age, had almost the same initials, and he too had connections everywhere. His hand had never gone into his pocket to settle a tab for dinner, either. They were alike in so many ways. There was equilibrium – they each balanced the other. Don had remembered watching episodes of *Batman & Robin* in the '60s and, in particular, seeing the character of Harvey 'Two-Face' Dent. When he was faced with any kind of moral dilemma regarding

Mickey – and there had been more than a few over the years – he liked to imagine that they were essentially the same person; both had an angel and a devil on his shoulders, wrestling for his soul.

He mused about this now, simply because such a dilemma was lying on his desk in front of him.

Terry Connolly had been apprehended by Don's officers on the fourth level of the multi-storey car park, allegedly selling heroin from the boot of his car. Don suspected that there was no absolutely *conclusive* evidence for this, but the report in front of him did contain a confession statement that Connolly had signed. This was of current interest to Don, as Connolly owned the vaulted spaces under the car park; spaces in which the copper knew Mickey Martin had an interest. Connolly had previous convictions for assault and drug offences – and had served time in Barlinnie. This latest accusation, providing a conviction was secured, could potentially send Connolly back to jail for five years.

He had previously resisted offers to sell the undercroft space at the Foregate multi-storey. He didn't like Mickey Martin and there was bad blood between the two businessmen. Don McAllister couldn't understand why Connolly didn't take the money. After all, he wasn't using the space for anything productive. But now an opportunity had presented itself for Don to do what he did best – broker a deal that made everybody happy. In truth, Terry Connolly wouldn't be happy; just *happier* that the charge against him had been dropped. But Mickey Martin would get the space for a mega-nightclub complex at less than he'd originally offered and, having been instrumental in securing it for him, Police Detective Chief Superintendent Donald McAllister would get his usual ten per cent cut.

Everyone's a winner.

So, a phone call to the Fiscal's office and a wee walk round to the Planning Department and the Licensing Board, and this would turn into yet another successful day in the life of the local Sheriff.

'There's nae chance. She's out on her fuckin' erse after aw this.' Harry was standing at the bar of the Kilmarnock branch of the Masonic Club. He was talking to Jock Newton, barman and all-round club good-guy. Jock booked the parties, took the money and organised most of the events; rumour was that Mason was actually his middle name. In fact, like many of his fellow Masons, you wouldn't need to go to the trouble of dissecting him to find *I'm a Mason* written through him. His identity was writ large on his arms in permanent blood-blue ink along with the words 'God Save The Queen,' giving no doubt about who might ultimately defend Queen and Country.

'Aye, so everybody seems tae be sayin'. But this fuckin' Falklands thing might gie her a way oot,' sighed Jock.

'Ach ah'm no sure it'll even come tae anything, Jock,' said Harry. 'Ah mean, naebody even kens whit it's aw about anyway.'

'Ah widnae put it past her tae fuckin' turn this intae a war just tae deflect attention awa fae aw the shite that's goin' on here, mate.' Jock pulled the last of the five pints that Harry had ordered. 'Is your boy no thinkin' he might be sent?'

'Whit, Bobby? Him ower *there*?' Harry glanced over towards the stage where Bobby was helping Joey manhandle a Marshall speaker column into place.

'Naw … the other yin. The Guardsman.'

'Ah dunno, Jock. Tells me nothin' that yin.' Harry put down a fiver, told Jock to have a dram with the change and lifted the tray of drinks. His lack of digits on one hand meant using his forearm to support the tray and his full-fingered hand to steady it. As he did so, the crashing sounds of The Jam's 'Heatwave' – the disco's newly adopted theme tune – nearly caused him to drop the lot. He looked over and glared at Bobby, who turned it down and continued with a sound check of whispered one-two, one-twos.

The Masonic Hall was a strange venue, but the acoustics were surprisingly good. A small stage area was set at the one end and the general layout and proportions were amenable to creating a good atmosphere. The baffling array of representations of the Queen, members of her family, and the *Great Architect of the Universe* – whom Bobby referred to a few times during the evening as Grandmaster Flash – allied to the multitude of stonemasonry symbols and insignia from other lodges made the hall seem cluttered. Joey, who didn't know much about the secretive codes and was suspicious of the Order as a result, had to admit that there was a fascinating heraldic order to it all. Harry had always resisted his son's questions about the Masons – never answering them directly; obliquely saying that when he was old enough to join, he could find out if he chose to. This had always irritated Bobby. Gary fed this irritation by telling his brother that they were all old perverts who drank goat's blood because they figured it gave their droopy old penises a much-needed boost. And, furthermore, they were mainly coppers, so they could *fit up* anyone who blabbed to outsiders. Harry had heard the two of them talking on a few occasions and knew of Gary's tall tales.

Overall, the night itself was a bit of a stroll for Heatwave. There were no women present, which made the choice of a disco seem a bit odd; these middle-aged, working-class Ayrshire guys would rather face a firing squad than get up and dance, particularly if the only available partners were other guys. Halfway through the night, Harry came over and reassured them that it was all going well. They had just wanted a bit of music, and the opportunity to request records by Frank Sinatra, Perry Como or Dean Martin, which the boys had with them thanks to Harry giving them access to much of his *own* record collection. Plus, Bobby had already detected the pride in his father's voice as he bragged to his mates that he was their manager and, more importantly, their financial backer.

So it had been an easy night. At almost exactly ten p.m., Harry approached the decks and asked for the microphone. He stood in front of the lightboxes and, with the lights flashing in sync with the sound of his voice, he addressed his fellow Masons.

'Lads, it's a big night for Chick McKenzie, an' on his behalf, cheers for turnin' out. Chick's been a lodge member for nigh on forty year … longer than he's been in his job, an' while he's leavin' the hospital, he'll always be a Mason.' Cheers and applause came back to Harry through the thick fog of cigarette smoke. 'Ah'm goin' tae let the boys go now, while we get sorted for the final ceremony, but while they're packin' up, Chick asked me tae say that there's a drink for aw ae ye'se at the bar.'

More cheers and louder than before, followed by a chorus of 'Wan Chick McKenzie, there's only wan Chick McKenzie … Wan Chick McKeeeennnzzziie …'

'Whit's goin' on, Dad?' asked a bemused Bobby.

'That's it. You'se can go up the road now. Did ah no tell ye we'd be by at ten?'

'Naw. Ye didnae. Jimmy's no due fur another two hours yet.' Bobby's tone was one of real annoyance. It was one thing to be playing the music of easy-listening crooners for three hours; it was another thing entirely to be hanging about in a cold back hall for another two – especially since Joey had already decided to leave him to it. Joey was going to head home since he wasn't getting paid for this one anyway.

By twenty past ten, Bobby was alone. The gear was packed and ready at the rear fire exits and he had been told to observe the rules of the club and stay in a back storage cupboard, out of the way of the 'ceremony'. There had been no point in using the club's phone to call Jimmy's house, as he'd already said he'd possibly be a bit late. He'd been hired to run a group of kids up to the Thin Lizzy gig at the Apollo in Glasgow and would pick Bobby up on the way back.

So Bobby hunkered down and prepared for a long and boring wait – which he'd make absolutely certain his Dad knew all about. He'd been in the cupboard for perhaps twenty-five minutes when a bizarre, repetitive sound made its way down the long winding corridor. Bobby listened intently; he couldn't identify its origin or discern its content, but it did appear to be a low, rumbling, monotonous chant. *What the fuck are these auld pricks on?* he thought. He waited and listened for another five minutes before tentatively edging his way closer to the source. The chant seemed to be 'One of us … one of us …' but delivered with such a lack of expression that it could have come from the cast of *Night of the Living Dead*. Bobby hesitated and then laughed to himself. There was absolutely no way Gary could've been right about this … *could he*?

He opened the door to the backstage area quietly, and climbed carefully over three drums, gingerly squeezing behind an upright piano. There was a glint of light coming from the tiny gap between the two drawn red-velvet stage curtains.

'One of us … one of us … one of us …'

Bobby couldn't make out what was going on. He'd have to get closer. He wished Joey had stayed. *They'd be pishin' themselves laughin' about this for years,* he thought.

'One of us … one of us …'

He got to the edge of the curtain and peered through the gap. Around thirty people, heads and upper bodies covered by white sheets – presumably Chick McKenzie's guests … and *Bobby's dad!* – were lined up in a circle. *This was too fuckin' much.* He was struggling to stop the laughter. They all had their left trouser-leg rolled up. *Joey'll never fuckin' believe this.*

'One of us … one of us … one of us …'

Bobby hadn't noticed it earlier, but there was someone lying under a sheet in the middle of the circle. He scanned the trouser legs quickly. Whoever it was, it wasn't somebody related to him. He could spot Harry's antiquated dark-brown cords a mile off.

'One of us … one of us …' *Boom*! The sound of a heavy bass drum, coming from the hall's front reception area, stopped everything; including Bobby's heart for a beat or two. The two heavy, red-panelled doors opened, and the drummer paced in slowly with a massive, marching drum on his chest, beating a slow pace with two large hairy drumsticks, one in each hand. Behind him was the clippety-clop of … yes, a goat.

Fuck me gently. Bobby's earlier mirth had evaporated as he caught sight of the shining machete in the goat-handler's grip. He couldn't believe this was all happening. How could they possibly keep this such a secret? Nobody he *knew* could keep secrets. Old Winker Watson had won the bingo jackpot at the Odeon and had given everyone there a twenty to keep schtum about it. He *still* woke up the next morning to find the house had been done over while he slept.

As Bobby deliberated anxiously over whether to declare his presence, the drummer had unhooked himself from the instrument and had gone behind the bar to pick up a cricket bat. Bobby noticed Jocky Wilson throwing a dart, *live* 500 miles away, in the box over the drummer's head. *Christ, they don't even turn the fuckin' telly off.*

'One of us … one of us …' The chanting started again as one by one; the guys lifted the backs of their sheets to reveal bare arses. The drummer worked his way round, thwacking each arse with the cricket bat.

'Thank you, Grandmaster,' said each consecutive owner of a reddened, smacked arse. As the drummer reached the arse belonging to Harry, Bobby stretched a bit further to see. In doing so he tripped over a Masonic marching pole and fell forward, grabbing at the edge of the curtain and falling headfirst through it. The batsman stopped in his tracks and all the other *ghosts* turned to look at Bobby. There was an eerie silence, which, for the prostrate interloper, seemed to last for ages. Even the goat was motionless. No one moved or uttered a sound until eventually …

'Fuck it … sorry about that,' said Bobby.

The Grandmaster cricketer turned and moved towards him.

'Ye shouldnae be here. Yer no … *one of us!*' he said calmly.

'One of us …' repeated the circle.

'Ye need tae become … one of us, now that ye've seen *this*. Gie him the machete.'

'*Eh!*' Bobby's heart was now beating a tiny bit faster. He looked over to the right.

'Dad?'

'Yer da' canny help ye now, son. He's … one of us,' said the Grandmaster, waving the bat in Harry's direction.

'One of us …' chanted the *still* bare-arsed followers.

'Get the goat,' ordered the Grandmaster.

'Ye can awa' an' fuck off,' said Bobby, as one of the circle handed him the machete and made an opening in the circle for him to go through. 'Dad!' he repeated, sounding like a little boy again, pleading for his father's protection; once more to no effect.

'It's the goat sacrifice or …' the Grandmaster paused for effect, '… shagging the virgin,' he said, nodding towards the concealed figure on the ground. Bobby was pushed in the direction of *the virgin*, and fell on top of whomever it was. He let out an embarrassingly high-pitched squealing noise as the virgin reached up and grabbed him around his middle.

It was a full hour before Bobby was able to laugh at the elaborate April fool's joke that his dad – and fellow Masons – had played on him, and all for the benefit of Chick McKenzie and his wife Betty; who played the virgin in tonight's little farce. As well as retiring, Chick and Betty were moving north to Aberdeen to be closer to their daughter and grandchildren. The boys at the Masonic Lodge had known Chick for most of his life and they desperately wanted to give him a good laugh as a send-off.

When Harry had been talking one night about the rubbish Gary used to tell Bobby about the Masons, the plan had started to form. It had worked much better than they'd all thought it would. When Joey left, Harry figured his son was far too much of a nosy bastard not to follow the sound of the chanting.

'See yer face son, when Betty grabbed ye? Ah swear ah near pished maself,' laughed Chick. He'd snorted a bubble of snot earlier and part of it was still hanging from his large, bulbous nose.

'Ah'm awfa sorry, Bobby, son,' said Betty, but she too failed to conceal her mirth. Her hiccups had only just stopped.

'Aye, Aye … yer a shower ah auld gits,' said Bobby finally allowing himself a smile.

'And hat's aff tae Ian Botham there, although yer beltin' wi' the bat wis a bit sore,' said Harry. Jock had come over with a pint for Bobby. 'Whaur did ye get the goat, Jock?' Harry asked him.

'Paddy McGarry's boy works up at a farm near Hurlford. He gied us a loan ae it. Cost me twenty quid mind ...' Bobby did allow himself a laugh at *that*.

AND SHE WILL WATCH OVER YOU, WHEREVER YOU MAY BE

3ᴿᴰ APRIL 1982

'The House meets this Saturday to respond to a situation of great gravity. We are here because, for the first time for many years, British sovereign territory has been invaded by a foreign power. After several days of rising tension in our relations with Argentina, that country's armed forces attacked the Falkland Islands yesterday and established military control of the islands.

Two weeks ago – on 19ᵗʰ March – the latest in this series of incidents affecting sovereignty occurred; and the deterioration in relations between the British and Argentine Governments which culminated in yesterday's Argentine invasion began. The incident appeared at the start to be relatively minor. But we now know it was the beginning of much more.'

Mrs Margaret Thatcher, the Prime Minister,
to the House of Commons

It is said that the Brecon Beacons were named after the ancient practice of lighting signal fires – beacons – on mountains to warn of attacks by the English. On this particular Thursday afternoon, Private Gary Cassidy and his three colleagues were lighting one simply to keep warm. It was absolutely freezing in the Welsh National Park, which was, because of its characteristic remoteness and harsh weather, used regularly for military training. The Special Air Service held their physically demanding selection exercises here and the fifteen-mile long-distance march known as the Fan Dance had become legendary amongst those new recruits who hadn't yet completed it. The soldiers had to carry an 18kg Bergen backpack, a rifle – weighing a further 5kg – and a water bottle. Miserable, relentless, horizontal driving rain seemed to be a constant as the young men – and on occasion women – set out to climb the *Pen Y Fan* and navigate their way down the other side in less than four hours.

Gary wasn't here for that exercise, though. He'd completed it in three hours and forty-seven minutes during basic training almost a year ago. His squadron was here for the far more demanding Long Drag: a march of forty miles with a 25kg backpack, to be completed in less than twenty hours, in a fortnight's time. Over the next two weeks there would be familiarisation techniques: basic survival tasks, like the one they were currently on, and an intense period of marches and runs. This exercise was borrowed from the SAS, and while it was better than domestic duties, initially all of Gary's squadron were perplexed as to why they had to undergo this most physically demanding of endurance exercises. When they had arrived in Wales a week before, almost all of them thought the Falkland Islands were in the North Sea, a few hundred miles beyond the Shetlands. Only recently had the squaddies been able to see the purpose of the Long Drag.

Gary had never been to the Highlands of his own country, but he imagined the peak of Snowdon – when he saw it – to be similar to that of Ben Nevis. Having understood their possible future deployment could be eight thousand miles away, near South America, it remained hard to imagine the environment being like this barren, inhospitable wasteland; and, furthermore, why it was of interest to Britain. The Scots Guards' base at the Sennybridge Training Camp reminded Gary of the Glaisnock Outdoor Centre in South Ayrshire he'd gone to for a school break in primary seven. He'd loved that week away, and had recalled it fondly in the dark times leading up to his decision to visit the Army Recruitment Centre in London last year. So when the four squaddies sitting around the fire, the curling flames licking their way around the pieces of wood, agreed to tell each other tales about their fathers, Gary – the oldest of the group – retold the Glaisnock story.

'It must've been 1975 cos' that fuckin' "Bohemian Rhapsody" was number one for about a fuckin' year,' said Gary, as if he was presenting an uncensored edition of *Jackanory*.

'Hey, don't be havin' a go at Freddie Mercury, now. Greatest frontman ever!' Private Kevin Kavanagh saluted as he said this.

'Fuck off,' said Gary, pointing at Private Kavanagh. 'He's a wanker … of *men!*'

'No he's not.' Kevin stood up for emphasis. 'That's just a daft rumour.'

'Yeah, ah'm with Kev there,' laughed Private Henry Buxton. 'Ah mean "Fat-Bottomed Girls"? Hardly the work of a bender, eh?'

'They're *aw* fuckin' bent! Mercury, Elton John … Gary Glitter,' said an exasperated Gary.

Kevin burst out laughing. 'What? The *Leader of the Gang*? Don't talk such shite, man!'

'Is this a story about bent singers, or your da?' Private Benny Lewis' deep growl made the other three turn round abruptly. He rarely spoke but when he did, the baritone sound that came from such a small person was remarkable. They all laughed and then settled down to listen. The lanky Scotsman's stories were usually good value.

'Aye, so we aw went tae Glaisnock; ma primary seven class … about sixty weans; the yins that's parents could afford it, ken? Glaisnock Hoose was a scary auld mansion in the woods near Cumnock, like out ae one ae they Hammer Horror films …' For the next twenty minutes, Gary created the setting, described the principal characters, and set up the premise for a hilarious reveal. He told how Glaisnock

House was absolutely bang in the middle of nowhere; hence, its resemblance to where they were currently billeted.

Rumour had it that the house was haunted, but kids' stories being what they were, there didn't appear to be any real foundation for such hearsay. The three classes in Gary's year were accompanied by four teachers – three women of varying age and attractiveness, and one man. The females were Miss Hardy, a well-liked and, at the time, heavily pregnant primary six teacher in her early twenties; Miss Peters, a middle-aged deputy head, prone to prolonged bouts of screeching at the boys, stoically using only their surnames. The third was a quiet woman of indeterminate age. Accepting that for a primary school child anyone over the age of thirty was ancient, Mrs Wallace was definitely a fossil, but from what prehistoric era was uncertain. The male teacher was a bastard. Gary was clear about that. And a Yorkshire one to boot, stressed Gary, much to Benny Lewis's annoyance. He was a throwback to the days when physical punishment was practically encouraged.

He thought nothing of reducing a child to tears in class by a hard slap to the head with the back of his hand. Not surprisingly, he was universally hated, even by those who didn't have to sit all day in his primary seven class, awaiting the latest outburst of unpredictable violence. He had a brutal, post-war, short back and sides, topped off with what looked like three Shredded Wheat sitting in a row from fringe to crown. The three Privates rocked with mirth as Gary described the old teacher, concluding that he wore a constant look of nervous anticipation that the State would eventually catch up with him; a *peely-wally* demeanour that suggested he lived in a subterranean cave when not occupied by the business of torturing eleven- and twelve-year-olds.

Gary got up to illustrate old Mr Copthorne's very pronounced limp – and confirmed that any attempts by pupils to enquire about its provenance were likely to be met with a projectile blackboard duster aimed at the inquisitor's head. Gary's classmates were all certain that he had a wooden leg. An awkward gait sustained the suspicion. His baggy, tweed trousers, held up by antiquated comedy braces concealed any indications of the point where wood met flesh but common consent amongst Gary's classmates had it just below the knee.

'Can ah just check, boy?' said Kevin. 'But what's this all got to do with yore fatha?'

Gary put his forefinger to his mouth.

'Glaisnock was fuckin' magic. It was excitin'. Most ae the weans had never been away fae home afore. But the instructors were a great laugh, ken?' Gary continued for another five minutes, describing a context that his three colleagues all knew well. He told of those who worked there being used to groups of boisterous, unruly and occasionally homesick kids – and demonstrating a great deal of patience. The five days there were filled with outdoor activities that, at first, resembled what Gary imagined National Service to have been like for Harry. He'd once heard Harry telling Hettie that he'd served in the catering division and, having spilled some suet pudding onto a higher-ranking officer's shoe, was told by that officer to run two miles, ladle still in hand, back to base. Once there, he was to say to a Sergeant: 'Permission to speak, Sir?' And upon the granting of said permission, 'I've come from the camp to inform you that I am indeed an idiot, Sir.' Then Harry was to salute, about-turn and march quickly out of the office, before running the two miles back to the kitchen. After Glaisnock, the young Gary figured he might have some similar stories with which to connect with his Dad.

Gary then told the story of Sean Tobin. He'd come to Gary's primary school a year earlier, in what seemed to be a bizarre free transfer from the Catholic school directly across the road. There were constant battles between the small soldiers from each school. To exacerbate the issues, the Catholic kids had to come to Gary's school at dinner time, because their building didn't have a kitchen. Every day, they were all marched single-file across the road and past the *Proddy* school's ground-floor classrooms. Forty-five minutes later, they were all marched back again, before the next session began, monitored closely by at least five teachers. Gary explained that Sean was known as 'Toblerone', after those bars of jaggy Swiss chocolate that were virtually impossible to eat without breaking a tooth or bruising a gum. Despite having been one of 'them', Sean adapted quickly and was quite a likeable kid, but one for whom trouble and chaos were magnets. Mr Copthorne, the one-legged Yorkshireman, was his nemesis. Gary had witnessed the man routinely abuse the boy, physically and verbally, particularly after finding out – through an essay Sean had written at the start of the year entitled 'How My family Spent the Summer Holidays' – that Sean's father had left his mum for another woman.

Sean Tobin appeared to take Copthorne's grief in his stride, but in the run-up to the Glaisnock trip, the voracity of the attacks seemed to intensify. Gary recalled being astonished that Sean was allowed to go at all as barely a day went by without some new outrage that had the playground gossips reeling. But he couldn't recall Sean ever being threatened with the no-Glaisnock sanction.

'So, on the last night afore we left, the teachers let us have a party,' said Gary. His three friends sensed the long digressionary set-up was finally coming to a point, although Benny was clearly still unsure of its relevance.

'Aw the supervisors had gone home, but the curfew was extended tae ten o'clock. There was loadsa jelly 'n' ice cream 'n' ginger …' Gary sensed clarity was needed on this final point. 'Lemonade, Cream Soda, Dandelion & Burdock, ken? Fae the Curries factory up the road.' The three squaddies understood. 'Everyboday was havin' a good time. Even that old prick Copthorne was laughin' an' jokin'. But then he starts fuckin' sloshin' about. It's obvious he's either pished or he's taken somethin'. He falls ower an' knocks the wee record player doon. Thank fuck for that, cos "Bohemian Rhapsody" was the only record they had wi' them.' Gary stopped and winked at Kevin, letting him know that he was joking about this last line.

'So the three other teachers have tae lift him an' help him out. Every cunt was pissin' themselves at this. Wee Toblerone rushes ower tae open the door for them aw' an' when they went out, he keeks back in an' gies us aw the thumbs-up.'

Gary took a drink from his water bottle. 'Ah fuckin' kent Sean had somethin' tae dae wi' it at that point there. Pit somethin' in the auld bastard's drink, most likely. Sean was in a dorm room wi' me an' four others. We'd aw been sent back to the rooms by Miss Peters. She kent somethin' wisnae right. She was angry but we didnae ken who with. We sat in our room wonderin' whit the fuck was goin' on. Sean had been awa' for almost half an hour, then there was a loud knock on the door, an' a gruff voice saying *"Right, lights out you little fuckers!"* Toblerone came in and ma heart almost missed a fuckin' beat. He had a widden leg in his hand.'

Gary was good at telling stories. He wasn't bad at lying either. He appreciated that sometimes they went hand in hand. The key to telling good stories was the pacing; the building of tension in order to accentuate the dramatic arc. He looked at the expectant faces of his audience and knew he still had it. Their *look* was one of: *Well what the fuck happened next?* Gary smiled, and then continued.

'Toblerone got a chair, lifted it on tae one ae the beds an' stuck the leg up through a suspended ceilin' tile. Ah was excited … an' shittin' it, aw at the same time. We *aw* were. Naebody could sleep. But we aw agreed, *Naebody was shoppin'*. So, next mornin', everybody's doon for breakfast an' the cops are there. Auld Copthorne's sittin' on a chair, wi' his left trooser leg flappin' away wildly in the breeze. The polis are tellin' everybody that naebody's leavin', an' there'll be nae breakfast until the leg's back. Naebody spoke a fuckin' word. Eventually, we aw went home. A week later there's a letter sent out tae aw the weans fae the school. It told aw the parents about whit went on. An' as a result ae the *leg business,* that was the end ae the trips.'

Gary stood up again and breathed in deeply, as if the story was finished. The other three looked bemused. Before Benny could lodge a protest …

'Ma dad got the letter an' immediately said he *kent* it was me. No interested in listenin'. Nae opportunity tae tell him whit *actually* happened. He just said, "Yer a bloody waster, an' ye'll never be anythin' different." Never spoke a word tae me after that fur about six months. Ah was twelve or thirteen.'

It was an unusual story, Kevin eventually conceded. Benny wasn't really sure what to make of it. Henry couldn't see how it fitted in with stories explaining *how your family reacted when you said you were joining the Army.*

'*That's* the reason why I'm here now,' said Gary, sensing the need to elaborate on the moral of the story. 'When ah was doon in London, ah realised ma dad would be thinkin': *He's just run away, and he'll just end up nickin' stuff and doin' drugs an' aw that shite.* So one day, ah thought *Fuck it,* dae somethin' that'll make the auld bastard eat his words. If we end up goin' tae the Falklands, he'll have nae fuckin' choice.'

Private Gary Cassidy of the Second Battalion Scots Guards stood up tall, saluted his comrades and then turned and walked away to look for more firewood.

5TH APRIL 1982

'I believe the British people are fully behind us in retaking those islands and sending the biggest fleet that's ever been mounted in peace time, with the most marvellous professionally trained, brave, courageous soldiers and marines in order to re-establish British sovereignty on those islands and to see that the islanders once again live under British rule.'

Mrs Margaret Thatcher, the Prime Minister,
radio interview for Independent Radio News

'Whit the fuck was that?' Mickey Martin was not a happy man. 'Brenda wanted a decent disco for her twenty-first. Ah fuckin' hired *you*, ya cunt … no yer fuckin' circus sideshow freaks. Where the Christ were you?'

Fat Franny was on the back foot here, of that there was absolutely no doubt. He'd taken a gamble and it had backfired spectacularly. Mickey Martin had booked him for this gig months ago and, in truth, he had forgotten about it. But his mum had a hospital appointment re-scheduled at short notice for the same day, and following it she'd been kept in for observation overnight. Her blood pressure had been incredibly high and the chest pains she'd been complaining about since Christmas had suddenly got worse. Franny was between a rock and hard place, and had finally decided that he wouldn't be back in time. So he made the decision to send wedding specialists, the Cheezees, and – as a bit of a back-up – Bert Bole, alias Tony Palomino, Lounge Singer. As he stood in front of a raging Mickey, last orders having just been called, it was a decision he now bitterly regretted.

'Fuckin' Peters an' Lee earlier … they were absolute shite,' Mickey ranted on. Having summoned Fat Franny to the Howard Park Hotel, he was determined to make sure he got the full picture. 'An' everybody fuckin' *kens* Bert Bole. He was the janny at the fuckin' school most ae them went tae! Comin' on in a wig and wi' an open-necked shirt an' tellin' every cunt *"I'm Tony Palomino … Welcome to Las Vegas"*? Whit the fuck are you on?' Mickey was secretly enjoying tearing strips off Fat Franny. His daughter had actually told him that her uni friends from Glasgow thought it was brilliant. A comedy cabaret for a twenty-first birthday was really different.

It had certainly been different. Jay and Jill Boothby had turned up thinking it was a wedding reception; a misconception reinforced by them having to pick up Bert Bole on the way there. They were dressed in tuxedo and white evening dress, like giant versions of the tiny couple that adorn the top of most wedding cakes. They had taken dancing lessons and – determined to show them off – normally started the first dance routine. Most guests found this a bit odd, but Jay's argument was that it would encourage reluctant grooms if the *entertainment* showed them how it was done. At Brenda Martin's twenty-first birthday party, though, it just seemed too bizarre for it not to be part of an elaborate joke; especially when Jill caught a heel in her dress and tripped Jay, sending them both crashing to the ground. Jay fell backwards, Jill fell forwards. When they finally came to rest, Jill's head was between Jay's spread-open legs in full *blow-job* position. As embarrassment turned to rage, Jill Boothy of Cheezee Choonz slapped her husband. The Glasgow University contingent cheered. Jay – ever the semi-professional – bowed. Jill, with angry tears welling up, lifted her white stiletto with pace in the direction of her husband's balls. The applause made no difference to Jill's pride and she stormed out, leaving her limping spouse to follow and Tony Palomino to carry the rest of the night.

Normally, Tony did two sets of around twenty-five minutes each; usually split by the bride and groom actually leaving. His repertoire was pretty limited: 'Take Me Home, Country Roads'; 'Pretty Woman'; 'Rhinestone Cowboy' … the most contemporary song he did was 'The Lion Sleeps Tonight', but with the same backing track as Tight Fit. Tony knew he was way out of his depth. The Cheezee disaster had struck early, at around eight-thirty. There were at least four hours to go and – by the looks of it – no buffet breaks planned. Unsurprisingly, Tony floundered. Shouts for 'Love Will Tear Us Apart', 'The Model' and – right before he was hit in the face by a beermat – 'Heart of Glass' had the Vegas lounge singer sweating profusely. Fat Franny had been contacted and instructed to appear before an irate Mickey Martin, after Tony had sung 'Chirpy Chirpy Cheep Cheep' four times.

'Ah cannae pay ye. No after that fuckin' fiasco,' said Mickey. He'd had no intention of parting with cash in any case. But he *had* been prepared to dangle the carrot of The Metropolis. Now he had an alternative approach. 'Dae ye ken how ah can get in touch wi' they Heatwave boys, Franny?' Mickey knew this would skewer the *fat fuck*.

His daughter wasn't unhappy with her night. For her it had been a cult success; and, besides, her father had just bought her an Austin Maestro that could talk to her and remind her to wear a seat belt.

Fat Franny left without speaking to Bert Bole, and pointedly left him to call a taxi to get home.

7TH APRIL 1982

'It is the Falkland Islanders' wishes that are paramount. In every negotiation – if the Right Hon. Gentleman calls it that, and I have called it that – that we had, we had some of the Falkland Islands Council with us. They were with us in New York. It is their wishes that must be paramount.'

Mrs Margaret Thatcher, the Prime Minister, House of Commons
Intervention

'I do not press the Prime Minister further this afternoon. I do not regard her answers as satisfactory. I shall come later to ways in which I believe that these issues must be solved and worked out. We have embarked on a most difficult and dangerous exercise which carries very great risk.'

Mr James Callaghan, MP for Cardiff, South-East

The conversation with Mickey Martin gnawed away at Fat Franny like toothache. He hadn't been able to sleep soundly for the two nights since. Admittedly, the party hadn't gone well, and although he'd initially attempted to defend his acts, deep down he knew that it had been his fault. There was no question of payment being offered by Mickey Martin, given their history, but it was the mention of these new *fuckers* – Heatwave – that had really got to Fat Franny.

'Ah'm gonnae gie these *Heatwave* boys the shout for the anniversary, big man,' Mickey had said in a phone call yesterday. 'It's nothing personal Franny, but that was a fuckin' shambles, mate. Ah'm no fuckin' havin' it.'

'We've kent each other for years, Doc. An' in aw that time, I've never let ye doon afore,' pleaded Fat Franny. This didn't come easy for him. Begging wasn't his style.

'Aye mibbe so … but we aw need tae move on,' said Mickey. 'Ah want tae gie them a shot, wi' The Metropolis comin' up an' that. Ah've heard good things about them, ken?'

The mention of The Metropolis cut Fat Franny to the quick. He'd known for a while that Mickey was planning a mega-nightclub with different bars and a resident DJ in place. Mickey was also rumoured to have secured a previously unheard-of four a.m. licence. Speculation was that it was now going to be located in the vast spaces under the Foregate car park, and that it would be open five nights a week. This was the Holy Grail to Fat Franny. An opportunity to cut loose all the charlatans who were dragging him down: *The Cheezees, Bert fuckin' Bole, That* Sunshine *walloper … all of them could go an' take a flying fuck to themselves … if he* landed this gig. Maybe even Hobnail – and the domestic carnage that always seemed to surround him – would be expendable. But at the moment, the dream was drifting away from him.

'Franny. Ye still there? Ah need tae go. Ah'll speak tae ye sometime … later.' Mickey Martin hung up.

Fat Franny was left holding the receiver, staring at it and trying to decipher the significance of the word 'sometime'. Eventually he pulled the bit of paper with the numbers written on it in red felt pen from the cork pinboard to his left. Time for a word with the new kids on the block.

→>-<-

'Bob, it's me. These two cunts have got a party at the Tory Club on the twenty-fifth.'

'Apwil?'

'Whit? Aye, this month. Get on tae Des an' the Painter.'

'Dith ye phwone him, th' Cassidy boy?'

'Eh? Aye, aye … ah phoned the cunt. Offered him a place at the table. Fuckin' walloper's no interested. He told me they were doin' a'right. Stupid prick also telt me the bookings they had.' Fat Franny could hear Hobnail sniggering, but the Fatman wasn't in the mood for humour. 'Listen. Gie Ally Sneddon a phone. He's the manager at the Tory Club. Owes me a favour. Tell him Des an' Wullie'll dae the door on the twenty-first. Free fuckin' gratis.' There was silence at the other end of the phone. 'Huv ye *got* it?'

'Aye,' replied Hobnail. 'Don'th worry. Ah've goath it.' The phone's tone flatlined.

Bob Dale hated Fat Franny at times like these. Ally Sneddon was *his* mate! Why could the Fatman not fuckin' phone him direct? He could be such a wanker at times.

25TH APRIL 1982: 8:45PM

Despite a difficult start, with all the early accusations from the punters that they didn't know what they were doing, unforeseen circumstances had intervened and their popularity was now definitely on the rise. That Heatwave Disco had *anything* in common with the Thatcher Government was surprising. That they should be here – at the Tory Party's Kilmarnock HQ – was, for Joey Miller at least, nothing short of shocking. Joey had been here with a group of colleagues from CND only five months ago. They had banged on the massive wood-panelled doors of the old Georgian building, supporting the Greenham Common Woman's Peace Camp in their demands to overturn the decision to site ninety-six nuclear cruise missiles in Berkshire. And now here he was – walking through those same black doors to entertain people who held views to which he was fundamentally opposed.

A *different* woman called Margaret phoned and made the booking for her husband's fortieth birthday party. Bobby had taken the call. He didn't care for the Tories either, but he reckoned their money would be the same colour as everybody else's. The venue was the Conservative Club in Kilmarnock. Bizarrely, the Conservative Club was immediately adjacent to the *Labour* Club.

Private functions were regularly held in both, as the alcohol was subsidised to Bowling Club levels. The Labour Club was an unusual building halfway up a very steep hill and perched on three levels on the banks of the river behind the Palace Theatre. It had a similar concept to Frank Lloyd Wright's famous Falling Water building in America, but resolved and constructed to a much poorer standard. Its stained, brutalist concrete was in stark contrast to its more refined neighbour.

The Conservative Club was at the bottom of the hill. Both buildings shared a car park and service area. The Tory retreat was a more conventional, two-storey sandstone villa, sitting on its own, out of context and severed from its original surroundings by the town's one-way traffic system. Only members of the Club – and therefore the Party – could book a function there. The Labour Club, on the other hand would take anyone's money.

Joey was in a bad mood. Bobby and he had recently left school in advance of their exams. This had gone down badly with Joey's mum, as her son's explanation that a career as second-in-command of a Kilmarnock-based mobile DJ business hadn't matched her aspirations. Bobby's initial dialogue with his own parents was similar, but his dad was an accomplice and had therefore given up the moral high ground weeks before. His mum was worryingly ambivalent about most things these days, including – it seemed – her youngest son's future plans.

'Whit the fuck are we doin' here?' moaned Joey, for the umpteenth time that day.

Even Jimmy Stevenson was getting fed up with the constant complaining.

'Christ's sake, son. You're like ma missus. On an' on an' on, til ye end up sayin', "Fuck it. Ah'm awa' tae the pub".'

'C'mon Joey. A coupla hours an' we'll be out ae here,' said Bobby. He patted Joey on the back as he got out of the van. Hamish May, who'd been sitting in the front with Jimmy, came out and put an arm round Joey. Jimmy reached over and shook Joey's hand.

'For fuck's sake ye'd think ye were goin' in for an operation, the way we're goin' on.' Bobby was laughing as he said this.

Hamish and Jimmy laughed as well. Joey could only offer a crooked smile through gritted teeth.

'Hello. You boys must be *Heatwaves*.'

'And you must be ... Andy?' Margaret McIntyre laughed nervously at Bobby's attempt to defuse the tension a bit.

'Oh, I'm Margaret. Andy's upstairs,' she said. 'You're a little bit late. I'd hoped you'd have been here earlier, before most of the people got here.' Her tone was polite, but her exasperation was detectable, even if it was mostly concealed beneath her veneered surface. 'But please just go quickly, right on up and to the left and you'll see the space at the end of the hall. You can set up there.'

'Right-o, Margo,' said Jimmy. He had heard what she'd said, but he had decided that her remarkable resemblance to Penelope Keith called for a different reference. He stopped himself from patting her tweed-skirted backside on the way past. *Maybe later*, he thought.

Andy – whose birthday was being celebrated – looked every inch the *true blue*. He was dressed in a blue pin-striped suit with a pale-blue shirt and a bright-yellow tie. He looked almost identical to every other male at the party. Only the ties seemed to offer any colourful contrasts.

'Bloody hell, everybody looks like they're at a political convention.' Joey's earlier annoyance had given way to bemusement and – Bobby could detect – disdainful pity.

'They aw look about fifty-five,' remarked Hamish.

No-one had paid the DJs and their crew any attention since they had walked into the upper-floor function room. But Hamish had spoken a bit too loudly and several men looked round sharply. They continued staring as the four made their way back out to the van for the remainder of the equipment.

'This is gonnae be shite.' Joey had convinced himself that the night would have no redeeming features.

Bobby sighed deeply, but said nothing. They'd arrived almost forty-five minutes late and were still a good twenty minutes away from sounds that entertained punters.

The function room was set up all wrong, with most of the buffet tables sitting across the small rectangle of dancefloor. There were already too many people there for the room and many were already demonstrating the *loudness* and bravado that are a frequent consequence of alcohol. In the two months that Heatwave had been in existence they'd had a few bad nights. Normally, Joey would just play out the boring chart music, the novelty songs that everybody hates but dances to anyway and the inevitable requests for '60s medleys of groups like Edison Lighthouse and Middle of the Road – who were actually from the '70s. Bobby spoke infrequently on these nights. He had assumed the persona of a performer and felt that such audiences didn't deserve his best work. Picking up the money at the end of the night was the sole stimulus for such evenings and so far – and with the exception of that traumatic first – they had been paid by generally contented customers. This night was different though.

'See they two weird lookin' stewards, watchin' us when we came in?' Hamish's agitation had been apparent on the final lift of the record boxes from the van. Nobody questioned why 'bouncers' had suddenly become 'stewards'; it just seemed appropriate in this context.

'Cannae say ah really noticed, mate,' replied Bobby.

'Aye, ah did,' said Joey. 'Looked kinda familiar, but not sure fae where.'

'Christ, will you two stop fuckin' lookin' for problems? "*There's too many Tories! Their suits are too blue! The bouncers are shifty! The stairs are too steep!*" Fuckin' hell, let's just get on wi' it an' get paid, eh?' The Heatwave leader had spoken, although Hamish felt it important to make one final observation.

'*You* were the one complainin' about the stairs, ya cunt!'

When Bobby, Joey and Hamish finally assembled the sound and light experience that was now known as Heatwave Disco, Margaret came over. She wasn't happy.

'More than three weeks have elapsed since the United Nations Security Council resolution was passed calling upon the Argentine forces to withdraw. During that time, far from withdrawing, the Argentine Government have put reinforcements of men, equipment, and materials on the island. If we have not yet reached a settlement, the blame lies at the feet of the Argentine Government.'

Mrs Margaret Thatcher, the Prime Minister,
to the House of Commons

'You'll have to move your van,' said Margaret McIntyre, tersely and in a way that suggested she'd been reprimanded by someone else. 'You're parked in a space reserved for the local party leader.' She turned and looked towards the two stewards.

'Is he comin' like, Margo?' said Jimmy.

'Eh! Sorry?' Margaret had been addressing Bobby and it had surprised her to hear the low, grumbling voice behind her. 'My name is *Margaret*,' she said and turned to face Jimmy. She breathed in, hands on hips, as if to deliver something profound but then sighed and turned back to Bobby. 'Could you just move the van? *Please* ... and then please get on with the music!' She turned and strode away.

'Oooh! Mrs La-Di-Da Gunner Graham,' said Hamish, waving his hand theatrically in her direction. It wasn't witnessed by Margaret, but Andy and four others at his table had seen it.

'Hey ... Larry fuckin' Grayson! Get a fuckin' move on.' Bobby's patience was being sorely tested. 'Jimmy, go doon an' shift the van an' then come back up.'

Jimmy walked over towards the door and noticed the smaller of the two black-suited stewards watching him intently. Almost an hour and a quarter after the party should have started, Heatwave's lights illuminated the function hall and were creating unusual effects on the elaborate ceiling cornice of the old Georgian room. The sound quality was better than expected, but when the distinctive riff of 'Should I Stay or Should I Go' kicked in, everyone froze due to its volume. Exactly the effect DJ Joey had anticipated.

'Joey, for fuck's sake! The Clash? *Seriously*?' Only one song in and Bobby was now regretting having taken this booking. Joey smiled suspiciously as the Angelic Upstarts followed. That new anthem of disaffected youth – The Specials' 'Ghost Town' – was already in his hand. Two songs in and the crowd was growing increasing disgruntled; job almost done.

Down in the car park, the VW campervan reversed slowly back into an alternative space against an adjacent retaining wall. It was dark and sheltered from the intrusive sodium illumination of the main street lights. Jimmy normally hung about and had a sleep in the back for a couple of hours, but tonight the darkness would allow him the joint he'd been coveting since finding it down the back of the rear seats at the start of the week. He'd head back upstairs later. A tap at the passenger side window startled him. He rolled the window down.

'Thanks for movin' the van, mate.' It was one of the stewards. The smaller one.

'Eh, aye. Nae bother, wee man.' The joint was still in Jimmy's hand below the sightline of the door. He was reluctant to let it go though for fear of losing it down the side of his seat.

'Ah think yer brake light's out,' said the steward. 'Is his brake light out, Des?'

'His brake light's out, Wullie.' A deeper voice from the rear of the van responded. Jimmy glanced furtively at rear and side mirrors but it was too dark to make anyone out.

'Need tae get that fixed, pal,' said the smaller steward, the one who'd just been referred to as *Wullie*.

Jimmy dropped the joint to the footwell as carefully as he could. He opened the door and slid out, pushing past Wullie and moving quickly to the rear of the van where the torch held by Des confirmed that there was indeed a smashed brake light. He left the driver-side door slightly open.

'Must've hit the wa' there, mate. Nae luck, eh?' said Des, shaking his head at this unfortunate mishap.

'Aye. Ye think ah'm a fuckin' eejit? Ah hit nae fuckin' wa'. That was you'se two that smashed it!'

'Hey, haud on there, Humpty Dumpty! We asked ye tae move yer van. Ye moved it an' hit the wa',' said Des calmly.

Jimmy was getting angry, but sensed that it might be better to accept bouncer's version. He also wanted to know where Wullie had gone, but Des had moved closer, towering over him and blocking both view and access to the driver's side of the vehicle.

'Ah'm no sure there's any point in takin' this further, pal.' Des poked his finger in Jimmy's chest. 'Awa' back and join Curly, Larry and Moe up there. Just mind and get that fixed now, eh?' With that he stepped back, allowing Jimmy to ease past him and catch Wullie leaning against the front of the van, smiling.

Upstairs in the flamboyant function room, things were getting worse.

'Where's ma pint?' said Joey, just as 'Alternative Ulster' faded out and the start of 'Eton Rifles' reverberated off the walls.

'Will you fuckin' gie it up wi' that music? Fuck me, every cunt's glowerin' at us. Ah cannae speak ower *this*. Get out the Lionel Richie and Phil Collins stuff.'

'Did ye hear me? Where's ma drink?' repeated Joey. He was secretly pleased that his choices of music were irritating the partygoers *and* Bobby. *He'll fuckin' think twice about bookings like this in future,* he was certain.

'Fuckin' cunty barman widnae serve us for being under-age.' Bobby was raging. Technically the barman was correct. Joey was still seventeen. But it worsened Bobby's deteriorating mood that he had broken the unwritten law of gigging: the band/performer/entertainer/DJ *always* got served.

Jimmy didn't return. He'd decided to stand outside, watching his vehicle. Wullie and Des had gone back up and no further threats had been issued. It was a pretty cold, late-spring evening, but at least Jimmy could see any approaches to the van from where he was standing. Upstairs, tempers flared when a request from one woman for 'Twist and Shout' went a-begging. She looked like Krystle Carrington and sounded like the Queen. Joey mocked her accent. Margaret McIntyre came over to intervene in the *contretemps*, threatening non-payment; birthday boy Andy followed, issuing threats of violence. Hamish May – assuming the role of minder – retaliated with a few of his own.

Bobby sensed a serious problem developing: they were at the opposite side of the hall – *and* up a floor – from the principal means of exit. The priority was becoming more about damage limitation than fee recovery. Hamish was prone to the great gesture without thinking of the consequences. He had achieved some local notoriety as the kid who had climbed out of a first-floor window onto the roof of an adjacent lorry for yet another common-room bet. The bet was for a fiver, and actually only required him to stand on top of the vehicle for thirty seconds. In the event, he was out there for so long, the vehicle eventually drove away with him clinging onto its top rails.

It was difficult to pinpoint what kicked it all off, but Joey later recalled seeing the two stewards over at a table of five males, gesticulating and pointing towards him. They all came over. Margaret McIntyre was in the middle of it. Her arms were outstretched, trying to keep order. There was some initial jostling, finger-pointing and a smattering of rebuttals in the form of abusive menace from the defiant figure of Hamish May. He stood tall, silhouetted against the flashing backdrop of Heatwave Disco's two main lightboxes. As the situation deteriorated and the first slap was issued, his *employers* for the evening instinctively crouched down behind the table holding up the decks. The main reason for this was to avoid the swinging microphone, which Hamish was whirling like a demented Roger Daltrey whenever anyone came within ten feet of him. Bobby was also trying to figure out a way to get to the one exit door undetected. When violence was in the air, both Bobby and Joey were firmly in the *flight* camp; Hamish could represent the primal *fight* instincts of the species if he wanted.

The microphone stand-off continued for about fifteen minutes, until Wullie the Painter came over, all windmilling arms and timing his advance perfectly to plough into Heatwave's man between rotations. Through a gap in the cabinets Joey saw Hamish stagger back a few steps on one foot, like Chaplin's tramp in *City Lights*. This resemblance was reinforced by the small strobe lightbox that had fallen over, landing on its 'on' switch. Its flickering, flashing light gave the action a monochromatic, slow-motion, filmic quality. But instead of boxing-ring ropes propelling him back into the fray, the rest of the lightboxes tumbled under Hamish's weight. The decks and their wobbly, trestled support followed, with the two trembling DJs underneath. Bobby couldn't see what was happening, but it was clear that things weren't progressing well for the disco's champion. It sounded to Joey like the blue-suited Tories were kicking the shit out of him and, apart from the odd, muffled squeal of 'Tory cunts!', it didn't seem like much resistance was being offered. And then suddenly there was quiet.

'I really think you should leave now,' screamed Margaret McIntyre, her head bent down to shout under the fallen table. Her eyes were moist and fully formed tears weren't far away.

'We're no' fuckin' payin', incidentally ... but any trouble and the police are getting called.' This was the first time birthday boy Andy had spoken to them, and his high-pitched Highlands accent took Bobby and Joey by surprise.

Hamish had been escorted outside by Des Brick and Wullie the Painter. As they did so, it had briefly registered with him that they were there on the night he had electrocuted himself. He said nothing to them about it, though, his guts in agony from an earlier kick that had caught him in the abdomen. Jimmy hadn't been aware of the chaos playing out upstairs, but he had heard the commotion of the first group of people heading down. Jimmy ducked behind a large solid-stone column that was helping to support a heavily indented portico. Jimmy had looked up at it earlier and had been impressed. *A lovely building ... for a shower ae' absolute cunts,* he'd thought.

A ceasefire had emerged up in the function room. No payment, but at least no further trouble or damage to the gear. Bobby reckoned that there was something of a result in this. Joey went down to let Jimmy know the story and tell him that they would be leaving early. Big Hamish was outside, vomiting over a wall into the river below. They assembled their gear in a neat pile at the unlit rear of the building and waited for Jimmy. Nobody spoke. Joey nipped back in to go to the toilet and – on the way back down the stairs, when he was sure no-one was looking – drew a small rectangular Hitler moustache and black side-shed on a new portrait of the current Prime Minister.

She was staring down, watching dictatorially over all who climbed the stairs from her exalted position inside a baroque frame – painted to reinforce the image of the contemporary Boadicea that her supporters believed her to be. When he got back outside Joey was stunned to see four policemen there, sniffing around the van and asking questions of the van driver and the equipment owner. Hamish May was being forcibly held against the wall he'd just vomited over by two of them. Joey was amazed that they had appeared before the ink was dry on the picture. Maybe Thatcher's boastful claims that the Tories had put more bobbies on the beat were actually true after all. One young policeman emerged from the darker side of the van with half a dozen large bottles of spirits. Jimmy's heart visibly sank.

'How did these get in the van, lads?'

'You're fuckin' jokin'!' said Bobby.

Joey burst out laughing. Des Brick and Wullie the Painter came out. Ally Sneddon, manager of the Conservative Club was standing between them.

'That booze got nicked during the night,' said the manager. 'There was a ruckus ... which *they* started ... an' while it was aw happening, they forty-ouncers went fuckin' walkin'.'

'Yer a fuckin' *liar*!' screamed Bobby. 'They fuckin' assaulted us!'

'... and they never fuckin' paid us either,' added Joey.

'Whit about you, fanny-baws?' The older copper who was holding Hamish addressed him directly.

'The two ae them fuckin' battered us, an' then pushed us doon the fuckin' stairs.'

Joey and Bobby looked at each other. Was he making this up? Had they really done such a thing? Des and Wullie looked impassive, eyes neither confirming nor denying. The bottles were placed in one of the three police cars in the car park. It did seem to Jimmy like a bit of *Regan and Carter*-type overkill, but he was determined not to speak. Nobody had so far referred to him and he remained partially hidden by the column.

'Intae the motors, boys,' said the most senior copper.

'Ah don't fuckin' *think* so!' replied Joey. About a minute later the three young Heatwave operatives were in the back of the cars.

'Hey, you ... Buster Bloodvessel! You tae. Yer gaunnae need a much bigger pillar if yer hidin' fae *us*. Ah'm assumin' you're the van driver?'

Half an hour later, and all four of them were each sitting in a small, bare cell at Kilmarnock police station; Police Detective Chief Superintendant Donald McAllister's police station. It was just after midnight.

26TH APRIL 1982

'I should make one point clear. These are not prisoners of war. A state of war does not exist between ourselves and the Argentine. They are prisoners, and they will be returned as soon as possible. We shall, of course, let their names and state of health be known to their relatives as soon as possible. I understand that the commander of the Argentine forces on the island is already grateful for the prompt medical attention that was given to the one Argentine marine who was badly hurt.'

Mrs Margaret Thatcher, the Prime Minister

For the following two hours, statements were taken during a series of individual interviews. What had seemed like a bad joke to start with was rapidly becoming serious for Bobby, and, more specifically, for Jimmy. It looked like they were all in a corner they couldn't escape from. Numerous people had come forward at the end of the evening to offer testimony that the DJs provoked everyone at the party and had actually started the fighting. The manager confirmed that a considerable quantity of alcohol had then been stolen and – in perhaps the worst crime of all – an extremely valuable portrait with sentimental attachment had been damaged beyond repair.

These were the charges facing Heatwave Disco's management and staff. At seven-thirty the following morning, they were all released, having been cautioned but not fed. Bobby was notified that formal proceedings might follow in due course. Jimmy was informed that he'd be requested to attend a separate interview the following Monday. He could have a solicitor present. Joey was in a state of shock. He elected not to tell his mother, lying to her that, as the party had gone on longer than expected, he'd gone back to Bobby's to sleep rather than run the risk of waking her and his young sisters. She suspected nothing. It was an excuse he'd used many times before – although this time it was covering up something potentially serious.

Having had his cigarettes returned to him, Hamish May offered everybody one. All accepted and lit up while still in the shadow of the imposing police-station building.

As they walked home, Bobby tried in vain to lighten the mood. 'At least we'll no be gettin' conscripted to go an' fight against Ardiles an' Kempes.'

'At the minute, ah think ah'd rather fuckin' huv *that!*' observed a pale Jimmy Stevenson.

PART III

AN ESCALATION OF HOSTILITIES

'What really thrilled me, having spent so much of my lifetime in Parliament, and talking about things like inflation, social security benefits, housing problems, environmental problems and so on, is that when it really came to the test, what's thrilled people wasn't those things, what thrilled people was once again being able to serve a great cause, the cause of liberty.'

Mrs Margaret Thatcher, the Prime Minister
Speech to the Scottish Conservative Party
Conference, May 1982

9

A WEAPON THAT WAS MADE IN BIRMINGHAM

4TH MAY 1982: 10.15AM.

GOTCHA

Our Lads Sink Gunboat and Hole Cruiser

The Navy had the Argies on their knees last night after a devastating double punch.

WALLOP: They torpedoed the 28,000-ton Argentine cruiser *General Belgrano* and left it a useless wreck.

WALLOP: Task Force helicopters sank one Argentine patrol boat and severly damaged another.

The *Belgrano*, which survived the Pearl Harbour attack when it belonged to the US Navy, had been asking for trouble all day …'

Tony Snow, news reporter for *The Sun,* aboard *HMS Invincible*

Harry folded his newspaper calmly, but inside he was raging. This jingoistic propaganda was obscuring the deficits of one of the most extreme and immoral governments in Harry's memory. Why couldn't others see it?

That morning he realised things would never be the same. He would never buy *The Sun* again. Harry knew this was an act unlikely to bring down Rupert Murdoch's media empire; he doubted anything ever would. But it was a personal stand at least, and for a middle-aged man in the early eighties, set in his traditional working-class ways, deep-rooted habits were extremely hard to break. Harry also knew that these headlines – and simply hiding the paper wouldn't avoid it – would exacerbate Ethel's fears for Gary when she turned on the television. An act as brutal, and as recklessly reported around the world as this, would force retaliation; of that there would be no doubt. And after that, the sabre-rattling would be over, and the country would be propelled down a route to war over a collection of virtually uninhabited islands that the vast majority of *Sun* readers couldn't have found on a map before the start of the month. He also knew he'd be seeing a lot more of the ridiculously cartoonish John Nott on the evening news programmes.

There were numerous Tories that Harry now hated with a passion – Francis Pym, that prick Lord Carrington, Norman fuckin' Tebbit (how he'd love to get on a bike and park it right up the crack of *his* arse), the Milk-Snatcher herself – but John Nott was rapidly rising to the top of the list. He recalled the hypocrisy of a Defence Secretary cutting back – correctly in Harry's view – on naval defence expenditure, then arguing for the launching of the most significant British Task Force expedition since the D-Day landings. But not before offering to resign following the Argentine Invasion. A series of decisive actions from a Minister of State? Hardly. Harry considered John Nott to be the lowest and most embarrassing component of a desperate government that was latching onto an unexpected event in a contemptibly opportunistic way, regardless of the inevitable human cost. They would propel a hitherto disgruntled population, still suffering from the severe economic recession only two years ago, towards a xenophobic culture of triumphalist aggression. And all aided by a ruthless media caught up in the Tory hype and hoodwinked by the false promotion of a Churchillian Bulldog spirit. Harry reached down and picked up the neatly folded newspaper. He tore it in half and walked towards the bin in the kitchen.

'Cunts!' he muttered under his breath as the swing lid spun.

Gary had also been troubled by the newspaper's front cover, but not for the same reasons as his dad. Benny had annoyed him by pinning it onto the wall next to his bunk at Wellington. He wasn't fully supportive of Thatcher's desire to 'Stick It up the Junta!' Gary's acceptance of his duty – and of the Battalion's likely deployment, now that mass deaths were being incurred – was one thing, but he couldn't fathom the media's bloody-minded desire for the whole thing to escalate. As it happened, both Gary and Benny didn't have long to wait to find out that their destiny lay on the other side of the world. Before British soldiers are committed to operations, they are briefed and prepared assiduously. At 19:00 hours, as Brian Hanrahan reported the events of the previous day live from the deck of the *Invincible* in an extended BBC News programme – and as Ethel paced the floor of her Kilmarnock home watching him – the Commanding Officers of the 2nd Battalion Scots Guards received notification by signal that the Battalion was to be on seventy-two hours 'Notice to Move', with effect from midnight.

The signal had kicked off an impressive chain reaction of British Army largesse. It had been almost six weeks since the first British death in the conflict, and the preparation for deployment was becoming well practised. All the standard peacetime restrictions were lifted and even Gary Cassidy was becoming aware of how quickly and dramatically the Army's routine bureaucracy dissipated. As a consequence, Gary and his closest colleagues experienced a tangible buzz and recognised the powerful sense of purpose that now flowed throughout the ranks. It was different from the occupations in Ulster, simply because those were essentially containments of an existing historical situation. This conflict – and he was well aware that war had not so far *actually* been declared – was much more in line with what Gary had believed Army life to be about. He still hated Thatcher and everything for which her vile and corrupt party stood; but his duty was first and foremost to his comrades. It was a feeling of belonging to – and participating in – something vital that he had been looking for all of his life. It finally became real to all of them in the following days, when the images of a stricken British Navy ship were broadcast around the world.

5ᵀᴴ MAY 1982

'In the course of its duties within the Total Exclusion Zone around the Falkland Islands, *HMS Sheffield*, a type-42 destroyer, was attacked and hit late this afternoon by an Argentine missile. The ship caught fire, which spread out of control. When there was no longer any hope of saving the ship, the ship's company abandoned ship. All who abandoned her were picked up.'

Ian McDonald, Ministry of Defence Spokesman,
Statement at an MOD press conference

'This empire's fuckin' crumblin'! D'ye *hear* me?' The opening line of Fat Franny's council of war meeting reverberated off the bare walls of the Ponderosie's double garage. A bare bulb swung gently like the one in the opening sequence of *Callan*, but apart from that there was no movement. The four figures sat at each side of the rectangular table were motionless. This was indeed bad news.

'We've run this fuckin' place for ages an' now these arrogant wee pricks come in an' just fuckin' take ower ... an' we're sittin' back lettin' the cunts dae it!' The door suddenly opened. It was Mrs Duncan.

'Hullo, son. Ah, just wondered if you and yer wee pals wanted a pot ae tea made?' She was wearing her bra over the top of her cardigan.

'Christ Almighty! Mam, this is really important,' said Fat Franny. His voice was much lower than it had been only ten seconds ago. 'We're fine. Naebody needs anythin'. Thanks, but. Awa' back in an' watch yer *Crossroads*. We'll no be long.' They all watched her go and Fat Franny waited a full minute from the point when the door closed behind her. He scanned the three faces for any signs of mirth. Satisfied, he continued.

'If we don't get a fuckin' grip here, every cunt in this room's gonnae suffer.' Fat Franny leaned back in his chair. 'Well? Ideas?'

'Why don't we just kick their cunts in?' enquired Wullie the Painter.

'Mibbe cos' the fuckin' cops have let them off wi' the Tory Club shambles. That means they've assumed some *other* cunt's nicked the booze an' mibbe afore long they'll be speakin' tae you two pricks. If the three ae them get a doin' it's gonnae look suspicious.' At least Fat Franny's volume had reduced, although the tone was still there.

'Why don't the three ae *us* just kick *your* cunt in then?' The words formed in Hobnail's head but they didn't make it out of his mouth. Something – more than just his inarticulacy – always stopped sentiments like these. Maybe someday though.

'It's got tae be somethin' that naebody can connect wi' me,' shouted Fat Franny before slamming a fist down on the table.

'They've got a thing comin' up wi' that daft fuckin' Mod group soon. There's tickets aw ower the place,' said Des Brick. He had succeeded in appearing to be the calmest man at the meeting.

'When's it on?' Fat Franny's interest was now totally focused on Des, to the exclusion of the others.

'End ae the month, ah think. Ah canny remember the date but ah'll find oot,' said Des, writing a note in ink on the back of his hand.

'There canny be any fuck-ups this time.' Fat Franny was now back facing – and addressing – all three men. 'This really is the last chance. We aw need this Doc Martin gig. Aw the other cost centres are losing money hand ower fuckin' fist. We're aw gonnae end up lookin' like that cunt Bobby Sands at this rate, but no through choice.' Fat Franny smiled at this, allowing the others to appreciate that a part of his rage had now passed. Des Brick smiled at the thought of the fatman *ever* looking like he'd been on hunger strike.

'Ah'm cuttin' the talent loose,' announced the Fatman. 'Huvnae told them yet, but ah need the Martin contract as a bit ae security first.'

Hobnail said nothing, but it was hardly surprising. Three weeks ago, Mr Sunshine was reported to the police by three mothers at a nine-year-old's birthday party for handing out balloon animals to each child that looked more like a cock and balls than the sausage dogs the entertainer proclaimed them to be.

Cheezee Choonz hadn't surfaced since the Howard Park Hotel fiasco and Bert Bole hadn't even been at work. Fat Franny's own bookings were also drying up in the wake of the seemingly relentless rise of Heatwave. He'd appealed to Mickey Martin for intervention and, despite their history – or perhaps *because* of it – he'd done nothing. In fact, it was now looking like Mickey was effectively encouraging Heatwave to break up Fat Franny's business. Well he wasn't going to stand idly by and watch these young *tossers* sail in and take away what was rightfully his.

'Here's whit tae dae.' He looked directly at Hobnail. 'Go an' see Nobby Quinn. Don't phone 'um. Take the motor doon.' Fat Franny was writing in a diary as he spoke, but none of the other three could see what he was writing. 'Go next Tuesday. That's his wife's birthday.' Fat Franny looked up. 'Nae Brummie gangster can refuse any request on his wife's birthday,' he said with all the certainty of the Don.

The Quinns were yet another in what seemed like an endless list of Ayrshire families who had criminality as their core ethos. Generally they all stuck to their own distinct areas. Although not a family in the truest sense, Fat Franny Duncan's group controlled

Onthank and the north west of Kilmarnock; Mickey Martin's extended family had the remainder – and much larger part – of Kilmarnock. The Wisharts ran Crosshouse to the west of the town, and the Quinns held an iron fist over Galston and the wider Cumnock Valley. The Quinns were different, in that they weren't indiginous. They were incomers from the Midlands. There was a bit of the Romany about them and they had recently become known as the 'Midnight Runners' after 'Come On Eileen' had gone to number one in the UK charts and Kevin Rowland's latest gypsy-inspired look had been widely mocked. Needless to say, nobody called the Quinns this in their presence. They had taken the Galston pitch by force and the war with the previous incumbents – the McLartys who had originally moved in from their base in the East End of Glasgow – had been prolonged, extensive and brutal.

Nobby Quinn was ideal for the sort of action Fat Franny had in mind. He knew from bitter experience that the Romanies were a fucking law unto themselves and up for a fight at the drop of a hat. His plan was for a crowd of them to pitch up early at the Henderson Church gig and wreck the place, destroying the Heatwave gear – and perhaps even the DJs – in the process. The seed would be planted that Heatwave were a liability – that there would be trouble wherever they went – and then he'd work on Mickey Martin for a second chance at The Metropolis. It all fitted, in Fat Franny's mind, and although it would cost him to engage the Quinns, he knew they'd do it if the price was right.

'Why canth *you* no go'th an thee Nobby Quinnth?' Hobnail shocked himself by saying these words out loud. All three of his fellow war-cabinet members turned to look at him with the same bemused look on their faces.

'Cos' it's your fuckin' job, ya cunt,' barked Des Brick. An opportunity to curry favour *and* boot the boss's number two squarely in the balls rarely presented itself, and he was quick to grab it.

Fat Franny put his hand calmly on Des's forearm. 'If yer losin' the bottle fur it, just say, Boab,' said Fat Franny. 'There's plenty linin' up for yer job … an' no just the two in here.' This took not only Hobnail, but also Des and Wullie by surprise. Fat Franny was a sharp guy and he'd noted the increasingly distant attitude his *consiglieri* had demonstrated over the last month or so. In fact, Fat Franny had put it at the top of the list of reasons why the business was currently suffering. Michael Corleone would have had him clipped weeks ago, but the Don's handling of a delicate situation would've been more subtle.

'How's that boy ae yours gettin' on?'

This enquiry caught Hobnail off guard.

'Heth's fine,' he responded, slightly fazed. 'Came tae see me last Friday. No aw that happy at home, is he? Wants tae mibbe dae a wee bit ae work for me, y'ken? Pick up a bit more cash, an' that.'

'Franny, ah fuckin' swearth …' Hobnail was on his feet, fists clenched.

'Sit doon, fur fuck's sake. How long have ye kent me? Ah'm no gonnae go behind yer back wi' Grant. Ah ken the trouble it'd cause wi' you an' Senga.'

Des saw the game unfolding and he had to hand it to Fat Franny. He had defused Hobnail's anger – for now at least – and reminded him that there are other ways to get what you wanted than brute force. Hobnail would go and see the Quinns. He would be unhappy about it, but he'd do it because of the ease with which his old 'friend' could manipulate the position with Senga. If Grant got anywhere near Fat Franny's business, it would be all over with Senga and that would cost him more than just money.

'Right. Let's get a fuckin' shift on an' get organised for The Anchorage the night.' Fat Franny stood up, signalling the end of the meeting. No papers had been presented and no minutes had been taken, but as far as Franny was concerned, the outcome was more conclusive than a United Nations resolution.

'Aw fuck. Fat Franny's the bastardin' DJ!'

It had looked like a promising night for Bobby Cassidy up to this point. Lizzie had been invited to a party at The Anchorage in Troon. It had come as a bit of a surprise, since Janice Fallon had been a friend of both Lizzie *and* Theresa. The three of them had been close until relatively recently. With the invite Lizzie had assumed that Janice had taken her side. She never thought for a minute the stupid cow would have invited *both* of them. But there she was. Theresa Morgan. Standing next to the DJ booth, all blond, layered feather cut and New Romantic make-up. The four of them – Lizzie had allowed Joey and Hamish to come as well – walked in to the small pub hall. Janice came over quickly, oblivious to the hard, driven stares coming from the DJ zone. The Heatwave contingent moved instinctively towards the bar, leaving Lizzie to fawn dramatically over Janice, her new earrings, her gold horn-a-plenty chain and other large pieces of brash jewellery which Joey felt certain must have come from the Jimmy Savile Collection, or the Mr T *House of Crap*.

The music was mundane and Bobby felt pleased with how far they'd come in such a short period of time, when compared with Fat Franny's hopeless vocal interruptions. After his first pint, Hamish went to the toilets. They'd been here for about twenty minutes and Lizzie hadn't yet returned to their table. Joey and Bobby sat together, looked over at Fat Franny – whose gaze had barely been away from them since they came in – and laughed. They weren't actually laughing *at* Fat Franny, but he assumed they were. Des and Wullie were despatched. Bobby was reminiscing about the time the eight-year-old Gary had played crazy golf with Harry on the esplanade across the road from the pub they were in. Gary had swung the club like Jack Nicklaus and had broken Harry's nose with the club head on the first hole.

'Hey! Whit the fuck?' The sack went straight over Hamish's head, causing him to pee all over his jeans and the shoes of one of his assailants.

'Ya fuckin' hoor, ye,' shouted Wullie the Painter, in violation of the no-sound edict from the Fatman. Des puts his forefinger to his lips and made a *shush*-ing noise. At the same time, he dropped the struggling Hamish to his knees with a kick to the balls. The restrained teenager was easier to man-handle when on his knees, and the Gaffa tape went round his body quickly. After only a few minutes – and despite looking like a Christmas present wrapped by Stevie Wonder – he was suppressed. In the adjacent female toilets, things were also starting to kick-off. Lizzie had been explaining the origin of the argument with Theresa to an uninterested Janice, who was more intent on reapplying another layer of deep scarlet lipstick.

'Well, ah'm no hiding in the bogs aw night. This was a daft idea. Her an' I have fell oot big style,' said Lizzie.

'Ah suppose apologisin' would be oot the question.'

'Ah've nuhin' tae apologise fur, Jan. It wis aw her dain'. She started it.'

'An' ah suppose, if ah asked her, she'd say the same? Best pals fae nursery and noo look at ye'se. No speakin' because ae a stupid argument.' Janice had started to warm to the role of potential peacemaker.

'Might seem stupid tae you. You've no got blonde hair … so you widnae understand,' said Lizzie. Janice would clearly have a job on her hands with these two.

'Whit difference does it make who got the *Princess Di* feather cut first?' Janice stood, arms outstretched, as if she was addressing the League of Nations.

'Well, it wisnae *that* fuckin' fat cow, anyway,' Lizzie said, laughing.

Theresa had been listening to all this from inside one of the Formica toilet cubicles and, on hearing Lizzie's laughter, she burst through the door.

'Aw aye … is that right, ya skanky hoor?'

If Lizzie was surprised at her nemesis having heard the invective, she hid it well and retaliated in surprisingly brutal terms. 'Ther's only wan skanky faced midden in here, an' we're baith staring at it … an' smellin' its manky fanny.'

'Ya gadgie cow,' screamed Theresa.

'Lassies, lassies … there's nae need f …' Janice tried to get between them, but was pushed to the side by both.

'Awa' an' get back tae blawing that fat dick that's attached tae yer sumo wrestler boyfriend,' laughed Lizzie, as she turned and walked out of the toilet to the hall. As she did so, Theresa ran at her, jumping on Lizzie's back and grabbing her around the neck. This momentum propelled both of them onto the dancefloor, where Lizzie eventually staggered and fell with Theresa landing on top of her. In one move, Lizzie righted herself and swung a punch of which Ali himself would have been proud. Perhaps fortunately, it didn't connect, but a subsequent, softer left hook did. It knocked Theresa onto her back. Quick as a flash, Lizzie was on top of her. Joey could instantly see that this wasn't Lizzie's first bout. She was moving like an alley cat, avoiding Theresa's wild kicks and clawing at her clothes. Buttons popped, as Theresa's cream blouse opened and a pale blue bra was on view, supporting heavy, hanging breasts.

'Quick, throw some fuckin' jelly on them!' shouted one onlooker, as others whooped and hollered. Bobby looked at Joey in amazement. Neither had any clear idea of what to do next. Intervene? Disappear? Applaud?

'She certainly disnae need hauners anyway,' said Joey.

Eventually, and only after both protaganists were reduced to similar levels of ripped undress, two doormen from The Anchorage pulled them apart. Due to Theresa's relationship with the DJ, it was Lizzie who was cast out into the balmy night air of Troon's Templehill. Bobby and Joey followed shortly after.

'Where the fuck were you'se two?' screamed an angry Lizzie, as they strode towards the taxi rank.

'Didnae seem like ye needed any help,' exclaimed Joey. 'Plus, whit the fuck did ye expect the three ae us tae dae? Jump in like an all-in wrestlin' tag team?'

Bobby wasn't sure which way to go with this discussion. Should he defend a girlfriend whom he liked, but hadn't even had sex with yet? Or side with his friend of almost six years? The Laurel to his Hardy; the Millican to his Nesbitt; the Bernie to his Mike … *Hold on a minute,* thought Bobby. *Where the fuck was Schnorbitz?*

→>-<-

'That yin there'll dae,' whispered Des. 'The wee yin wae the oars in it.'

Wullie the Painter reached into the cold, black water and grabbed at the rope that was connected to the small rowing boat.

'Stroke ae fuckin' luck, eh? That fight kickin' off like that,' said Des. '*And* a Brucie fuckin' bonus that they diddies were even there, eh? We'd ae struggled tae get out without aw that commotion.'

'Aye, although ah wish we could've stayed to see it aw.' Wullie stopped wrestling with the top half of the parcel and looked up. Des urged him to be quiet. Wullie swung a leg at the end of the struggling body. His boot connected with a dull thud. The body stopped moving. 'That should make it easier to shift the cunt,' he said.

'Fuck sake, Wullie. Ye mighta killed him.'

'Naw ah huvnae. Just knocked the prick out a wee bit. Anyway, like ah was sayin', Theresa's tits are fuckin' magic … an' we'd have seen them if we'd hung on a wee bit longer. Many's the time ah've had a rerr auld soapy-tit wank in the bath thinkin' about them.'

Des couldn't help but laugh. 'Well, let's get this yin in the boat an' run back up. Mibbe we'll catch the last round.'

Hamish's taped-up body was rolled into the small vessel. Wullie pushed it gently away from the wooden boardwalk and watched it drift with the outgoing tide into the calm night beyond the stone breakwater.

'Ach, fuck it,' exclaimed Wullie. Des looked back suddenly.

'Whit is it?'

'Ah forgot tae take the oars out.'

10

HIGH NOON

'How's things, Harry?'

'They're fine.'

'Ah got told that yer boy Gary's away tae the Falklands.'

'Aye that's right. Sailed on the *QE2* last Tuesday.'

'Did ye go doon tae see him off? Southampton, wis it?'

'Naw. We didnae. He didnae want us tae come doon. He kent Eth– … he kent it wid be too much for his mam.' Harry was uncomfortable with this conversation, and not just because he was deep inside Kilmarnock's Eastern Bloc-style police station. Don McAllister sat, hands clasped, on the other side of the laminated desk. There was a manila folder sitting in front of him. When Harry had been shown into the room – just after he'd ignored Don's outstretched hand – he'd noticed four surnames written in black ink on a notepad. One of them was his.

Harry stared around the room. There were flickers of things that prompted him to think of the time he'd first met Don McAllister: a Kilmarnock Order Masonic Lodge pennant on the wall; a British Rail ticket stub next to the bin on the floor; the photographs of the copper and his wife on the desk.

It's 1960. Hogmanay. Twenty-year-old Ethel Fleming is going to a New Year Dance organised by three of her new friends from work. She doesn't know them that well and this is making her dad, James, uncomfortable. Ayr is a dangerous place at night, he warns his youngest child. He knows from bitter personal experience that there are plenty of greasy corner-boys wandering about the town centre, blades at the ready – especially at this time of year, when exuberance can so quickly turn to aggression. Anne, his wife, is more willing to let Ethel go. It's been a hard year for everyone in the family and she feels that her youngest daughter should be encouraged to go out and enjoy herself.

Robert – Ethel's eldest brother – contracted polio as a child and the condition had deteriorated dramatically over the last year. Anne feels that Ethel has sacrificed a lot for her brother and deserves a bit of time to have fun. Ethel's other brother – also James – is currently serving his National Service and was never close to Robert, mocking him constantly for the metal calipers he had to wear when they were boys. Mary – Ethel's older sister – was already something of a party girl and an almost constant cause of concern for her father as a consequence.

So, reluctantly, James lets his daughter go to the dance at the Station, Hotel on the corner of Burns Statue Square. It's an obvious choice for a British Rail staff dance, as the hotel is part of Ayr's railway station, where many of them are employed. Ethel has just started working in the typing pool immediately above the function room where the party will be held. The condition that James accompanies Ethel on the 45-minute bus journey in from Kilmarnock where they live doesn't please her, but since it seems to be non-negotiable, she agrees. Robert's various ailments mean that no-one is allowed to smoke in the house, so both Ethel and her father welcome the sanctuary of the upper deck of the red-and-orange number 33; Ethel with her favourite Embassy Regal and James with his pipe.

'Ach, ah'll catch up wi' a coupla auld mates in the Pot Still,' says James to his daughter. She says nothing but turns to look out the window, mainly to conceal a sigh. God, the Pot Still's just across the road from the station. That'll mean he'll be staying to take me home as well, she's thinking. James also works for the Region's Transport Department as a conductor on the local buses, but the friends he's talking about aren't workmates. They are fellow Masonic Lodge members of whom Anne, Ethel's mother, doesn't approve, so James is glad of the diversion.

Ethel has bought a new frock for the evening. It is pale-blue sleeveless dress with a fitted bodice and a plain round neck. She loves the dress. It was bought with her first pay cheque and she feels it is the first thing that is truly hers. She would keep it forever, due to the significance she would later attach to it. A string of pearls given to her by her gran is the only accessory. It is a freezing, foggy Ayrshire night and Anne has made her wear a heavy coat – which doesn't really go with the dress or the shoes – but, again, Ethel conceded. Earlier, Anne said she looked pretty; like Shirley MacLaine. Ethel took this to be a compliment because she knew her mum loved Shirley MacLaine. Although Ethel wished she'd said Doris Day. Shirley was unconventionally attractive, but Doris was beautiful.

The dance begins at seven o'clock and is due to finish at ten. This would give the revellers time to catch the last buses from Fullarton Street and be home well before the Bells. James walks his embarrassed daughter right into the hotel's reception, where her friends Betty and Eileen are patiently waiting. He leaves her with a reminder to be outside the front door of the hotel at exactly ten. He does have the tact to whisper this to her, knowing her older friends may make fun of her later if they hear him. A third friend, Sadie, is late. She has told Betty earlier in the day that she might be coming with her new man and just to go in. She'd catch up with them later.

The three girls enjoy the night, dancing with different lads and sipping from their gin and tonics. The conversation is relaxed and easy and Ethel begins to feel that she will grow close to Betty and

Eileen. She is less sure of Sadie, and is quietly glad that it appears she isn't coming.

At around nine-thirty, Sadie finally arrives. The dance hall is busy but Ethel catches sight of her immediately. Her blue-and-white spotted dress is one that Ethel has considered for herself, but she decided that it was a bit outlandish. She also vaguely recognises the man with Sadie, but can't remember from where. Sadie comes over, but it is clear she isn't going to stay. Her man has headed in the opposite direction, towards the bar and presumably some people he knows.

The night ends with a chorus of 'Auld Lang Syne' and everyone links arms under the dance hall's sparkly glitter ball. Some coloured balloons are still defiantly circling the dancefloor – their end-of-evening impact lessened by the netting that was holding them having fallen during the early part of the night. As she looks round the circle of drunk but jovial British Rail workers, Anne notices that the man who was on Sadie's arm is no longer there. Sadie is gazing into the eyes of Don McAllister, a young police sergeant and Sadie's married boss.

Before leaving, Ethel goes to the toilet on the upper floor. When she comes out five minutes later, an argument involving a few people has broken out on the stairs. A spotted dress is clearly visible at the centre of it all. Ethel manages to squeeze past the commotion and, although it doesn't look too threatening, and mindful of her dad's finger wagging, she makes her way quickly out into the sharp, cold air of the street.

Most of the revellers leave while she waits impatiently for her dad. She is annoyed because he stressed how important it was that she didn't hang about on street corners at night in the city, and here she is kept waiting by him and his cronies in the old pub over the cobbles. She has been waiting for around fifteen minutes when Sadie's man – the one she came with, not the one she left with – comes out of the hotel's revolving door. He is clearly in pain, holding a left wrist that doesn't look like it is set at the same angle as his right. Ethel asks him if he is all right. He says, No, he doesn't think so. He's taken a swing at Don McAllister, missed badly and fallen down the stairs, landing *awkwardly on his arm. He thinks his wrist might be broken.*

Ethel says that he should maybe go the hospital. It is New Year's Eve, he reminds her. If you've broken your wrist, you'll need to get it looked at tonight, she tells him. The man says he has no money to get to hospital and, slightly ashamed, admits that Sadie has his wallet in her pocket book.

James Fleming is decidedly less than happy to be sharing a black cab to the town's Seafield Hospital on Hogmanay – far less paying for it – with a man that his daughter barely knew, but he's lost a bit of the moral high ground, since it is his fault that Ethel has got into a detailed conversation with him in the first place.

→-◄-

This was how Ethel Fleming met her future husband, Harry Cassidy; and also how Harry Cassidy first met Don McAllister – a man whom he would see again two years later, when Don turned up on the arm of Mary, Ethel's elder sister, for a strained Christmas Day dinner at James and Anne's house. Strained, principally because Ethel had just suffered a miscarriage, which she was trying to conceal for fear of it spoiling everyone else's day. Only months after this, Don was a man who'd had a brief but devastating affair with Ethel. He was a man to whom Harry hadn't spoken for nearly eighteen years. Ethel had not spoken to Don's wife Mary for even longer.

'It's been a while, eh?' said Don, snapping Harry out of his temporary paralysis.

'Mmm,' mumbled Harry. The names on the notepad were holding his temper in check. Plus, a scene now – after all these years – did seem a bit pointless. He'd resolved to keep out of Don's way since the day Gary was born. Harry's only condition for the reconciliation of his marriage was that there be no contact between Ethel and Mary, or, more obviously, Don. Ethel acceded to this harsh demand more willingly than Harry had expected. Burying the memory seemed marginally less painful for her than acknowledging and addressing her debilitating shame. For his part, Don had moved to the Masonic Club in Hurlford, although this was mainly at the insistence of James Fleming, who was secretary at the Kilmarnock Order when his son-in-law was introduced into the membership.

'Look, ah ken things have been rough in the past between you and me ...'

'Aye,' said Harry.

' ... but ah felt ah owed ye this at least.' Don waited a moment for another interruption, but none was forthcoming. 'Bobby and three other yins got lifted a coupla' weeks back. Ah've got the report.' Don tapped the manila file.

Harry looked down at it but still sat impassively. Don was a good detective but he couldn't read Harry. In fact, he'd *never* been able to read him.

'They were at the Tory Club. A fight broke out. Some booze got nicked and ma boys found it in their van.' Don straightened in his seat and delivered a summary quickly and professionally. 'CPS are pushing for a conviction an' there's a lotta top Tories in there.'

Harry still remained silent. He was unsure if Don was angling for some sort of a deal here.

'Ah can make it go away for Bobby and his two mates, but the van driver's gonnae get fucked unfortunately.' Don saw Harry's eyebrows rise at this. 'Stevenson. D'you ken him tae?'

'Aye. Ah dae. He's a good lad. Ah'm sure he'll no be involved.'

'Harry, the stuff was in his fuckin' van! An' wi' his record, he's the obvious Lee Majors here.'

Harry look bemused.

'The fuckin' Fall Guy ...' said Don. 'Look, ah'm lettin' Bobby off wi' this ... an' afore ye say it, ah'm no wantin' anythin' back.' Don sat back in his large leather chair. 'Ah just wanted the opportunity tae set the record straight wi' you ... an' wi' Ethel. Mary forgave her years ago. And me, for that matter. For *everythin*'. No' comin' tae the weddin', an that tae ... She still misses her.' Don could almost see

Harry's hackles rising. 'Ye cannae put yer arms around a memory, Harry.' It was well intentioned, but way wide of the mark.

Harry stood up abruptly. 'Don't you talk about ma wife. *Ma* wife, ye hear it? No yours … mine!'

Don also stood up, closing the manila file as he did so.

'*Forgiven*? Whit you did left Ethel too fuckin' ashamed tae look her sister in the face.'

'Harry …'

'Don't fuckin' *Harry* me, you!' Harry's voice was getting louder. Don's hands were faced down in a patting, calming motion. It wasn't working, though.

'Ye fuckin' took advantage when me and her were at the lowest ebb. She'd just lost the wean, an' you were goin' wi' her fuckin' sister! Jesus Christ, how dae ye think ah'm gonnae react even after aw this time? Ah'm fuckin' staggered Mary took ye back ya cunt …'

'Right, Harry that's en–'

' … ye destroyed our lives, an' yer ain wife's. Although she should fuckin' ken how it feels at least, since *she* did it tae yer first yin …'

'Too far, Harry … yer goin' too …'

'It took us the best part ae a year tae get back on track. Tae when *he* was born … an' even then, things have never been the same. Ethel will never get ower it, she's a fuckin' nervous wreck … an' ye fuckin' ruined any chance ae her an' Mary ever speakin' again. *Forgiven*, ya bastart. Ethel cannae forgive *herself.*' The rage in Harry's voice was matched by the reddening of his face. He had waited a long time for all of this to come out and even though he could sense that he *would* actually go too far, he still wasn't fully aware of what that boundary constituted.

'Ah kent that Mary couldnae have weans, in fact, ah probably kent that before you did.' Harry's voice was calmer now. He'd struck a blow. It was a low one, but he'd definitely scored a hit. He walked over to the door. 'Look, you dae whit ye have tae dae wi' Bobby. If he's done somethin' wrong, then he deserves tae get punished. If he husnae, then let him off, but don't bring him intae any situation wi' you an' me.'

Harry paused at the door with his back to Don. His hand was on the door handle.

'Ye ken this … ah still cannae speak tae him … tae Gary, even though he's a better man than me. Ah cannae find the words or the way tae tell him that … an' for that more than anything else, ah fuckin' hate you McAllister.' Harry opened the door and walked through it, closing it gently behind him.

Don stared at the door for a few minutes and then stood up slowly and walked over to the window. He watched Harry cross the road and walk up John Finnie Street. Don watched him walk the whole length. Harry never looked back. Don loosened his tie, poured himself a large Scotch and sat down at his desk. He lifted the phone receiver and dialled five numbers.

'Mary, hen? It's me …'

11

OH BONDAGE: UP YOURS!

With Hamish May still in hospital, and the threat of some Fat Franny-funded violence now lurking in the shadows of every gig, Bobby figured Heatwave required a new level of security. The last few functions had gone off very quietly – and successfully – but this was due to Joey's inspired idea of self-promoted, 'secret', one-off nights at the Killie Club. The Club was located in the spaces under the terracing at Rugby Park, home of Kilmarnock Football Club, and was promoted by the music-loving manager, whose cut was an acceptable twenty percent. With the nights advertised locally at forty-eight hours' notice and populated by mates of the DJs and local Mod band The Vespas, there was little chance of trouble. But The Vespas had asked Heatwave to support them at a gig on the fifth of June. It was going to be held at the large Henderson Church Hall in the town centre and, with tickets circulating widely, Bobby was growing increasingly anxious about his own level of personal protection.

'Whit about havin' a word wi' Malky MacKay? See if he'd dae it?' suggested Bobby.

'Aye. That's no a bad call, mate,' replied Joey. 'He's no a bad lad, once ye get tae know him a bit more.'

'Right. Let me ken later how ye get on, eh?'

'Whit? Awa' an' fuck yersel'.' Joey nearly choked on his Cabana bar. 'Ah'm no fuckin' askin' him. He's mental!'

'Ye just said he was a good lad! And ye ken 'im better than me.' Bobby's palms were outstretched. Joey intuitively knew what was coming. 'C'mon, get in there.'

→>–<←

It was true that Joey knew Malky more than Bobby, but the basis of this knowledge was now almost three years old. In the early part of his fourth year, Joey had been going through a phase of picking up regular detention punishments at school. These were mostly for ridiculous things, like passing notes in class, or laughing out loud at an old female teacher's ridiculous attempts to administer the belt to a boy almost two feet taller than her and her ultimately having to stand on a box to do it. During this period Joey had even copped a detention slot for 'repeatedly sneezing'. He wouldn't have needed Perry Mason to get him off on that one, had he attempted to make an issue of it, but the truth was, Joey actually enjoyed detention. It was marshalled by a groovy English-teaching hippy who evidently considered the short straw of detention duty to be as much a punishment for him as for the detainees. Given that it was generally the same miscreants populating the detention chamber night after night, something of a shared group mentality kicked in and they all passed the time talking about football or, more significantly, music. The hippy brought in a Dansette record player and forced his captive audience to listen to stuff like 'Bug-Eyed Beans from Venus', 'Dark Side of the Moon' or 'The Lamb Lies Down on Broadway'. Joey emerged from this phase with a love for the first, a respect for the second but nothing other than outright, lasting contempt for Genesis.

Back then, detention for Joey began to feel more like an after-school record club and, although the class was populated by the misbehaved, the boisterous or, on occasion, the downright violent, short-term friendships inevitably prospered. One of these unlikely pairings was between Joey and Malky Mackay. As early as second year, it was accepted wisdom that Malky was the best fighter in the school. How this had happened was unclear. As far as Joey was aware, there had been no qualifying bouts before a shot at the title. No mandatory defences against leading contenders of the day. Malky was just assumed to be the heavyweight champion. That he'd achieved this while still only fourteen didn't say much for the youths in the upper school, but it did give him an undeniable air of invincibility. If, indeed, heavy was the head that wore the crown, Malky certainly didn't show it.

Their main connection was through Subbuteo. Malky invited Joey back to his house to see his set-up. Poorer kids were obsessed by the game. Slightly better-off ones had moved onto Scalextric. Malky had amassed an impressive collection of accessories, from the dugouts and touchline fencing to the much-envied stadium, complete with politely seated supporters. It looked great, and when he switched on the battery-operated floodlights, Joey was suitably awed and initially a little envious. Impressive though the stadium was, Malky only had one battery-operated pylon and the empty seats outnumbered the static punters by around twenty to one.

Joey only had the basic components. He did, however, have some glamorous teams. He had River Plate from Argentina, Cagliari from Italy and the Brazilian national team. Malky, on the other hand had only ever needed two: Glasgow Rangers and Glasgow Rangers in away strip. His house was a temple to all things bluenose. A smiling portrait of the Queen greeted everyone upon entry. Framed pictures of famous goals lined the route upstairs to the bedrooms. Posters of the team and individual players fought with pennants for space on Malky's bedroom walls. A Rangers alarm clock, bedspread and lightshade kept up the theme. Curtains, carpet and a dressing gown completed the ensemble. Although he'd apparently taken enough of a liking to Joey to invite him back, there was an undeniable tension when Malky wasn't happy. To Joey's relief, their game was going well. Naturally, he was Rangers reserves, and he was getting hammered. It *was a price worth paying. When Malky's mother shouted up the stairs that his dinner was ready and that Joey needed to go home, he stood up abruptly, tripped over the black elastic strips of his home-made bondage trousers and collapsed onto the field like some stumbling, drunken Gulliver, crushing half of the Rangers first team, and destroying the mini-terracing, sending the shocked and motionless fans flying across the room. Joey was a punk-like tsunami.*

'*Ya fuckin' stupid cunt! Look at the state of Davie Cooper! You're fuckin' gettin it!*'

And that was just Mrs *Malky.*

→►◄←

'Twenty quid,' said Malky, in what was fast becoming the standard rate for any service. He glugged from the large Alpine bottle of American Cream Soda.

'Aye. OK, although it's Boab that'll pay ye.' Joey was grateful that Malky hadn't borne any grudges from the day the tiny Cooper had been forced into early retirement. They parted, agreeing for Malky to meet them at the church hall the following night.

5TH JUNE 1982

'What a pity we ever had the hostilities, what a pity there was ever the invasion. Once we have repossessed the islands then of course we have to try to mend fences and we shall do that, but the integrity of the islands must be respected just as the integrity of each country in Latin America ought to be respected, otherwise we shall go to international anarchy and none of our peoples will profit from that.'

Margaret Thatcher, the Prime Minister,
radio interview for the Central Office of Information

There were four in The Vespas band, including two brothers playing guitar and drums. Bobby didn't know the names of the brothers or that of the stand-stock-still bass player, but he was reasonably friendly with their singer, Dale Wishart, whom he'd known since primary school. The Vespas' repertoire was limited and their need for some form of support act for their gigs was obvious. Early in April, Heatwave Disco became that support, topping and tailing the live music with a vinyl mix of Mod standards, Stax and Motown classics. Songs from the new Mod revivalists such as The Chords, Secret Affair, The Lambrettas, The Vapors, The Knack and Nine Below Zero made up the general playlist.

When the emerging 2-Tone label artists and the slightly less definable Dexy's Midnight Runners were added to the playlist, it was a pretty impressive line-up. There was a real sense of belonging within this group of kids who followed the band. Concerts by favoured bands were generally few and far between, and almost always restricted to the bigger cities. Watching a Mod tribute band comprised of people they knew and liked, and in a small venue, from which they could stumble home drunk, was a pretty good stop-gap. Heatwave had now completed five such gigs with The Vespas and they had all been pretty great.

Bobby liked Dale and, despite his often-ludicrous on-stage behaviour, Joey also couldn't find it within himself to avoid speaking to him on the rare occasions when their paths crossed. Dale's more outlandish persona had emerged when the band secured an unlikely late-night radio session in January on Ayrshire's independent radio station, West Sound. The grapevine promoted the theory that the band had only got the spot because Dale's dad had threatened Mac Barber – a club DJ from Ayr who had landed a nighttime slot on the station. This seemed highly plausible, as the Wisharts were fairly regular visitors to Kilmarnock's police station and sheriff court. Assaults, money-lending and drug-dealing were among the most frequent topics of conversation when the family dropped in to Don McAllister's office for tea and a chat.

The Vespas had built a small but loyal local following by doing the pub gigs around Ayrshire, but the radio session had been a disaster. During the pre-recording of their first original song, the bizarrely named 'The Legomen Are Here', Dale – in full-on performance mode at this point – unhooked a microphone and swung it in an arc, knocking out the front teeth of Steven 'Stera' Dent, his band's bass player. A major studio mêlée ensured that the session remained unrecorded and therefore unbroadcast. It had also given birth to the strained relations within the band and led to an inevitable parting of ways.

Following the first night at the Killie Club in May, Dale phoned Bobby. It was very much out of the blue. His call was to ask if Heatwave would do the DJ sets for some gigs leading up to a farewell show at the Henderson Church. The event was to support a local charity close to Jimmy Wishart's heart. Jimmy was the singer's father and it was clear from Dale that this wasn't a request to be answered negatively. In the spirit of charitable endeavour, Heatwave would also be doing this *pro bono*. Things had been going well with bookings for the disco lately, and, with the target of travelling to Spain with the rest of the Tartan Army for that summer's World Cup campaign now almost within their financial grasp, Bobby decided to let this one go for free. However, he ducked out at the last minute, opting to spend the evening with Lizzie and leaving Joey in sole charge.

'A'right Malky?' Joey tried not to smile as he saw Malky standing at the main door waiting for Jimmy's van. The former undisputed champion of the James Hamilton Academy was wearing a suit – his dad's perhaps, judging by the cut – and a tie. The tie was a James Hamilton Academy one. *Thank fuck he didnae wear his old school blazer*, thought Joey.

'Got the twenty there?' Malky had always been a man of few words. Joey took the two notes from his pocket and handed them over. Malky examined them as if they were forgeries before eventually putting them in his inside jacket pocket. Joey didn't even ask him for assistance with the gear, knowing it would cost more if he did, and since Jimmy no longer even came into the venues, Joey resigned himself to a long night of heavy lifting for no reward.

The night started quietly. Few people turned up and those who did were either Wishart family members or associates under orders to be there. Joey played some new records as a warm-up. He'd picked up some rare vinyl at a record fair in Glasgow's Merchant City, and a run of old classics including Eddie Floyd's 'Big Bird', Madeline Bell's 'Picture Me Gone' and Lee Dorsey's 'Get Out of My Life, Woman' had the small group of assembled Mods in raptures. Joey was really enjoying the power. He also debuted some brilliant new songs, like Odyssey's 'Inside Out' and The Associates' 'Party Fears Two'. Many of these were elongated twelve-inch mixes in order to avoid him having to speak and run the risk of patronising or offending the Wisharts.

Dale came over to say that his band would be on stage at nine, in around thirty minutes. The singer looked thoroughly defeated. Gone were the sharp Fred Perrys and Lonsdale shirts of old. Now he was all floppy hair, batwing shirt and lycra trousers. He wore legwarmers and gleaming-white patent shoes. Joey felt for him. It was apparent that there were some considerable musical differences at the core of The Vespas. There was a faint glimmer of a smile when Dale said the band would be starting with their *own* version of The Jam's cover of 'Heatwave', and that the DJ should activate the smoke machines and the strobes 'for old time's sake'.

Just before The Vespas entered stage left, a large mob piled into the church hall. There was no immediate commotion. They all paid and made their way to the middle of the hall. Joey whispered to Malky that perhaps there would be a decent atmosphere for The Vespas' farewell after all. Malky couldn't care less. At five to nine the main lights went down and curling, dense smoke began to fill the church hall. Joey could still see the tall, skinny singer through the fog. Even from the opposite end of the smoke-filled hall, there appeared to be a sparkle in his eye as he stood front and centre-stage, clocking the half-full venue, rather than the embarrassing turnout he'd anticipated twenty minutes earlier.

'Hiya, Kil … nock … we're the …. and we … go … build a … of music … love … you … ight!'

It was hardly 'Hello, I'm Johnny Cash', but nevertheless Joey had to admire his enthusiasm. From his postion on stage, though, Dale was unaware that his microphone wasn't working fully and he sounded just like Norman Collier.

'We … Heatwave!' shouted Dale. The opening bars of the first song were terrible. The sound was was tinny and mono-tonal. It was like Ultravox heard under water. Even though the events that followed were regrettable, Joey Miller was almost grateful to the punter in the front row who threw the empty bottle that hit the singer in the face, stopping the song before the end. It quickly became apparent that this was no protest act from an insulted music fan. The large group who had come late to the gig took the bottling as a signal to attack the stage and those on it, prompting a counter by the surprised Wisharts and their followers. A full-scale riot ensued.

Joey missed most of it as he had bolted for a side door and found himself at the back of a female toilet. If he was going to be beaten to a pulp, several heavily made-up females would either be ahead of him in the queue or would be responsible for it. As Joey cowered at the side of a cistern, the noise from the main hall was incredible. Stained-glass windows that had survived for more than a century were sure to be among the victims; as was the majority of Heatwave Disco's sound equipment and record stocks, Joey figured. A twelve-inch single, carefully thrown, could be a handy weapon, and Joey envisaged emerging into a scene of carnage where casualties lay with 'Let's Start the Dance Again' or 'The Message' embedded in their skulls.

At nine-thirty, Joey was still ensconced in a girl's toilet cubicle. The noise had died sufficiently to hear the more welcome sounds of approaching sirens. He unlocked the door and, along with his cautious fellow deserters, ventured carefully back into the main hall and towards the only available exit beyond. The scene was a familiar one, but its familiarity was associated with last year's scenes from Ulster. Windows were indeed smashed. The injured were nursing wounds, and the recently arrived cops were lifting those left standing. The Heatwave gear was in better condition than Joey was entitled to expect. It was apparent that Malky had earned his twenty. A few lights were out and the speakers were on their side, but there were no shattered fragments of black plastics lying around, looking as if they'd been targets at a clay pigeon shoot. The focus of the crowd's anger had been directed towards the stage end of the hall, whereas Joey had set up at the rear. As for the actual stage itself, the band was gone, their instruments strewn all over the place. Apart from a synth that, although still upright, was on fire.

In the days that followed, it transpired that there *was* no charity. The gig was an attempt by the Wisharts to raise money to pay off a Glasgow gang from whom they had taken a large amount of drugs that they had been unable to move on. The Quinn rent-a-mob was hired by Fat Franny, but badly briefed by Hobnail. He had only mentioned the word 'Heatwave' and when the heavies misheard Dale's opening introduction, the leader simply launched his bottle in the direction of the code word. To make matters worse, they'd all got there late, due to the bus drivers' strike.

Dale Wishart, formerly of The Vespas, was in intensive care at Crosshouse Hospital. He had been opportunistically walloped by Stera's bass, while trying to get his bearings following the bottle's impact. Bobby visited him only once in hospital the day after the gig – on the way to see Hamish May – but it was still once more than Joey.

→><←

At the same time as many in the Henderson Church Hall were getting their balls booted, Bobby was getting his fondled. He'd taken advantage of the limited supporting role Heatwave would be playing in Dale Wishart's last stand to suggest that this gig didn't need both him *and* Joey. That this was a charity gig in more ways than one further lowered his interest. But he had an ulterior motive. After the night at The Anchorage, Bobby had fallen out with Joey on the walk back down Templehill. He hadn't been comfortable doing it, but he felt obliged to defend Lizzie rather than support Joey's daft theory that Hamish had been abducted as a result of Lizzie being unable to control herself. Bobby did feel a bit of subsequent regret when it transpired that their friend had, in fact, been *Shanghai-ed*; a fact that only came to light after the unconscious teenager's tiny rowing boat had been snared by an Irish fishing trawler near the Mull of Kintyre. Hamish had been in Kilmarnock Infirmary suffering from hypothermia since that day.

Lizzie had slipped off her bra in the taxi back home from Troon and had encouraged him to feel her up in the back of the car. Her nipples felt enormous and Bobby had almost shot his load when Lizzie reached down and rubbed the bulge in his jeans. In the days that followed, it became clear that they'd be having sex at the next available opportunity. With Hettie staying with her friends and Harry and Ethel due to go to an anniversary party at The Clansman, the Friday of The Vespas' gig was that opportunity. Bobby said nothing of this to anyone, least of all Joey. Joey was a bit strange around girls and most of them – including Lizzie – found him a wee bit too intense and serious. They had gone out to The Broomhill for a pint to throw Harry and Ethel off the scent. But also to provide the necessary Dutch courage for a sexually inexperienced young man desperate for his equipment to work in the way that God intended.

As they walked back up Almond Avenue, Bobby spotted *auld* Sadie Flanagan about fifty yards up ahead. It was a warm evening and Lizzie was dressed very provocatively with a ridiculously short pleated ra-ra skirt riding all the way up her muscular thighs. If *auld* Flanagan saw the two them and noticed – as everyone in the pub had – that Lizzie was wearing no bra under that skimpy white vest-top, Bobby would've faced the parental Spanish Inquisition the next day concerning where they had been that night. Bobby took evasive action and they climbed over the fence at the back of the school. He'd intended to go in through the back-garden gate; actually that very phrase had gone through his mind and had been the origin of the rapidly developing hard-on that was now bursting up through his Y-fronts.

They reached the rear hedge at Bobby's house, but in a crushing blow to the evening's romantic plans, he could make out the unmistakable silhouette of his father through the curtained kitchen window. As they approached, it was apparent that an argument was in progress, and that his mother was on the receiving end. If they had gone out at all, it hadn't been for long. Although this wasn't a massive shock given the way things had been between them lately, Bobby was still annoyed.

'Ach, fuckin' bollocks.' Bobby's angry tone had been louder than he'd intended. Lizzie saw the silhouette turn towards them. She pulled Bobby down behind the large timber shed, where Heatwave Disco's equipment was housed. The kitchen door opened, throwing some additional light into the gloom. Harry stared out across the garden. He was sure he'd heard something out there. There was nothing, though, and at least it had broken the momentum of an ongoing dispute with Ethel that had no resolution. Gary was *that cunt McAllister's* son and no amount of crawling over the coals of a twenty-year-old situation would change that. Harry had made his decision decades ago. For better or for worse, there was no erasing that now.

Out in the garden, Lizzie had ensured silence by clamping her mouth over Bobby's. After the door closed and the kitchen light was extinguished, her warm, soft tongue worked its way all around Bobby's. He liked it a lot, but he did have a very sensitive gag reflex and when she almost touched his tonsils, he had to push her back slightly.

Fucking hell, Bon Scott died from choking on his own vomit, Bobby remembered. *Bet his head was bent backwards at the time as well!*

'C'mon we'll go in there,' whispered Lizzie, nodding towards the shed. She took his left hand and lifted it up the inside of her vest. He could feel those massive, plate-sized nipples standing to attention. His hand worked its way around Lizzie's tit like a baker kneading dough. *Fuck me, that felt fucking fantastic.* For a moment, Bobby thought that he was actually saying these thoughts out loud.

'Aye … OK,' he said finally. 'It's where ah keep the gear but it's got a carpet an' it'll probably be a'right.'

Lizzie stood up. She looked quickly towards the house. It was now illuminated only by the clear moonlight. Everything else was quiet. Bobby reached under the black plant pot and found the padlock key. He opened the wooden slatted door carefully and stood back, allowing Lizzie to step inside. Although the equipment in the shed had not been arranged with all the considered attention to detail and diligence of Hairy Doug's, there was an order of sorts to the composition. Bobby reached for his father's torch and flicked the switch before placing it upright in the corner of the shed. He turned to see Lizzie pulling off her vest-top. Bobby'd had a few pints and thought she looked gorgeous. The bizarre perspective of the light source made her cleavage look even bigger. Lizzie arched her back, forcing her breasts forward and pushing hard against him. Bobby fell backwards and had to put his right hand out to stop himself falling over a small lightbox at his feet. His face was smothered in Lizzie's hot, heaving tits.

'Kiss them.'

Bobby lifted them up so that he could speak. 'They're really big.'

'They're no as firm as ah'd like them tae be.'

'Ah think they're fuckin' brilliant.'

Lizzie took his left hand and pulled it slowly up her thigh, across her pants and inside the elastic. He was still looking straight at her, as his hand found its way around the hairy mound and his fingers finally worked their way easily inside the soft, full lips of her fanny. With his right hand, he clumsily undid his belt buckle and, with Lizzie's help, Bobby's jeans and Y-fronts were rapidly down at his shins.

'It's big tae, Bobby.'

'Ah was near the front ae the queue when they were gettin' gied out.'

'Here, put this on.' From the small slit pocket in her skirt, Lizzie pulled out a condom.

'Christ, Lizzie, ah never even thought aboot a *johnny*.'

'Jist as well one ae us is thinkin' ahead then. Here, bring it ower.'

Lizzie took hold of Bobby's prick and, with her free hand and her teeth, tore open the packaging and then deftly placed it over the top of his cock, rolling it down the shaft with both hands.

'Thank fuck ah went for a wank earlier.'

'Eh?'

Bobby *had* let that one escape from his inner monologue, but to cover this affront, he pulled Lizzie close and then lifted her up onto a small bass amplifier. He slipped inside her easily. He knew he wouldn't have been the first, but at that moment it didn't matter to him in the slightest. As his primal bucking and heaving got going, Lizzie made a lot of noise and, conscious of the close proximity of his parents, Bobby reached up to try and *kiss* her quiet. But she fought free of his mouth and screamed as though she was in pain. Bobby bucked harder and felt them both gradually sliding backwards off the amplifier box.

With his cock still inside her, Lizzie's arse slipped onto a much smaller, metallic box. Her legs had tightened around the base of his back, keeping them locked together. Bobby jerked as a blast of cold smoke came up between his legs from the box. Lizzie's arse cheeks were slapping against the box, flicking the switch of the Heatwave Disco dry-ice canister machine on and off, blowing smoke – literally – up Bobby's arsehole; not a totally unpleasant experience. By the time they both came, shuddering to a dramatic climax, the shed looked like it was on fire. Smoke had seeped out of the cracks in the door and was drifting freely across the school playgrounds.

Sated, they lay there in each other's arms on the blankets and tarpaulin sheets until about four a.m., when it started to get lighter. Bobby woke first and leaned awkwardly back, resting his head on his hand. *She's alright,* he thought. They had had an inauspicious start to their relationship, but she *was* pretty cool. And – in Bobby's mind at least – she'd stood up for him at The Anchorage in a way that few of his mates had ever done. Lizzie hadn't told him about her history with Theresa and was enjoying the reflected glory of having taken on the Fat Franny troupe … and won.

20ᵀᴴ MAY 1982

'The House has before it the draft agreement, and I turn now to its main features. Article 2 provides for the cessation of hostilities and the withdrawal of Argentine and British forces from the islands and their surrounding waters within fourteen days. At the end of the withdrawal British ships would be at least 150 nautical miles from the islands. Withdrawal much beyond this would not have been reasonable, because the proximity of the Argentine mainland would have given their forces undue advantage. Withdrawal of the Argentine Forces would be the most immediate and explicit sign that their Government's aggression had failed and that they were being made to give up what they had gained by force. It is the essential beginning of a peaceful settlement and the imperative of Resolution 502.'

Mrs Margaret Thatcher, the Prime Minister,
House of Commons Statement

12

DISPATCHES

Queen Elizabeth 2
The English Channel
13th May 1982

Dear Mum,

Didn't get much chance to write yesterday. Sorry. The bus was late in leaving and there was a real panic on with the Command. Southampton docks was absolutely mental, though. It felt great to finally be going and everybody cheering and waving banners. It was like being one of the Bay City Rollers.

Never ever thought I'd be on a cruise. I know it's not like a holiday, but it's really exciting. We should reach Ascension in a couple of weeks and then get new orders there. I'm in a decent bunk with three of my mates and even the officers are all mucking in and having a laugh with us. It's been good on the boat with five Infantry, the Gurkhas and the Welsh lads.

We were up early this morning at 06:30 hours for a run round the deck then breakfast. Weather was great, really calm seas, and for all of last night there was wee boats following us but they've all gone now.

Hope you're OK and give everybody my love.

I'll try and write as much as I can but, you know me … I'm not the greatest with the words.

Don't worry about me.
Love
Gary x

Queen Elizabeth 2
At Sea
14th May 1982

Dear Hets,

How's it going? Things are great here. The weather's brilliant and even I'm getting a tan. You should see me now. No white pale skin anymore … now I look like Michael Jackson! Hope the exams are going OK and that you spoke to Dad about your art highers.

Don't worry about all the stuff on TV and in the papers. This is probably going to be over by the time we get there. The Argies have only got a few catapults and three air rifles …

I'll write again soon but it's time for lunch now.

All my love,
Gary xxx

Dear Mum,

I went for a run around the deck on my own yesterday. Ten times round the upper deck, which is about four miles. It's really warm now so I was sweating like a pig and totally knackered by the time I stopped. Had a quick shower then some of the other boys had a wee birthday thing for Benny, one of my mates. It was his nineteenth and he was a wee bit down because there was no letters or cards from his mum and dad.

I don't know if you're sending me anything but a lot of the boys have been complaining that their post is getting censored. I really hope this gets to you soon.

The bunks are now getting piped music and the BBC World Service, which is good. None of that rubbish that Bobby likes but we think it's alright. It's air conditioned as well, so it's really comfortable. Apart from the noise of soldiers running round the decks above us – and there's a medical training film getting shown constantly next door to us.

Have to go now. Inspection's coming.

Love you, Mum. Say hello to Dad.
Bye for now.
Gary x

Hi Bawface,

Been at sea for a week now and I'm bored fucking rigid! Haven't seen land since the day after we left Southampton. There's bugger-all to do but run round the bloody boat. I could beat Steve Ovett and Sebastian fucking Coe running in a relay!

How's things with you anyway? Still nicking that Lizzie one? What about Dopey Joey? Still spouting all that Bruce Kent shite?

We all watched *Knight Rider* last night. It's fucking brilliant, that programme. I seriously want a car like that when I get back. Maybe Hammy's old man could sort me out, eh?

I missed the end of it though cos' Kenny my mate started spewing and I went back to the bunk with him. The waves were a bit crazy last night. You don't really feel it most of the time because this liner's bloody massive, but even I had to admit last night was a bit rough.

Still don't know what the plans are and nobody tells us anything, but there's rumours we're all going straight to the Falklands now rather than Ascension Island. News came through last night about the twenty Special Forces boys that died in the Sea King crash. The mood here's beginning to change a bit. Not as much laughing and joking.

Sorry you didn't get the money together to go to Spain. I wish I could've helped you.

Anyway enjoy the Cup Final. I'm assuming you and Joey are in the Rangers end? Tell him I hope Aberdeen hump them ...

I miss you, mate.
G

Debbie,

Sorry it's taken so long to write. To be honest, I'm not great at writing letters and especially a letter like this one. It was great to see you at Southampton. I know I told you not to waste your day off coming all the way down there, but I'm really really glad you did. Things are beginning to get pretty serious now but I think the Navy have got it well covered so far. Last night we heard that the United Nations talks had failed. We're hearing a lot on the World Service, but that's really the only place we get told anything.

I hope you're not worrying about me too much. I still don't know what the actual plan is, but it looks like we'll be landing at San Carlos in about a week. I still find it incredible that I'm actually here. I've never been abroad before and here I am on the *QE2* in the South Atlantic, eight thousand miles away from home … and you!

I wonder what you're doing, and if you're thinking about me as well. I'm feeling a bit lonely now. Mates are good company but everybody's a bit depressed at the minute. There's been no post since we left so I'm not even sure if this letter will get to you.

It was only last night when I couldn't sleep and all sorts of weird things started going through my mind … I got really irritated.

It's not until a time like this when you're not here and I don't know when I'll see you again that I realised how much I love you.

I hope you feel the same Debs.

I love you and I'll write again tomorrow …

G xxx

'In view of the confident assertion yesterday – some people might think over-confident – that the days of the Argentine garrison are numbered ...'

Mr Martin Flannery, MP for Sheffield Hillsborough

'They are.'

Mr Nicholas Winterton, MP for Macclesfield

' ... may we now have a cessation of hostilities? I know that the bloodthirsty hooligans on the Tory Benches do not want that, but could we not discuss future sovereignty of the Falklands under the aegis of the United Nations, especially in view of the fact that the Tory British Nationality Act has deprived at least a third of the islanders of British nationality? What shall we do with those islands once we have them? Are we to have a permanent fleet on a vast scale there indefinitely, and are we to have an army down there indefinitely to protect them?'

Mr Martin Flannery, MP for Sheffield Hillsborough

'That is about seven questions. I wonder which to start on. The Hon. Gentleman referred to the phrase in my right Hon. Friend's speech that the days of the Argentine garrison are numbered. Does the Hon. Gentleman not want those days to be numbered? We wish them to be numbered. He then called for a ceasefire while the invader was kept in occupation. We totally reject that. It would leave the whole paraphernalia of tyranny in place. Perhaps two answers will be enough for the Hon. Gentleman.'

Mrs Margaret Thatcher, the Prime Minister

'Is my right Hon. Friend satisfied with the flow of mail to and from the Falkland force, because I have received one or two complaints from my constituents about delays, and mail is important for morale?'

Miss Janet Fookes, MP for Plymouth Drake

'I am sure that everything possible under the circumstances is being done to get mail both to the Armed Forces and from them. I recognise the importance of mail, and I am confident that everything is being done.'

Mrs Margaret Thatcher, the Prime Minister

Queen Elizabeth 2
At Sea, South Atlantic
26th May 1982

Dear All,

A lot seems to have happened in the last few days. We have continued to head south towards the islands and the weather has been good. A Hercules flew over yesterday and dropped mail and I got all your letters so I'm feeling really good now. Hope mine are getting through to you.

The whole ship is blacked out at night and on the way back to the bunk I fell over one of those bulkhead steps at the door. I rattled my shin off the edge of it and it's come up in a big welt this morning. Hettie, you would have killed yourself laughing at me.

A couple of nights ago we had a good church service up on deck. I know you won't believe this, but I really enjoyed it. I even went to communion afterwards. There were loads of soldiers who turned up for it and all the Welsh lads chose the hymns.

We were all allowed to have drinks after the service. The drink's incredibly cheap here … Dad, you'd love it. It's cheaper than the Masonic. I bought a round of four vodkas and it cost me 86p! I couldn't believe it!

Anyway, better go now. We've got the cinema tonight. It's a film called *Porky's* which sounds like it should be a good laugh … but then we're up at 07:00 hours for emergency drills. Not looking forward to that …

Lots of love to everyone, and I'll write again soon.
Gary

Queen Elizabeth 2
At Sea, South Atlantic
28th May 1982

Dear Mum,

I miss you and I hope you're coping with all the news coming from the Islands. I'm fine and everyone here is really calm. There's a real feeling that it's all coming to an end now and that Galtieri's going to give up any day. I think that by the time we land at San Carlos in a couple of days there'll just be time to swap jerseys with the Argies before coming home again …

I hope Hettie told you about my girlfriend Debbie. I can't wait to bring her up to Killie and for you to meet her. She's really great.

Mum, don't worry about me in the next few days. I know you will though, but I'll be fine.

I can't wait to get back for some of your lentil soup …

I love you, Mum.
Gary xxx

Dad,

I know we haven't spent much time talking together over the years and I'm really sorry about that now. I never ever thought I'd be any good at writing letters … or anything else for that matter … but since I started writing a couple of weeks ago, it's got a lot easier.

I know Mum will be worried but I'm not sure what to write to make her feel any better. We all watched the TV footage showing the 2 Para attacks at Goose Green and Darwin. Some of our officers knew H. Jones and it's really shocked a lot of us here. It brought it home to me that in a few days I might actually be fighting in a war. Everybody's really quiet now. My three mates spend all of their free time writing. I've even started a sort of diary. Hettie would be proud of me …

We're due to sail to San Carlos Water on Tuesday but it's too dangerous to take this liner in further so all the battalions are getting disembarked at different times. At the minute, it looks like we're going to be last. The 5th Brigade are going on the Canberra tomorrow. We've still to be briefed but I think we're going on the Intrepid. We saw a couple of Mirage fighter planes last night so the Argies know we're here.

I'm actually scared, Dad. It's not that I wish I hadn't signed up. It's just that I'm scared I panic and do something stupid or I let somebody down. I've been thinking back to all the stupid things I did as a kid, and that I now wish I hadn't. I wish I'd told you how I felt more and that I hadn't caused you as much heartache.

I hope you'll be proud of me, whatever happens … and that we can go for a pint together down at the Masonic.

I love you, Dad.

Bye.

Gary

Bluff Cove Base Camp
Falkland Islands
5th June, 1982

Debs,

I love you and I miss you so much. I won't get the chance to write again for a while. We landed at Bluff Cove this morning. There's been Skyhawk fighters all over the place and we've had to move everything pretty quickly. We were due to wait for the Galahad but orders were changed and we went ahead of the Welsh Guards.

We'll be moving towards Stanley in a few days time. The weather's taken a turn for the worst. It's freezing and it's been raining since we landed.

I hope you're fine and not worrying too much about me. Hope you've been getting my letters.

Can't wait to get home to you, and to cuddle you again.

I love you …

Gary xxx

'On a point of order, Mr Speaker. May I give the House the latest information about the battle of the Falklands? After successful attacks last night, General Moore decided to press forward. The Argentines retreated. Our forces reached the outskirts of Port Stanley. Large numbers of Argentine soldiers threw down their weapons. They are reported to be flying white flags over Port Stanley. Our troops have been ordered not to fire except in self-defence. Talks are now in progress between General Menendez and our Deputy Commander, Brigadier Waters, about the surrender of the Argentine forces on East and West Falkland. I shall report further to the House tomorrow.'

Mrs Margaret Thatcher, The Prime Minister

'Hear, hear!'

Hon. Members

'Further to that point of order, Mr Speaker. First, may I thank the Right Hon. Lady for coming to the House to give us the news, particularly because the news is so good for all concerned, especially because it appears from what she has been able to tell us that there will be an end to the bloodshed, which is what we have all desired. There will be widespread, genuine rejoicing – to use the word that the Right Hon. Lady once used – at the prospect of the end of the bloodshed. If the news is confirmed, as I trust it will be, there will be great congratulations from the House tomorrow to the British Forces who have conducted themselves in such a manner and, if I may say so, to the Right Hon. Lady. I know that there are many matters on which we shall have to have discussions, and perhaps there will be arguments about the origins of this matter and other questions, but I can well understand the anxieties and pressures that must have been upon the Right Hon. Lady during these weeks. I can understand that at this moment those pressures and anxieties may have been relieved, and I congratulate her on that.

'I believe that we can as a House of Commons transform what has occurred into benefits for our country as a whole. I believe that that is the way in which we on the Opposition Benches will wish to proceed. There are many fruitful lessons in diplomacy and in other matters that we can draw from this occasion, and that will be the Opposition's determination.'

Mr Michael Foot, Leader of the Opposition, MP for Ebbw Vale

15TH JUNE 1982: 9:45AM

The British Army is the ultimate procedural organisation, especially in times of war. Although the families of those involved in the fighting would be aware from every broadcast that their husbands, fathers, sons, brothers, boyfriends were now fully engaged in war, they also knew that the Army – after its years of experience in Northern Ireland – was never drawn on the subject of casualties until every possibility of doubt was eliminated. In the British Army, next-of-kin should only learn of a death through official channels. With a few notable exceptions, the media cooperate in this respect. The Army adheres to another strict procedure: bad news should never be broken to next-of-kin in the middle of the night. And so, on the morning of 15th June, almost twenty-four hours after their son had been charging across the light-snow-covered slopes of Sapper Hill towards the Argentine defences with a bayonet attached to the end of his rifle, Ethel and Harry sat in their living room with Bobby standing behind them, facing a very official-looking Scots Guards officer, who was accompanied by two chaplains. The elder of the two chaplains spoke first; the other comforting Ethel as his colleagues broke the news.

As soon as they had approached the front door, Hettie had run, screaming, up the stairs to her room. Gary had once told her about all of the formal procedures that happened in wartime. From this, Hettie knew that if two *padres* came to your door, it meant there had been a death. If it was one, it meant an injury. Ethel had barely moved from her seat for two days. Harry had paced the floor between the radio in the kitchen and the television in the living room. And Bobby had tried to take his mind off everything by making tea and answering the countless telephone calls, enquiring if there had been any news. The officer had some official business first. He handed over a collection of letters written by Gary in the last month. Procedural mix-ups had prevented them from getting through to their intended recipients. The Army was officially sorry for any distress that this had caused. Ethel was in complete shock and, although she heard it, she took in nothing of the official story relayed by the officer. He told the following expansive account:

On the morning of 13th June, Gary's Battalion was moved by helicopter from their position at Bluff Cove to an assembly area near Goat Ridge, west of Mount Tumbledown. The British plan called for a diversionary attack south of Mount Tumbledown by a small number of Scots Guards, assisted by the four light tanks of the Blues and Royals, while the main attack came as a three-phase silent advance from the west of Mount Tumbledown. In the first phase, G Company would take the western end of the mountain; in the second phase, Left Flank would pass through the area taken by G Company to capture the centre of the summit; and in the third phase, Right Flank – of which Gary was part – would pass through Left Flank to secure the eastern end of Tumbledown. A daytime assault was initially planned, but was postponed at the British battalion commander's request. In a meeting with his company commanders the consensus was that the long uphill assault across the harsh ground of Tumbledown in daylight would be suicidal.

At the time of the battle, N Company held Mount Tumbledown.

Mount William was just south of Tumbledown and the Marine battalion's O Company was on its lower slopes. B Company 6th Regiment was in reserve behind N Company. M Company occupied Sapper Hill. The Argentine defenders held firm under the British 'softening up' bombardment, which began at seven thirty p.m. local time. At eight thirty p.m. on 13th June, the diversionary attack began. The 2nd Battalion Scots Guards' Reconnaissance Platoon, commanded by Major Richard Bethell and supported by four light tanks of the Blues and Royals, attacked the Argentine marine company entrenched on the lower slopes of Mount William. On Mount William's southern slopes, one of the tanks was taken out of action by a booby trap. The initial advance was unopposed, but a heavy firefight broke out when British troops made contact with Argentine defences. The Argentines opened fire, killing two British soldiers and wounding four. After two hours of hard fighting, the British troops had secured the position.

Fearing a counter-attack, the British platoon withdrew into an undetected minefield, and were forced to abandon their dead. Two men were wounded covering the withdrawal and four more were wounded by mines. The explosions prompted the Argentine troops on Mount William to open fire on the minefield and the likely withdrawal route of anyone attacking Mount William. The barrage lasted for about forty minutes and more British casualties would have been suffered if the mortar bombs had not landed on soft peat, which absorbed most of the blasts.

The fighting was hard going for Left Flank. The Argentinians had well dug-in machine guns and snipers. At two thirty a.m., however, a second British assault overwhelmed the Argentine defences. British troops swarmed the mountaintop and drove the Argentinians out, at times fighting with fixed bayonets. By six a.m., Left Flank's attack had clearly stalled and had cost the British company seven men killed and eighteen wounded. On the eastern half of the mountain the platoon of Argentine conscripts was still holding out, so Colonel Scott ordered Right Flank to push on to clear the final positions. Major Simon Price sent 2nd and 3rd Platoons forward, preceded by a barrage of 66mm rockets to clear the forward RI 6th platoon. Major Price placed 1st Platoon high up in the rocks to provide fire support for the assault troops. Lieutenant Robert Lawrence led Gary's 3rd Platoon around to the right of the Argentine platoon, hoping to take the Argentinians by surprise. They were detected, however, and the British were briefly pinned down by gunfire before a bayonet charge overwhelmed the Argentine defenders.

Advancing out of the central region of Tumbledown Mountain, the British again came under heavy fire from the Argentinians, but by advancing in pairs under covering fire, the British succeeded in clearing those RI 6th Company platoons as well, gaining firm control of the mountain's eastern side. Right Flank had achieved this at the cost of five wounded, including Lieutenant Lawrence. The Argentine sniper with a FAL rifle had helped cover the Argentine retreat, firing shots at a Scout helicopter evacuating wounded off Tumbledown and injuring two Guardsmen, before the Scots Guards killed him in a hail of gunfire.

Gary had been confirmed as one of the Guardsmen who had killed the sniper. Shortly after this there was some final shelling from the Argentine encampment. This had disorientated and scattered 3rd Platoon and, although his remaining comrades hadn't witnessed their deaths or been able to recover their bodies in the aftermath, Gary – and one other private, Benny Lewis – was now officially Missing, Presumed Dead.

Just before Ethel collapsed, the officer informed them that Gary had been recommended for the Distinguished Conduct Medal.

PART IV

DENOUEMENT

'With permission, Mr Speaker, I should like to make a statement on the Falkland Islands. Early this morning in Port Stanley, seventy-four days after the Falkland Islands were invaded, General Moore accepted from General Menendez the surrender of all the Argentine forces in East and West Falkland together with their arms and equipment. In a message to the Commander-in-Chief Fleet, General Moore reported: "The Falkland Islands are once more under the Government desired by their inhabitants. God Save the Queen."'

Mrs Margaret Thatcher, the Prime Minister
House of Commons Statement,
15th June 1982

13

THE LAST POST

'Ethel. Ethel, love? C'mon, hen. We need tae get ready.' Harry was struggling to get through to his wife. For the majority of the last week, she had sat in the chair nearest the window of her house, watching as people walked past, staring in; some even pointing. There had been a lull in the number of photographers camped outside and most had gone on Tuesday – after Bobby's pleading, and Harry's anger. Last night though – the night before Gary's memorial service – a significant number had returned.

'Bobby, can you go and see tae yer sister?' Harry was struggling to hold it together, but he knew it was his final duty to Gary. 'Bobby, dae ye hear me?' he shouted. He was desperately trying to keep his anger in check. Harry knew that his youngest son wasn't coping well with his brother's death, but disappearing to his girlfriend's house for three days midweek, while her father had taken his expanding family to a caravan at Butlin's, didn't help. Harry suspected Bobby was away watching the Scotland v Brazil game – he couldn't really criticise, as Harry had watched it, too, and he couldn't deny that, for a wee while after David Narey had scored, it had distracted him a bit. Nothing short of regularly administered industrial-strength Valium was able to do the same for Ethel, though, and Harry was seriously concerned about her ability to make it through the day. In the first forty-eight hours after the Scots Guards Family Liaison woman had left, Ethel said little other than implying it was all her fault.

Hettie had similarly crumpled into a shell, stepping out of her room only to go to the bathroom or, on the few occasions that Harry had had to nip out, to sit downstairs with her mother. She felt absolutely empty, bereft of any feeling. She felt that she had no more tears left to cry. There didn't seem to be any point. Up until a week ago her entire life had been focused on passing her O levels, and she had had high expectations of passing all seven with very good grades. A brief conversation, months ago with Gary, had helped her with the momentum required for concentrated studying, but now all of that seemed totally pointless. She couldn't think straight, couldn't rationalise the events of the last week. She had no concept of time. It all seemed so fluid at the moment. Minutes into hours into days, unpunctuated by sleep. Hettie was – understandably – emotionally exhausted.

The first time she answered Mickey Martin's telephone call, she accidentally put the phone down before she heard the whole message. When it rang again, she let it ring out. Her dad was out at the shops, Bobby was away – *somewhere* – and with her mum almost catatonic there was only her to respond to the incessant ringing. When Mickey phoned again the next day, he immediately apologised and offered his condolences for Gary. Hettie had burst into tears at this and again the remainder of the message was lost in the fog of her despair.

Bobby had also received a phone call during the week, but it was one intended for his dad, which he'd intercepted.

'Could you let him know that Chief Superintendent Don McAllister would like tae speak tae him, please? It's about his son,' the female voice had said. Bobby had panicked at this and bolted to Lizzie's for a couple of days, to give him time to break more bad news to his father during this, the most difficult week of his life.

'Dad, there's been a guy looking for you all week. Doc or *something* … It hasn't been a great line. An' ah wisnae really listenin' properly. Ah'm sorry, Dad.' Hettie had come downstairs. She was wearing a short purple dress and some make-up, and looked much better than she had since well before the news about Gary had been broken to her. Bobby jumped to attention at hearing this information.

'Eh, Dad. Ah ken this isn't the best time tae tell ye this but that phone call was about me.' Bobby was nervously making a knot with the black tie Harry had given him earlier. He turned to face his father. 'That phone call she's on aboot … it's fae the polis … a guy called Don McAllister.' He inhaled deeply. 'A while ago, we aw got lifted after a stramash at the Tory Club when we were out wi' the disco.' Bobby walked over to his dad who now had his hands over his face. 'Dad, ah'm really, really sorry. Ah hidnae heard anythin' an' …' As tears had began to roll slowly down Bobby's face, Harry put an arm around his son's shoulder.

'It's a'right, son. Ah've spoken tae him already. It's fine. He was phonin' tae say they'd dropped any charges.' Harry could see the relief in his son's face but he was struggling to contain his own rage. Of all the weeks to phone and hassle his family, Harry couldn't believe Don McAllister would have chosen this one. He put his other arm around Hettie's shoulder. 'Right c'mon … let's try and help yer mam get through the day, eh?' Harry kissed his daughter on the cheek and walked out of the room. He had a few tears of his own to conceal.

The service itself was extremely difficult for the Cassidy family. Although many young men had died in the brief battle on the other side of the world, Gary's death had special resonance for the Scottish media in particular. A young war hero who had been killed on the last day of a conflict that had not been universally popular north of the border was big news. That his body had not been found and buried along with his colleagues where he fell added a significant emotional poignancy. When the Distinguished Order Medal was part of the story, journalists started dreaming of BAFTAs. But the event had taken the Kilmarnock Police by surprise and camera crews and TV news teams had virtually blocked the cobbled route down Bank Street to get to the Laigh Kirk. It was by far the biggest church in the town, and had been chosen to accommodate the multitude of people who had turned up to pay tribute or simply to be seen.

'I knew a simple soldier boy
Who grinned at life in empty joy,
Slept soundly through the lonesome dark,
And whistled early with the lark.

'In winter trenches, cowed and glum,
With crumps and lice and lack of rum,
He put a bullet through his brain.
No one spoke of him again.

'You smug-faced crowds with kindling eye
Who cheer when soldier lads march by,
Sneak home and pray you'll never know
The hell where youth and laughter go.'

Bobby struggled to get through his reading of the Sassoon poem, but he knew it would have meant a lot to Gary. When he and his dad were sorting through Gary's stuff, they found this poem ripped out of a school textbook. When they found the same text written out several times in Gary's jotters, they both recognised that it must have had an effect on him. Although the second verse told of a different outcome, Bobby felt that its sombre tone summed up that painful disunion between selfless heroism and pointless sacrifice.

At the end of the short service, the Reverend MacNeil – who had christened Gary nearly twenty years before – led the Cassidy family past the large, framed photograph of a smiling Gary taken on the day of his passing-out, and along the flower-bedecked aisle. As she walked haltingly, supported by her daughter, Ethel looked up and spotted a vaguely familiar female face.

'Aw, God. *Mary, no!*' Ethel fainted right after she said this. The tall man to the woman's right instinctively leapt forward. He called out her name.

'Get back, you!' shouted Harry. 'Don't you fuckin' touch her!'

Bobby didn't think too much of this at the time. With the full blast of the media outside, his dad had been on edge all morning. Many people had crowded around his mum and although it seemed a strange thing for his dad to shout, it *had* been an unbelievably stressful week for him and, in any case, it wasn't entirely clear whom he had been addressing. A doctor had taken Ethel back to the vestry, along with Harry and Hettie. Bobby had been asked by his dad to go on with Joey and Hamish – and Hamish's dad, Stan – to the Masonic Club for the customary wake. Jock Newton had sorted out enough food to have kept all of the Scots Guards going while they were in the Falklands, and, even more magnanimously, he'd organised a free bar.

'He was a guid lad, your Gary,' said Jock.

'Thanks mate,' replied Bobby.

'Lazy fucker, mind you.' Bobby looked up sharply, but he conceded a smile when he saw Jock Newton wink at him. 'In fact, ah heard his Sergeant was speakin' tae Gary's Platoon. He says, "I've got a nice wee easy job for the laziest man here. Put up yer haun if you're the laziest." Nineteen outta twenty men raised their hauns, and the sergeant asks the other man, "Why d'you no raise your haun?" Gary says, "Too much fuckin' trouble, sarge."' Bobby looked around before laughing.

'Thanks, Mr Newton. Ah appreciate everythin' ye've done for ma dad.'

'Hey, it's nae problem, son. Look, aw this'll get easier, ken? Yer ma and yer da'll take a while tae get ower it aw, but Gary's done a great thing. It'll no be forgotten, an' it'll gie ye's aw real comfort in future.' Bobby pursed his lips, nodded and carried another tray of whiskies and vodkas away to distribute for the toast to his dead brother.

Harry only made a fleeting appearance at the Masonic Club, and many people had left after the soup and the sandwiches. The hardcore of Harry's own mates were settling down for a long night, and Harry felt obliged to show his face for them at least.

'Sorry lads,' said Harry. 'Ethel finally went doon. She's had more sedatives than ah could count this week, but Hettie's watchin' 'er now.'

'Mate, there's absolutely nae need tae apologise. Everyb'dy kens whit an ordeal this has aw been for ye, whit wi' aw the papers an' that.' From the nods and winks, it was clear to Harry that Chick MacKenzie spoke for everyone. At that moment Harry dearly wished he could go and lock the doors to the club and just stay there for the next few weeks, surrounded by people he loved and trusted. But he knew he had to go home. He knew the situation with Ethel was going to get worse and, most of all, he knew he had to speak face-to-face with Don McAllister. When he finally opened his front door, ten hours after he'd initially opened it to take his family to a memorial service for his dead son, he found a letter posted through the letterbox. There was no stamp and no postmark, and only one five-lettered word hand-written on the envelope. Inside, the brief note read:

Harry,

I'm truly sorry about today, but I need to speak to you. I'll be waiting for you tomorrow at one o'clock at the Cochrane out near Gatehead. Please come. We need to sort some things out.

D.M.

Harry screwed up the paper and threw it at the bin.

Harry buttoned his sports jacket, looked at the bags under his eyes in the mirror at the front door, and shouted up the stairs. 'Hettie, ah need tae go. Ah'll be back in a coupla hours.' There was no response from the teenager's room. Harry felt bad about leaving her in charge of Ethel yet again. He resolved to sit Bobby down and make him appreciate that he had to pull his weight a bit more in terms of looking after his mum and taking some of the pressure off Harry, and especially Hettie.

'Hettie? Did ye hear me? There was still no response. Harry sighed deeply and started to climb the stairs. He first looked into his own room and saw Ethel still sleeping the sleep of one whose senses have been medically numbed. Harry then passed Bobby's empty room to the smallest bedroom at the end of the hall. The door was only slightly open but by looking at the reflection in the small *Coca-Cola* mirror at eye level on the wall next to the door, Harry could see that his daughter was lying slumped across the bed, still fully clothed.

'Aw My *GOD! HETTIE!*' Harry burst into the room as soon as he saw the brown pill bottle lying discarded on the floor at the side of her bed. '*NAW*! No ma Het ...' Harry's heart was pounding as if it was going to vault straight out of the cavity in his chest.

'Wha ... Whit izzit? *DAD*! Dad, whit's wrong?' Hettie jumped up, make-up stained down one side of her face, and all over her bed covers. Harry began sobbing as he threw his arms around his daughter and pulled her close to him. 'Dad? Is it Mum? What's wrong?' Hettie was also now crying.

'It's just ... ah saw the bottle there. Ah thought ye'd taken the pills.' Harry wiped his eyes and turned to look at her. 'Ah couldnae cope if anythin' happened tae you tae.'

'Aw Dad, ah took them out of your room cos' ah was worried about *Mum*. She was actin' really strange last night.'

Harry sat on the edge of Hettie's bed with his head in his hands. It was Hettie's turn to comfort him.

'I'd never have done anythin' like that, Dad. Ah'm strugglin' to hold it together here but we'll aw get through this, eventually.' Hettie got up and looked at the image that presented itself. 'My God, look at the state ae me! Ah must've fell asleep the minute ah lay doon. Ah'm absolutely knackered, Dad. You must be tae.'

Harry got up and wiped his face. He was embarrassed at his daughter's maturity in the face of his despair. 'Hettie, ah need tae go out, just now.' Harry was breathing heavily, but he had recovered his composure. 'Ah'll be away for a wee while.' Harry turned towards the door.

'Wher' are ye goin', Dad?' said Hettie

'Ah've jist got tae go and see somebody. Just a message tae dae,' replied Harry. He paused and then turned to look back at his youngest child. 'Ah love ye, Hettie. Ye ken that, don't ye?'

'Aye Dad. I do, I really do.' And with that he was gone, down the stairs and out the front door.

14

SYNCHRONICITY

The two men staggered across the swampy grasslands. In fact, only one of them was staggering, and he was doing so partly through exhaustion, but also because he had the other, smaller man on his back. The smaller man was breathing lightly, but he *was* still breathing *and that, frankly, was a fucking miracle.*

It was amazing how calm everything seemed. The weather was still flexing its considerable muscles. Icy, driving rain ripped into the pair and, with the treacherous conditions underfoot, it made the job of the carrier far more difficult than he had anticipated it would be when he finally decided to leave the shelter of the old stone barn earlier that morning. The terrain was uncannily like that of the Brecon Beacons, where they'd completed their final training exercises. In fact, when Gary Cassidy first regained any kind of consciousness, he initially assumed that he was in Wales. That was days ago.

EIGHT DAYS EARLIER …

'Gary … *GARY*! Fuck … GARY!'

He recalled a story that involved his dad, and three of his mates sitting around a fire. One of those mates was still here, but Gary could only hear him, and not particularly clearly. It was as if he was underwater. Evidently there had been some sort of explosion that had occurred close to them. It must have caused the partial deafness in Gary's right ear.

'*Gary*, for fuck's sake. Can you hear me? I'm *hit* … I've been fucking hit by somethin'.' Gary pulled himself up onto his haunches. Instinctively, he kept low. He tried to quickly take in the surroundings. There was smoke or was it a low, misty fog? It was hard to be certain. Gary still hadn't determined the origin of the voice. He stood up, heart pounding, and looked across the mountainous landscape. This wasn't Wales. Fires were ablaze all across the skyline. But there was no movement other than his. And then suddenly – in the corner of his eye – he saw his stricken colleague. Benny Lewis was face down in a shallow slurry of reddish-brown mud. His head rested on what initially appeared to be a smooth rock. On closer inspection, it was his helmet. Benny's skin tone and his green-and-brown fatigues made it virtually impossible to see him in the rapidly disappearing light.

'Wha … *coughs* … whit the fuck's goin' on? Where are we?' whispered Gary. He dropped down to his knees. Instinct still played its part in telling him that whatever had caused this was likely to still be around.

'Gary!' Benny was struggling for breath. Gary reached him by crawling through the sodden undergrowth and knelt down, trying to establish where his colleague had been injured.

'Benny. Where are ye hit mate? We need tae shift fae here. Whit fuckin' happened anyway?' Gary pulled Benny's backpack off and turned him over. 'Aw fuck!'

Benny was shaking. 'GARY! What? What is it? I don't wanna fucking *die*!'

'You're no gonnae die, mate. I'm here. I'm here, Benny.' Gary looked at the two most obvious sources of the blood stains on his friend's jacket. It didn't look like there were any more, but Gary couldn't be entirely sure. The light was fading fast and he didn't want to use his small torch to investigate properly. There was a smallish hole at Benny's upper left shoulder. It looked like a bullet hole, but there was no evidence of any exit wounds when Benny had been lying on his front. The other larger and more worrying wound was low on Benny's left-hand side at approximately appendix level. Gary looked all around them and then again at Benny's wound.

'Fuck, Benny. We need tae move awa' fae here. We need tae get tae some cover. This is too exposed.' Gary stood up again and looked around. 'Dae ye think ye can move?'

'I don't think so, Gary. I can't feel my legs.' Benny began sobbing. 'Aw fuck, Gary. I've got no feelin' in my legs, man.'

Gary's hearing was becoming slowly clearer. As this most vital sense was returning, Gary's feeling for the need for shelter intensified.

'C'mon. Let's go.'

'*Aaaaghhh!*'

Gary dragged the smaller man up and held him with his right arm. He pulled his rifle over to him with his left foot and, noticing the bloodied bayonet, picked it up. Gary had no sense of the direction in which they should be heading. His compass had smashed and, other than the flickering lights of the various fires on the hillside, there was no indication of movement anywhere. Logic dictated that they head downhill, although at this point, safety seemed no more likely in that direction than in any other. Gary reckoned that they'd haltingly covered about four miles before he spotted the small structure at the base of the hillside below them. Gary had set Benny down and crawled through the soaking undergrowth to reach a post and wire fence. When he was as satisfied as he could be that there was no-one inside the small stone outhouse, he went back for Benny and manhandled him towards the black timber door.

In the days that followed – Gary figured it had been four but he was having trouble sleeping and couldn't be entirely sure – Benny drifted in and out of consciousness. Between them, the two Scots Guards worked out that they had become detached from their unit after Lieutenant Lawrence had been hit. Three – Gary, Benny and

Kev Kavanagh – had progressed and had taken out the snipers. The remainder must have stayed with their commanding officer. Benny Lewis had taken cover when a surprisingly intense barrage peppered the area around them. He saw Kev going down and then Benny got hit in the chest himself. Benny remained unaware that Gary had survived the bombardment until he moved into the periphery of his vision in its aftermath. By that time, Benny reckoned their colleagues had either advanced and unwittingly left them behind, or the Argentine forces had re-grouped and retaken the original British bases. Since this scenario would've effectively placed the two survivors well behind enemy lines, the former seemed more likely. The lack of any kind of personnel supported this conclusion, but Gary still went warily as he explored a little bit further each day in a quest to identify their location and work out a plan to get help for his friend.

He had a feeling that Benny's wounds weren't immediately life-threatening, but would become so if he didn't get attention soon. Gary cleaned and dressed the wounds as best he could every day. The small outhouse had a sink with an intermittently running cold-water source, but Gary used it sparingly. He assumed there was a storage tank somewhere, as opposed to a more natural supply. He had walked for miles and found no signs of any farm or small holding of which their current shelter might be part. Gary astonished himself during a surreal seven days: his intuitive actions that had stabilised his colleague; had made and maintained a fire each night in the small shed when the smoke would be less evident; had hunted, caught and then cooked two hares. There had been a couple of times when Gary felt that he had been looking down at someone else performing these tasks. Like many people who undergo training for a job or a vocation, Gary had an underlying belief that the circumstances of the training were just extreme examples of scenarios that had very little chance of actually happening. Yet here he was – survival instincts to the fore – coping with far more than anything three weeks in the Welsh mountains had been able to throw at him. Only three months ago he had been concerned about the level of boredom in the Army. Fast forward and he had fought in a war and, more significantly, he had killed several young men who were just the same as him. Just as disorientated; just as scared and perhaps just as desperate for their father's acknowledgement and respect. Maybe it was best not to think about these things too much.

Eventually, Gary had decided that they should move again. Benny was getting weaker by the day and, although his blood loss had slowed, it was apparent that there was some form of shrapnel still lodged in his stomach. Gary knew his friend would die without proper medical attention. So, seven nights after they had arrived, Gary lifted his friend onto his back and set off, broadly in the direction from which they had originally come. He left all of their equipment, including his rifle. It was his intention to find the nearest encampment and either return to his unit or surrender; whichever the situation required.

Having staggered for miles in as straight a direction as he could manage, Gary eventually came to a road. After only ten minutes following it, a Range Rover approached. It stopped suddenly about forty yards in from of them. Two elderly civilians got out and shouted towards them.

'Are you English?'

22ND JUNE 1982: 1:32PM

Bobby normally hated going to Joey's house. Onthank was full of arseholes who'd give you a doing just for looking at them the wrong way. Plus, Fat Franny Duncan's tentacles reached far and wide across north west Kilmarnock, and since it seemed certain Hamish May had been hospitalised as a result of the Fatman, it was fair to assume that *he* was also a prime target. The other, more pragmatic reason Bobby rarely went to Joey's house was that he was scared of dogs. Joey didn't have a dog, but on the principal route to his house along Knockinlaw Road, everyone else seemed to have at least two. They seemed, uniformly, to be big Alsatians – or *Al-fuckin-Getyes* as Bobby referred to them. And since they were all allowed to roam free like it was a Safari Park, Bobby was convinced he could've given Allan Wells a run for his money on the few occasions when he'd had to sprint along *Alsatian* Road.

Today though was different. He was simply enjoying the respite of lying on the bed in his best friend's upstairs room, listening to music and trying to forget the events of the last week. Joey appreciated that his friend was looking for an escape from it all, even from Lizzie. He hadn't spoken to his friend since before the news of Gary's death, and he instinctively knew that the last thing he'd want to do was talk about it now.

'Listen tae this, Boab. It's fuckin' brilliant.' Joey sat next to his old record player and pulled the needle across. A two-note riff eventually gave way to crashing drums and shortly afterwards, Ian McCulloch's distinctive vocals. Bobby didn't rate Echo and the Bunnymen – or any other of these wierder *arty* bands like New Order, Wire or U2 that Joey was currently into – but he had to concede their new single, 'The Back of Love', was pretty damn good. Bobby lay back on the bed and looked at the mosaic of posters and newspaper clippings that concealed the walls and ceiling. It was an odd mix indeed. A life-sized poster of Debbie Harry was pinned to the zone directly above the bed. As she stared back down at Bobby he wondered how many times his friend had filled his bin with Kleenex while looking upwards. *Turning Japanese right enough, eh, Joe?*

Less easy to fathom were numerous, large pictures of Govan socialist, Jimmy Reid, and father of the welfare state, Nye Bevan. Photos of Weller, Costello, Che Guevara, Jimi Hendrix, Ian Curtis and a whole host of headlines about the death of John Lennon were all grouped together in one space. Bobby remembered Joey being really upset about the former Beatle dying. He'd gone on and on about them having the same birthday and also about that fucking book *The Catcher in the Rye* – which Bobby had absolutely detested – being involved in the murder.

'And whit about *this* yin?' said Joey, as Simple Minds' 'Love Song' emanated from the tinny speakers.

Joey's large wooden, coffin-like box of a record player sat on its four sturdy, foot-long legs at the side of his bed. It was designed to hold long-playing records in horizontal storage to the left-hand side of a centrally placed turntable with an automatic arm mechanism. The final third of the box was given over to the controls for sound, radio-station selection and waveband frequency. The records had to sit in a stacked, holding formation, like Harrier Jump Jets waiting for the signal to descend to their circular, black landing target. Sometimes two would drop at a time. When this happened Joey's impatience would often cause him to force the next record down by manually moving the arm across. More often than not, a low persistent grumble from the speakers would follow this action. To Bobby, it sounded like Max – the elderly butler from *Hart to Hart* – recorded backwards.

'*Stoapfuckin'dain'that, Stoapfuckin'dain'that*', over and over again. Bobby laughed out loud. This bizarre sound was the result of Joey attempting to play a record by The Fall, one by Killing Joke and 'Is Vic There?' by Department S. Joey eventually laughed as well. He was irritated at *that stupid fucking box* but also pleased to see his friend happy again, even if it was only briefly – and at his own expense.

'Listen, ah ken ye might no want tae think about this yet but whit's the plans wi' the disco?'

Bobby stopped laughing and covered his head with Joey's pillow.

'Ah'm only bringin' it up cos' ah've got an idea. Ah could dae aw the alternative yins. Y'ken, just tae keep it going.'

'Ah dunno, Joey. Ah canny think aboot anythin' tae dae wi' the disco at the minute. We're supposed tae be doin' Doc Martin's anniversary thing next week. Ah'd dae it but ah think ma Dad would go daft.'

'D'ye no think Gary would want everybody tae be gettin' on wi' their life?'

'Aye mibbe. But it's nothin' tae dae wi' whit ah want tae dae. At the minute it's aw aboot no upsettin' ma mam, or our Hettie. Ah can't cope wi' it aw though. Ah just want tae get out and get fuckin' miroculous, aw the time.'

'Let's dae the Doc Martin gig then! Dae it properly ... in Gary's honour.' Joey was trying to be as upbeat as possible. 'Remember that time he got us fired fae the job at the Tennis Club?'

Bobby sat up and leaned back against Leon Trotsky. 'Aye.' Bobby smiled at the memory. 'Stupid bastard.'

At the beginning of June, more than twelve months ago, an interesting – if short-term – opportunity presented itself for both Bobby and Joey. They had each been offered the position of 'temporary groundsman' at the Kilmarnock Municipal Tennis Club, which was buried in the cleft behind the Henderson Church. The club had four clay courts and they ran parallel to the gently flowing Kilmarnock Water. The datum of the courts was around ten metres higher than that of the river's normal surface level. The courts themselves had a coating of red *blaes* on top. A chain-link fence surrounded them, creating a safe internal oasis that Joey remarked would be forever middle-class. The fence was damaged only at its southern edge; an edge it shared with the far more working-class pie-and-a-pint outdoor bowls club. The damage was due to overuse as a route onto the flat, asphalt bowling club roof when stray tennis balls had to be recovered. A small, red-brick, single-storey tennis clubhouse was under construction at the northern end. It was moving forward at the slow-motion pace of a brick course a week. This clubhouse was partly functional, but some people still made use of an old tongue-and-groove timber-slatted garage that sat just outside the fenced enclosure, on the upper edge of the riverbank.

The job was offered due to the enforced absence of the existing incumbent. His name was Jeffery. He'd been there since leaving school three years earlier but had to give up on this particular summer as a result of recuperation from an eye operation. His recovery from this procedure would rule out his usefulness to the club for the absolutely mental period leading up to and just beyond Wimbledon in early July. This three- to four-week stretch traditionally saw hundreds of kids, who had evidently never lifted a tennis racquet for anything other than pretending to be Jimmy Page, throw on a headband and a FILA polo shirt and head for the courts.

Temporary memberships almost doubled in this period, and consequently someone prepared to be there at the crack of dawn to open the gates was essential. This was to be one of Bobby's tasks. Joey would take other responsibilities, such as locking up at night. Sweeping the courts and lines, repairing the damaged fence, and operating the tuck shop would be shared equally between both. The recovery of countless yellowish-green Wilson tennis balls with a tadpole net – which all the *would-be* Borgs had skied into the river – was an expectation that hadn't been made clear to them at the beginning, though.

Bobby was good at tennis and took on the additional unpaid role of coaching several useless and unenthusiastic kids. The weather that summer was glorious and most of the girls who came to play were dressed like Tracy Austin.

Admittedly, there were a few growlers who resembled Betty Stove, but, as Bobby and Joey now reminisced, these were good times. The only blot on this sylvan landscape was the assumption made by the committee that they were doing this work for the unremitted enjoyment of it. To be fair, they held this view because Bobby's geography teacher, who had approached him in the first instance, hadn't cleared the position or agreed any payment for it with anyone. Two events brought those halcyon days to an end. Gary was involved in both and they occurred during the same week.

A middle-aged female lawyer had been due to play a competitive singles match against a young student. After a number of abortive attempts to arrange the game, it was suggested that they try to play at eight on a Tuesday morning. The remainder of the tennis tournament was being held up by this tie and a great deal of pressure was being brought to bear by the all-powerful committee members. Bobby had been out with a girl the night before and, having come home late, had offered his brother two pounds to take the key and open the courts for him. Since Gary was still asleep in the same room at ten, when Bobby finally woke, the furious Ayrshire legal eagle was forced to forfeit the match due to her inability to find an alternative date, or anyone else with a key for the padlock.

Bobby and Joey were reported to the committee and dismissed days later. The other issue, which no doubt had a bearing on this decision, was the abuse of the position of tuck-shop manager. Gary had come down a few times and, with Bobby's knowledge, had been robbing the tuck shop for weeks. Texans, Wispas, Spangles and a wide selection of other confectionary, had steadily been going missing from the timber garage since the two of them had started the job. The takings weren't accounting for it. Bobby's theory was that good old Angus, the timid geography teacher, had been making up the difference on a weekly basis to avoid any suspicion falling on the two working-class teenagers from the council estates whom he'd appointed. On the particular Tuesday night of the locked courts, Gary went home with three full boxes of twenty-four Cadbury's milk-chocolate bars and a full box of cheese-and-onion crisps. These were smuggled covertly out of the garage, through the tree cover of the Kay Park and up into the Cassidy boys' bedroom for onward sale to the wee lads around Almond Avenue. At a price that undercut the numerous ice-cream vans prowling around the scheme at night, of course.

Sometimes opportunity for a seventeen-year-old outweighs judgment or conscience. Old Angus was devastated. He'd privately trusted his pupil and publicly suspected others. A parting of the ways was inevitable and only his intervention with the committee prevented it becoming a police matter. Unsurprisingly, no payment was proffered for three months of genuinely hard work. They *did* sweep the courts, they *did* repair the fence and they *did* recover an incredible number of previously disregarded tennis balls. Unfortunately, Bobby did open the courts every day, but rarely at the required time and, with Gary's help, they did manage the tuck shop, but not in the way the committee had envisioned.

Despite the possibility of criminal action, Joey still felt extremely hard done by with the lack of any payment. On the last night there, Bobby and Joey sat outside the courts, defiantly attempting to justify their perspective. In their self-righteous, selfish teenage minds, the work they'd done equalled freedom to help themselves. The positives outweighed the negatives. They were due remuneration. As they made their arguments, Gary appeared. Prompted by the eldest, anger and annoyance built, and the three took their frustration and revenge out on the timber garage against which they had been sitting. After a fair bit of shoving, they dislodge it from its concrete base. To Gary's astonishment and utter delight, it came away from the base in one piece. The weight of the carcass gave it a momentum all of its own and it tipped up onto one side of its pitched-tar roof. It then slid slowly but gracefully down the bank and into the river. Like one of the massive ships moving down the slipway at John Brown's Dockyard on the Clyde, it was an impressive sight, despite suffering by comparison of scale.

'Ah still canny believe it came awa' in wan bit.' Tears of laughter were rolling down Bobby's cheeks. 'The look on his face, man … fuckin' brilliant!' Bobby looked over at his friend. 'Fuck it. Let's dae the Martin thing. For Gary. Then we're finished, eh?'

'Aye … fur Gary,' said Joey.

22ND JUNE 1982: 1:32PM

'Ye be watchin' the gemme the night, pal?'

'Eh, ah'm no sure.'

'Whit! Biggest gemme in history, an' yer no sure! Ye no intae the fitba, then?'

'Just had a lot on, mate.' Harry had intended to watch the match, but he just didn't want to discuss tactics – or the likelihood of Scotland beating the Soviet Union – with a taxi driver. 'Mate, just let me off up here, on the left.'

'The pub ye wanted is still about half a mile up the road.'

'It's fine. Ah'm a bit early anyway,' Harry lied. 'I'll walk the rest.'

'Well, a'right mate.' The car pulled over to the kerb. 'That's two twenty-five, pal.'

Harry paid the driver three pounds and closed the door before the change was offered. He was almost forty-five minutes late. He'd walked around the bus station, deliberating on whether to go and meet Don McAllister for so long that he missed the hourly bus service. When he finally convinced himself that not showing up would only lead to more *approaches,* the only option was a cab from the stance behind the bus station.

Harry was sweating profusely as he walked up the hill towards the small, village pub. He wasn't a fit man, and the weather – for the umpteenth day in a row – was ridiculously hot. A multitude of thoughts bounced around the inside of his overheated brain. All involved Don McAllister – Harry's nemesis for more than half of his life. Despite his anger at Don's phone calls, which Hettie had intercepted, Harry was determined to keep his temper in check. He was equally determined to say as little as possible. As he advanced towards Don McAllister's outstretched hand in the deserted car park of the Cochrane Inn, both of these objectives were quickly abandoned.

'Why are ye hasslin' ma family, ya bastard?' shouted Harry.

'Whit?' Don seemed genuinely confused.

'You fuckin' heard me, ya cunt! Phonin' the house an' leavin' messages wi' Hettie. Of aw' weeks, for Jesus sake!'

'Hey, whit the fuck are ye *talkin'* aboot?'

'Ye just canny fuckin' leave us alone, can ye? The boy's fuckin' deid. He's no comin' back. Whit possible fuckin' difference does twenty years ago make now? Why can ye no just fuckin' let it go?'

'Whit the fuck are ye on about? I tried to fuckin' help ye out wi' Bobby. You were the yin that told *me* about Gary. If ye'd kept yer mooth shut ah'd never of kent ... an' besides, it's no me that's pushin' here. Mary needs tae see Ethel again. She's worried about her.'

'Aye, that'll be right. She didnae gie a fuck about Ethel twenty years ago. She kent Gary was yours an' *still* fuckin' took ye back. How wis Ethel meant tae act after that, eh? Wi' her sister obviously takin' your side.' Harry's face was becoming drained of its colour.

Although Don was sure no-one was watching them – that was the main reason he'd picked the location – he felt the need to defuse the situation.

Harry continued ranting. 'Mary's no seeing Ethel. Ah told ye aw they years ago that ye were tae stay awa' fae us. An' ah fuckin' mean it even more now. Don't phone. Don't come round. Just fuck off. *Get it*?'

'Harry, ah canny promise that. Mary ...'

'*Fuck Mary!*' Harry lurched forward to punch Don with his full-fingered hand, but Don was too quick, and, stumbling, Harry hit only fresh air, and then, with his head, the dry-stane dyke wall.

22ND JUNE 1982: 1:32PM

The toast popped up. Hettie walked over to it with the butter in one hand and a knife in the other. She hadn't eaten much in days, and her mum had eaten even less, but she felt that perhaps a bit of toast and a cup of tea would help them both. She picked out one slice, buttered it and promptly dropped it face down on the floor. *Shite,* she muttered under her breath. The swing bin in the kitchen was full so she took the hairy toast into the living room and dropped it into the smaller bin in there, bending down to pick up the screwed-up ball of paper that was lying behind it.

She read the note.

'Aw *Dad*. Whit are ye *doin'*?'

15

ASHES TO ASHES

'Jesus fuck, yer a hard man tae get a hold ae.'

'Well, it's no been the easiest of weeks, ken?'

'Aye. Aye, sorry about yer brer an' that. But life goes on, y'ken? Time tae get back on the horse an' aw that shite.' Mickey Martin didn't really *do* condolences. That was what Hallmark was for. But he felt he should say *something* profound. That done, it was back to business. 'So. Fenwick Hotel, Saturday night. It better be fuckin' good. The wife's shitin' herself that it'll be like the wean's twenty-first. A great night though, an' ye'll be in The Metropolis in a coupla weeks.'

'Aye, about that Doc. Everythin's fine for Friday, but ah think we're gonnae call it quits after that,' said Bobby, moving to one side to avoid Mickey's cigar smoke. 'It's been good wi' the disco an' that but there's been far too much hassle. The fuckin' polis are phonin' ma auld man now, an' wi' everythin' else that's happened, it's no fair on him an' ma mam.'

Mickey Martin scratched at his stubble. He looked unconvinced. Bobby continued, 'Plus, ma mate Hammy's had a doin' offa Franny Duncan's crew, he's ended up in hospital wi' hypothermia, and he got electrocuted tae!' Bobby sniggered. 'Although that was his ain fault, tae be honest.' Mickey Martin didn't laugh, though. Bobby looked nervously around the portacabin that Mickey's lackeys had brought him to after tracking him down to Joey Miller's house in Onthank.

'Ah've picked *you* fur this Metropolis gig. Could've gied it tae that fat cunt but ah don't want tae. Needs brought doon a peg. Ah'm no used tae takin' no for an answer, ye should ken that, Bobby.'

'Aye, Doc. Ah dae, but ah'm in a tough spot here. Ma dad paid for aw' the gear an ….'

'Dae the fuckin' job then, an' pay him back!' Mickey was losing patience with this conversation. 'Look, leave Fat Franny tae me. Ah'll deal wi' him an' make sure he disnae bother ye again.' Mickey reclined in a big leather seat that looked totally out of place in a builder's hut. 'I'll make a phone call, an' afore ye can say *Tommy Cooper's a cunt*, it'll be sorted. Just like that.'

'Aye,' said Bobby falteringly. 'A'right, then. I'll speak tae Joey.'

'Dae that.' Mickey stood up, signalling the discussion was over. 'Get there early on Friday, an' don't fuck it up, cos' ah ken where ye live.' Bobby turned back at this to see a wicked Dick Dastardly smile beaming back at him. 'Ah'm fuckin' jokin', fur Christ's sake. Whit dae ye think ah am?'

23ᴿᴰ JUNE 1982: 10:11AM

'Des? *Des!*'

'Whit is it, boss?' Des Brick rolled his eyes. He was in the Ponderosie's kitchen and had just submerged the teabag into the sugary, boiled water.

'Get in here.' Fat Franny's tone had all the excitement of a child who had just been informed that Santa Claus was a lazy bastard who left all the presents at the first house he got to, and this year it would be *his*.

'Where's the joy, big man?'

'The Doc's just off the phone, Desi Boy! The Metro gig's back on. Fuckin' *yes!*' Fat Franny punched the air three times. 'At last, mate. At fuckin' last!'

'That *is* guid news. Whit changed his mind then?'

'Ah made him an offer he couldnae refuse,' said Fat Franny with the smuggest of smug looks all over his face, which only slipped when Des Brick eventually said:

'Naw *really* … whit changed his mind?'

Fat Franny glowered.

'We're finishin' off the work at the Metro, an' cos' we're doin' that we're gettin' a long-term contract.' Fat Franny was a bit irked at having to explain this to a subordinate, especially since it wasn't entirely true. Mickey Martin *had* indeed phoned Fat Franny about fifteen minutes ago. He *had* indeed asked for some help in finishing off the joiner work, some electrical installation and all of the painting at his new club. He *had* indeed dangled a carrot of 'help me out wi' this wee problem an' ah'll gie ye the first weekend.' However, Fat Franny was unaware that Mickey Martin had no intention of using the Duncan crew for his new venture beyond getting the place finished for free.

'Thought he wis fur usin' the Cassidy boy?' asked Des innocently.

Another one who might be sleeping with the fishes if his attitude don't fuckin' sharpen up. 'Ah told ye. He changed his mind. Now dae ye want tae be workin' wi' me or no? Fuck sake, Des, yer gettin' as fuckin' negative as that brother-in-law ae yours!'

'Sorry, Franny. Nae sweat man. It's just a wee bit ae a surprise, ken?' Des recognised Fat Franny's irritation and moved quickly to defuse it. 'So whit's the plan, boss?'

'Right. Well, first of all, ah'm firing they cunts the Cheezees, Bert Bole and that fuckin' paedo Sunshine. Ah want ye tell get Wullie tae go round an' tell them aw later, an' while yer at it, ye can gie the fuckin' magician a good pastin'. Ah got huckled in by the polis after that fuckin' *balloon* shambles.'

'Nae problem. It's done.'

'Then you, Wullie and a couple of his boys need tae go down tae the Foregate and get on wi' The Metropolis work. The Doc's lads will meet ye there later on the night tae sort ye oot wi' keys an' let ye ken whit's needing done.'

'Whit about Hobnail, Franny?'

'He's out, Des. Finito.' Fat Franny knew this would shock Des. 'He's been on the take, mate. Ah ken he's family ... fuck, he's been like family tae me *tae*. But ah canny have that in the ranks.'

Des was even more shocked.

Franny felt the need to keep talking. 'Senga's been on his back about Grant comin' tae work for me ...'

'Is he? Ah didnae ken that!'

'Aye, he is. In fact, pick him up later as well. He's gonnae be useful. Ah'm gettin' him on tae the money collections round the streets here.'

'Does Hobnail ken aw this?'

'Naw,' said Fat Franny. 'But ah'll deal wi' that later, eh. Phone the boy at this number.' Fat Franny handed Des a small square of paper with some numbers written on it. 'His maw's thrown a fuckin' fit, so he walked out. Ye'll get him there.' Fat Franny reached for his jacket. 'So are ye clear on everythin'?'

'Eh, aye. Ah think so,' said Des.

It was a lot of information so Fat Franny let Des's hesitation pass this time. 'Phone me later at the Portman, when yer headin' down tae the Metro. Ah'm awa tae get Theresa. Let yerself out, an' wash that cup.'

And with that the Fatman walked out the front door and down the gravel drive away from the Ponderosie, considerably happier than he had been when he'd got up that morning. He'd lost a *ton* last night because of those two *fannies* – Miller and Hansen.

'Jesus Christ, Bobby, son … where have ye been? We've been lookin' everywhere for ye.'

Bobby was perplexed. Normally nobody bothered much about his comings and goings, yet here he was, having heard virtually the same phrase twice in just over an hour.

'Gary's no deid!' proclaimed Harry.

Bobby sighed. 'Dad, ah ken this is tough for ye but …'

'Naw. Naw Bobby. It's the truth. He's turned up. He'd went missing in the fightin' an' …'

'Whit d' ye mean! We had a bloody funeral thing for him an' a … an' a wake!'

Harry put his arms around his youngest son. 'Ah ken, son. It's hard tae believe. But it's the truth. The officers are just away. Gary's gonnae phone in a wee while. They had tae come first an' tell us face tae face, cos' ae the shock an' that.' Harry wiped a tear from Bobby's face. 'They're tryin' tae keep the story quiet because aw the papers will be back, but they think there'll be loads more ae them now.'

Bobby felt his knees buckle. He slumped backwards into his dad's chair. 'My God, Dad. Ah cannae believe this. It's just … fucking unbelievable!'

Harry laughed. 'Right, ah'll let that wan go, but mind yer language fae now on, eh?'

'Where's Mum … an' Hettie?'

'Yer mum's no copin' well, son. She stayed wi' Sadie Flanagan last night, mainly tae gie us a break. The chaplain thinks we should wait a coupla days before tellin' her about Gary. Hettie's in wi' her just now, but *she* couldnae believe it either.'

Harry moved over to the window and opened curtains that had been constantly closed for days. Bobby saw the multitude of deep cuts on his dad's face.

'Jesus Christ, Dad, whit happened tae yer face?'

'Ach, it's nothin'. Ah went out for a walk tae clear ma head an' ah tripped an' fell. Ah scraped it down a brick wall. It's fine. It looks worse than it is.'

Bobby slumped into Harry's armchair. He felt totally drained. 'By Christ, it's been some fortnight, Dad, eh?'

'Aye, son. In more ways than one!'

16

ONE SINGER, ONE SONG

28TH JUNE 1982: 6:52PM

'Ye heard anythin' else fae Gary? Any idea when he's gettin' back home?'

'Aye, he phoned again this mornin'. He isnae good, though. Loadsa nightmares an' that, ken?'

'Mmm.'

Joey wasn't a supporter of the war – of *any* war, in fact – and found it hard not to jump in and lecture on the futility of it all. Bobby had already pulled him up about it twice in the days since they had realised Gary had actually survived. The euphoria of his Lazarus-style resurrection was now being tempered by the concern that Gary's mental state was never going to be the same again. Bobby hadn't known what to say when Gary had admitted to an initial feeling that he wished he'd died on the battlefield along with Kevin Kavanagh. His happiness at Benny Lewis's stabilisation in a field hospital was now tempered by deep-rooted doubts that it might feasibily have been Gary's action – or inaction – that caused him to get injured in the first place.

Bobby had confided in Joey that, as the days had gone on, he was becoming more anxious about Gary's homecoming. It was the same voice that spoke to Bobby from the other side of the world, but there was a resigned weariness that he couldn't equate with his brother's personality. Bobby also couldn't comprehend Gary's guilt about emerging physically unharmed. His was a little dehydrated, perhaps, but his physique had managed to withstand the ferocity of the bitingly cold Falklands environment much better than his medics could've expected. He was also rightly lauded for his courage in protecting and ultimately saving his comrade.

Gary couldn't see any of this though. Ten of his fellow Guardsmen had died in the battle for Mount Tumbledown. Three of them had been to his left in the darkness as the advance across the wet, jagged rocks began. After Lieutenant Lawrence had been shot in the head by a sniper, confusion reigned, and then the final Argentine shelling splintered the platoon. This much had come back to Gary in the forty-eight hours after he'd been driven to Port Stanley by an elderly couple out in their 4x4 for the first time since the Argentine surrender. The rest of his recollections were viewed through the haunted prism of his dreams. In them, he saw the crudely shaped limbs of what appeared to be tailors' dummies sticking out of the marshes and the mud as he advanced – bayonet out – towards them.

As he got to them, they weren't mannequins but real people; kids barely out of their teens, just like him, crying for their mums. It was Gary's job to silence them. As he stabbed at them, they didn't just fall and die like they did in *The Longest Day*. They grabbed desperately at the blade. They wriggled and rolled to avoid its rough action. It got one in the face, another in the chest; it took ten thrusts to silence the desperate screams of the third. All of them were so close to Gary he could feel their hot breath on his face. Every time Gary had closed his eyes and slept in the last five days, these terrifying images had invaded his subconscious.

Rehabilitation was going to take a substantial amount of time. He had informed Harry – in a long and emotional phone call – that he'd be home soon. He had been debriefed almost immediately and, due to the nature and misreporting of his 'death', the Army had relaxed its rigid protocol and would be flying him home to Prestwick Airport well in advance of his unit, who would return in the same manner by which they'd gone.

But as Bobby drained the remainder of his pint, sitting in the corner of the Fenwick Hotel's Snug Bar, he wanted to put the last two weeks to one side, just for tonight. Although Joey had – bizarrely, given his initial reservations – wanted them to agree unreservedly to work for Mickey Martin at The Metropolis, Bobby still intended this to be the final night for Heatwave Disco. He'd worry about breaking that to Mickey Martin after what would hopefully be a decent night.

'Right. C'mon mate. Let's get through and get sorted out, eh?' said Bobby, standing up. He'd made sure they were at the hotel two hours earlier than usual. He was treating it like a *proper* gig, making sure a full sound check and lighting tests were carried out. Joey had been really impressed. Even Jimmy Stevenson – with his court date pending – had been persuaded to come back for this swansong. Only Hamish May had declined. Perhaps this was understandable. The law of probability had decreed that there was more chance of him suffering some form of painful mishap when out with Heatwave Disco than not. He had rejoiced when Bobby had decided to call it a day.

The Fenwick Hotel was a great venue. The shape of the room – a well-proportioned rectangle – was perfect for a function. The long bar was at the opposite end of the room from the slightly raised stage; the step up itself providing a defensible space, which kept the punters and their drinks on the right side of the electrics when asking for a record. One entire side wall was fully concealed by a rich velvet curtain that, when working in tandem with the deep-pile carpet, absorbed a lot of the reverberation that the high-volume speakers generated.

'It's gonnae be good, Boab,' muttered Joey. He'd already mentally compiled a playlist in his head. There would still be room for the spontaneity necessary for a great gig. The ebb and flow of people's responses to the music; that building of atmosphere in a series of mini-crescendoes; the brilliant vibe associated with that *haven't-heard-that-song-for-ages* moment; and the unmatched satisfaction of introducing new records that people haven't heard before but keep them on the dance floor. All of these eventualities seemed not only possible, but likely on this particular evening.

As the first guests started to appear around seven – greeted by Mickey, his wife and their two daughters – Joey noticed another encouraging sign.

'Good mix of ages, Boab. And everybody looks up for a good night anaw.' He didn't mean they were all drunk, but there was definitely something in the air. It might've been the extended period of great weather that Ayrshire had been experiencing of late. It was probably also a result of the impending Kilmarnock Fair holiday, which started next week and would no doubt see the vast majority of the hall's inhabitants heading off to exotic places like Magaluf or Playa de las Americas for a well-earned break from either work or (equally likely) manipulating the benefits system.

The party was due to finish at one. Under normal circumstances, Heatwave would've strung out the pre-gig background music routine until around nine-thirty. But Bobby was determined to milk every last drop out of tonight. At precisely seven-fifty, he indicated to Joey to start their rehearsed introduction. The main hall lights went down and a small steady stream of smoke began to flood the dancehall. As it did so, a recording of 'Ride of The Valkyries' filled the air. People stopped their conversations, turning around in their seats to look. A strobe light kicked in, illuminating the previously ridiculed spaghetti-light Heatwave sign. Weller's rasping guitar riff bludgeoned its way through the fog and out of the urban townscape of Marshall Amps, and, simultaneously, a pin spot shone directly onto the hotel's own mirror ball, casting snowflakes of dappled light onto everyone in the room.

'Fuck me!' whispered Joey. 'That was fuckin' brilliant!'

As the Heatwave signature tune ended, Bobby put his hand on Joey's arm. 'Wait,' he said.

This unnerved Joey as he knew that the run-off from the Heatwave record was immediate rather than gradual. Still Bobby held, and the sound disappeared. There was briefly *dead air* and everyone was watching the stage, waiting to see what would happen next, especially a slightly anxious Mickey Martin.

'The twenty-fifth anniversary is called the silver anniversary an' it's celebrated wi' gifts of silver. The reason twenty-five years ae marriage is celebrated wi' silver is cos' it's a precious metal. Nowadays, few couples make it twenty-five years th'gither, an' for them that do, they deserve a celebration of their love and commitment to each other and their family.'

Joey caught on quickly to Bobby's speech and, with great timing, started the long, gospel-inspired introduction to the first song of the night.

'Please raise yer glasses to this amazing couple who've made it through twenty-five years ae happiness an' joy, sorrows and losses, an' remained committed tae each other *and* in love through it all. Their marriage is an example tae us all of what true love really is and that, if you're dedicated, you can realise a marriage until death do you part.'

Cheers and applause rang out throughout the hall. Mickey pulled Ella to him and kissed her. But Bobby wasn't finished yet. There were still about fifteen seconds to go before George Williams started singing about Ms Grace.

'Doc … eh, sorry, *Mickey* and Ella, thanks for allowin' us aw to celebrate this beautiful occasion with you tonight as ye celebrate twenty-five years of togetherness. Here's hopin' we'll aw meet back in another twenty-five years for yer golden anniversary!'

Again, loud cheers met the raising of Bobby's glass, and as the song's mellow groove got into its stride, almost all of the guests followed their hosts onto the large central dancefloor, filling it completely. Joey looked at his watch. Its digital display read *7:58 p.m.* 'Holy fuck, Boab! Where did *that* come fae?'

Bobby looked like he was in a trance. 'Eh, ah dunno. Whit did ye think tho? Too much?'

'Naw,' replied Joey enthusiastically. 'It was absolute fuckin' genius, mate. Look at it!' At the end of the song, the dancers actually stopped and applauded in the direction of the stage. Bobby didn't speak for the next three songs, allowing momentum to build and for the impact of his introductory valediction to last as long as possible. The Tymes were followed by Van McCoy's 'The Hustle', The Emotions' 'Best of My Love' and Chic with 'Good Times'. All songs with an immediacy that makes people *want* to dance; sometimes despite themselves and their rhythmic shortcomings. Even this early, it was evident that a memorable night was in front of them.

By ten o'clock, everything Bobby and Joey attempted had worked perfectly. Even Joey's determination to add some abstract music into the mix had paid off. After 'Once in a Lifetime' by Talking Heads – a notoriously difficult song to move to, which Bobby had dedicated to his brother, drawing yet more applause from the guests – two young black-clad girls made a request for 'Song from under the Floorboards' by Magazine, and something by The Birthday Party. Delighted though he was to play the former, even Joey had to admit Nick Cave's demented vocals had no place here.

'It's goin' well, boys. The wife's lovin' it,' said Mickey on the stroke of ten. 'Mibbe, cool it for half an' hour or that. Just tae gie everybody a break an' let the auld yins get a sandwich and a bit ae cake.'

'Nae bother, Doc,' said Bobby. 'We'll jist stick on an LP or somethin'.'

'Aye, fine. Awa' an' get yerselves a drink anaw, on me.'

'Cheers, man.' Bobby put the main hall lights up slightly and headed off to the snug, where he was very pleasantly surprised to see Lizzie waiting for him. Concerned about the growing rift between Lizzie and Joey – and his developing role as umpire when they were in the same room – he suggested a plan to his girlfriend with which she seemed to have gone along. The pretty blonde-haired girl next to her was intended for Joey. It was a risky strategy;

his friend would surely see through the set-up, and his disdain for Lizzie might surface in front of them all. But there was some form of weird magic in the air that night.

Lizzie stood up and kissed a shocked Joey on the cheek as he came in. 'Joey, this is ma pal, Katie.'

'Hi Joey,' said the sweet-voiced Katie. 'You guys were great in there. We were watchin' through the doors.'

Bobby could see that Joey was instantly hooked. He was beginning to think that anything was possible on this exceptional summer evening. *Perhaps if Thatcher had called* him *rather than Perez de Cuellar, or that fuckin' idiot, Reagan?* Bobby smiled at the thought.

'Hullo, son. You're Harry Cassidy's boy, aren't ye?' Bobby turned round from the bar to see Bert Bole standing behind him with his hand outstretched.

Bobby shook it, noticing the strange grip. 'Aye, mate. D'ye ken ma dad?'

'Ah do, son. Ah used tae work wi' him at the school.'

'Aw … ah *kent* ah'd seen ye before.'

'But ah was also there the night ae yer … the night ye shagged the virgin.' Bert winked, and eventually Bobby dissolved into fits of laughter. 'Tell yer dad ah'm askin' for him. Canny have been easy for him and yer mam, this last wee while, eh?'

'Naw. Thanks, though. Whit ye drinkin, mate?' asked Bobby.

'Yer fine, son. Ah couldnae get ye wan back, the now, so … it's a'right.'

'Listen, don't be daft. Ah'm a bit flush the now. Pint ae lager, is it?'

During the following five minutes of animated chat between his friend and the older man at the bar, Joey could see a familiar look developing on Bobby's face. It was one he knew so well and, predictably, it was followed by the words *I've just had an idea* when he came back to the table.

Bobby and Joey left the girls sat in the snug bar, and went back to the hall, where a snaking queue had formed for the buffet.

'Have ye got it, Joey?' said an excited Bobby.

'Aye, it's here!'

'Whit about the other two?'

'Eh, aye … one ae them, an' ah've definitely got the other yin as well here somewhere.'

'Right, let's go then. Put the lights down but just a wee bit an' get the first yin lined up.'

Joey did as requested, prompting some turned heads from the assembled guests.

'Ladies and gentlemen, while you enjoy yer food and a wee break from the disco, Heatwave is proud to present – singing a couple of well-known classics – Kilmarnock's ain, Mr Bert Bole!'

There was only a ripple of applause this time, and Mickey glanced over with a worrying *What the fuck is this?* look on his face. When the instrumental version of 'You've Lost that Loving Feeling' started up, Bert emerged from the back of the stage and began singing, right on cue. It was a hesitant beginning for Bert but, by the end of the song, virtually everyone else in the hall was singing along. This was followed by a more confident version of Patsy Cline's 'Crazy' and a triumphant rendition of 'Can't Take My Eyes off You'. By the final refrain of this last song, people were again out on the floor and turned as one to cheer for Bert when he had finished. Again, it had worked brilliantly.

Shorn of his curly Tom Jones wig, Ronseal-toned stage make-up and open-necked frilly shirt, Mickey hadn't initially recognised Bert as the same Tony Palomino who had disgraced his daughter's recent party. But Bobby's alchemy seemingly knew no bounds. Mickey paid Bert £50, mainly because his old mum had told him to.

'Aye, nice idea, Bobby,' said Mickey. 'Cost me a fifty spot, mind.'

'Sorry about that, man. Ah didnae mean tae …'

'It's a'right. Other folk have come up tae me an' asked if *they* can sing anaw. It's fuckin' bizarre!' said Mickey Martin, shaking his head in disbelief that people would even want to sing along to an instrumental backing track in front of a hall full of strangers. 'If we could get them tae pay for doin' it, then we'd really be ontae somethin'.' Mickey winked at Joey. 'We'll keep it in mind for The Metropolis, eh?' An arm was put round Bobby's shoulders and its significance wasn't lost on him.

'Aye, Doc. A'right. We're in.'

'Ye ken it makes sense, son.' And with that, he was gone. Back to join guests and relatives who were undoubtedly having one of the best nights they could remember.

In the very early hours of the morning that followed, Bobby looked up and winked at the poster of Rod that was looking back at him. He reflected on a truly memorable day. His girlfriend was lying beside him, looking beautiful. His best friend had gone home with a girl with whom he seemed besotted, and more crucially, she didn't appear likely to alert the relevant authorities as a result. They'd just delivered a truly brilliant night and had decided to continue in the less stressful context of a nightclub residency. Hettie had been granted a dispensation to retake her exams during the summer, and Harry – after some rollercoaster emotions – was back on an even keel again. Most significantly, Gary was coming home, back from the dead. Only fears about his mother's health and mental state remained, but, as his dad had recently acknowledged, the seeds for that concern had been sown well before Gary had even set sail.

As Bobby lifted the covers of his single bed to cop yet another sly look at Lizzie's deliciously full breasts, he conceded that – at that precise moment – life was pretty fucking good.

17

THE HARDER THEY FALL

30TH JUNE 1982: 1:58PM

The anticipated media bombardment of Almond Avenue hadn't materialised. There may have been a few extraneous reasons for this. The national UK media had been encouraged to move on somewhat by a government determined not to seem triumphalist in the wake of criticism from Margaret Thatcher's *left-wing, loony* opponents. The *Scottish Sun* had drawn local public opprobrium with a thinly veiled suggestion that Gary Cassidy *wasn't* a hero, but actually a deserter who'd run in the face of the battle. High-profile figures, such as Roy Jenkins – the newly elected MP for Glasgow Hillhead – had poured such scorn on this that the paper backed off after the one ridiculous headline to concentrate on a week-long debate about what names Prince Charles and Lady Diana Spencer would eventually settle on for their first-born child.

Harry also suspected that the higher-than-average police presence outside his door had something to do with Don McAllister. If that was his atonement for leaving Harry lying dazed in the car park of the Cochrane for the kitchen staff to come out and find, then frankly that was the *least* Harry would've expected. But he also hoped it would be the last event in a truly bizarre month-long game of cat-and-mouse, during which Harry sought at all costs to maintain the status quo for everyone's sake, particularly Gary's.

Harry had cursed himself for the slip of the tongue that had alerted Don McAllister to the fact that he was Gary's father. But, in more private moments, he had been astonished that it had never dawned on the copper before. Admittedly, his surreptitious dalliance with Ethel was brief. According to Ethel – and Harry had elected to believe her – they'd only slept together twice. Of course, Don wouldn't have known that Harry and Ethel were sleeping in separate beds at that difficult time. The miscarriage of their first baby had hit Ethel very hard and Harry – never the most tactile of men – couldn't give her the understanding and emotional comfort she needed. Don was a practised ladies' man and saw the signs. Don knew he had taken advantage – Harry had been right about that – but his growing sense that he was untouchable in those days blinded him to the wider dangers. It was all too exciting, and therefore too tempting, for the young policeman. But it had proved to be a pivotal lesson for Don. In realising how close he had come to losing *another* wife, his resolve to change his ways had been genuine. Ethel had barely seen Don and her sister Mary since the day after Harry had caught them together. He hadn't actually caught them in the act. Harry had come home early from work and Don had been in their living room, drinking tea with Ethel. But his police shirt was opened at the neck, and his police tie was still up in the bedroom. Ethel had burst into tears the minute she saw Harry walking up the path. It didn't take too much detection on Harry's part. As time passed, positions became entrenched and, for Ethel at least, it was simply less painful to re-open wounds that were more psychological than physical.

As Harry walked up to the main entrance of the hospital where his wife had been admitted two days earlier, he reflected that, with Gary's return, it was unlikely that Don's attempts to contact him would stop. In fact, Harry was sure that they would intensify. Although he'd made a breakthrough in talking directly to Gary in ways that he'd never been able to before, this wasn't something with which he could burden the boy over the phone, especially not now. Four of the five phone calls between them had been brief, and restricted to general updates about how Gary was feeling, how his family back home were coping and Gary's concerned reports about his friend, Benny Lewis. The last call had been longer, though. It had taken place in the middle of the night for Harry, but he had been unable to sleep in any case. The older man had been surprised but pleased by the interruption.

Harry hadn't contributed much to the conversation, as it turned out. His role was to be that of a sympathetic ear. It suited him well that night. He sat in the darkness, whisky in hand, listening to his son – and at that moment he'd never felt so strongly that Gary was *his* son – confront his fears, his nightmares and his attempts to rationalise the traumatic, life-changing experience that he'd just come through. In the end, Gary had tearfully admitted that he'd only joined the Army in the first place to earn his his father's respect. He didn't mean to imply that if it hadn't been for Harry, this mental torment that he was going through would have been avoided. But that's how Harry interpreted it, and it made him feel loathsome. Harry was desperate to tell the boy that for almost twenty years, it was *he* who had craved *Gary's* esteem. But the words didn't come. They'd have to wait until they were face-to-face, and that wouldn't be long.

→-◄-

'Hello, Mr Cassidy.'

'How is she today, nurse?'

'She's been comfortable. She hasn't eaten anythin' so she's had to go back on the drip, but I'm sure she'll be pleased to see you.'

Harry thanked the young staff nurse and walked towards his wife's single room.

'Oh, by the way, Mr Cassidy,' said the nurse. 'I nearly forgot. Ethel's sister came in to see her this morning. It wasn't visiting time, but Doctor Shapoor said we could make a wee exception.'

Harry was stunned.

'Ethel got a wee bit of a shock and she was crying so we had to ask Mrs McAllister to come back later.'

Harry didn't know what to say. All of a sudden, he could feel himself gasping for breath. It was already too warm in the ward, but it seemed to be getting hotter. Harry felt like he was going to be sick. A burning pain was beginning – and rapidly developing – across Harry's mid-chest and up towards his left shoulder. As it radiated into his left arm and up into his jaw, Harry knew what was happening. So did Nurse Mackintosh.

'Margo, *Margo*!' she shouted. 'This man is having a heart attack.' These were the last words Harry heard before collapsing to the linoleum, feeling as if a Clydesdale horse had just kicked him, full-force in his rib-cage.

30TH JUNE 1982: 4:23PM

'Ah told ye months ago, that if Grant ended up wi' that fat bastard, after aw you've been through wi' him, then you an' me were finished.' Senga stood in her kitchen. She was as calm as she could manage, determined not to prolong this or to allow her better nature to give the man she'd once loved a second chance.

Hobnail, for his part, had already known it was over the minute he saw Grant at Fat Franny's side. There was no possibility of appeal, no Joe Beltrami sitting in the wings waiting with a cast-iron alibi to get him off.

'Ah don't care if this is aw *your* doin' or no ...'

'How'th could it be ma dain'th, Thenga?' He knew he was on the way out but that didn't mean he'd go meekly. 'The fat bathdard fuckin'th thacked us yethderday!'

'Aye, ah ken Bob. Disnae say much that ye couldnae even haud

238

down a job wi' the local gangster, does it? Or that ye were replaced by yer ain son!' This was a bit underhand and a small part of Senga regretted saying it. But she'd lived a life of broken – and hidden – dreams, and since Grant had walked out on them ten days ago, saying he wouldn't be back, Senga saw no point in continuing with this sham of a relationship any further. In a relatively short time they'd grown so far apart it was unbelieveable. She couldn't now fathom how they'd stayed together for so long. It was a cultural expectation that people like her just *put up and shut up*. But Senga had changed much more than Bob had and, as a consequence, the action she was now taking was more opportunistic than last straw.

'Ah want ye tae go, Bob. Ye canny say ye wurnae warned. We've talked about this afore. For the sake ae the weans ah dinnae want a fuss. Just pack a bag and go, eh?'

'Go where, Thenga?' pleaded Hobnail.

'That's no ma concern, now. Mates? Yer mam's? No ma problem.' Senga had her arms crossed and an impenetrable scowl that suggested even a Beltrami *on-top-of-his-game* would be wasting his time. Again, Senga knew she'd score a direct hit. Outside of Fat Franny's crew, Hobnail had *never* had any mates; and as for his mother, he wasn't even entirely sure she was still *alive*, such was the length of time since he'd spoken a word to her.

The door closed quietly behind him. Out with a whimper as opposed to a scream. That just totally summed up his life. It was a life of servitude to more charismatic people, and the only way of making his prescence felt was with his fists. Throwing his weight about – it was the only thing he knew, the only way to retaliate. As he walked aimlessly around the Onthank area, where he'd lived for the majority of his life, his mood worsened. He was utterly alone. Betrayed by his childhood friend and disposed of by a son he'd never even attempted to get to know. Hobnail knew he had major failings, but he wasn't the only one.

He wandered past the old Mount Carmel Chapel, pausing to stare at the large Christ nailed to the stone cross over the front door.

He walked up Todhill Avenue and past the house where – as a man barely out of his teens – he'd administered a beating to a middle-aged man who owed Fat Franny a tenner. He walked on past the house in Amlaird Road where on Christmas Eve he'd taken a TV, a cooker and a collection of wrapped presents from a family whose repayments on a loan to the Fatman had been two weeks late. And on down into Onthank Drive, where he'd set fire to an ice-cream van because the old man inside wouldn't pay the fat cunt thirty percent protection money. He kept walking. Senga was right. His life amounted to nothing. He kept walking. His kids didn't know who he was. His wife didn't want him. His only use was in battering people. Perhaps he should just accept this. And put it into practice one last time. He walked on. And on.

When he stopped, he was at the very top of Redding Avenue, outside the black-metal gates of the Ponderosie. This gaudy temple of shite, and an example of the worst of Thatcher-driven capitalism. The fat bastard had forced out the next-door neighbour as if he was J.R. *fucking* Ewing. He'd 'bought' both semi-detached ex-council houses, bludgeoned them together without permission and then *lorded* it over every tenant in the street, forcing most to seek a move and the others to pay a small fee for the price of the security his residency would afford them. Hobnail figured he could take Fat Franny, no problem. But he was rarely alone, and if Hobnail was to succeed in taking him out, he'd almost certainly have to get through Wullie the Painter's men, Wullie himself, Hobnail's kin Des Brick and, most worryingly of all, possibly even Grant.

On this balmy Monday evening, though, there were no vehicles in the driveway. Maybe the fat prick was out. What should he do? Wait? Come back later? He'd psyched himself up over the last three hours of aimless wandering. *Too late to go back now.*

'Oh, hullo, Andy, son. Come on in. Francis isnae here just now, but c'mon in, anyway. It's lovely tae see ye. How's yer mam keepin'?'

'Eh … em … ah'm fine, Mithus Duncan.'

The old woman walked away, talking to herself and leaving the door wide open. When she turned round, Hobnail could see her floral skirt was partly tucked inside the waistband of her worn, greying knickers. He felt instantly sorry for her, and knew that he should leave, that he shouldn't be doing any of this. But then he caught sight of something intriguing. It was Fat Franny's safe, visible through the two hallway doors and beyond, in the recently completed kitchen extension. Hobnail stepped in. Fat Franny's mum had wandered away, but Hobnail could still hear her – in a wee contented world of her own, having conversations with people long dead. Hobnail envied her this insulation from such a brutal life.

'Andy? *Andy!* C'mon back tae bed. It's nearly midnight!' The voice from the other room jolted Hobnail into action. Fat Franny couldn't have gone out for long. He wouldn't have left his dotty old mum alone for any length of time, and he certainly wouldn't have left the safe exposed with the framed picture that had concealed it – *a fucking horrible mawkish picture of a crying six-year-old* – lying discarded on the worktop. Some emergency must have drawn him away in a real hurry. Hobnail stared at the safe's central dial. He gave it a hopeful turn in one direction, then again clockwise and finally a small one counterclockwise. The safe door opened. He had no gloves on, but was Fat Franny *really* going to report this to the cops?

'Andy! The bed's gettin' cold. Hurry up …'

Stupid fat cunt, thought Hobnail. Stacks of pound notes sat in the hole in front of him. The number of times he'd listened to the fat bastard going on about that fucking *Godfather* film: 'Dae ye ken the importance ae forward planning? Thinkin' ahead? Well, let me tell ye this. When Coppola started shootin' the part one, he asked fur eighty days. The studio *gied* him eighty-three. He did it in seventy-seven!' Fat Franny had delivered this analogous tale so many times, those figures were ingrained in Hobnail's memory. 'An' that goes tae prove the value ae making proper plans.'

Serves ye right ya fat prick, thought Hobnail as he headed for the back door. He looked up at the pinboard on the wall next to the door, with its line of keys along the bottom edge. He took the set labelled 'Metropolis' – *another wee problem sorted for later* – and headed out the back way, over the fence and away across the fields.

18

I THINK IT'S GOING TO BE A LONG, LONG TIME

1ST JULY 1982: 3:52PM

Fat Franny Duncan strode purposefully towards the ten-storey monolith that dominated his town's skyline. He fucking hated that building. Hated the people that used it. Hated the stone aquaduct in front of it that carried the West Coast rail line to the South. Hated the whole fucking town. Somebody knew something. Had some information. Could point a finger. Fat Franny's mind was racing. Was it someone in the Inner Circle? Was it one of the younger boys working on instruction? Was it a complete fucking stranger?

As he paced down the narrow Foregate, furtively looking right and left, Fat Franny couldn't stop thinking that *everyone* was a potential suspect. Fat Franny had a simple code: *Fuckin' Ten Commandments? Ther' wis only five in Kilmarnock and three of them involved no' starin' at yer mate's burd!* The two that really mattered were 'Nae nickin' fae the Boss' and 'Don't shit wher' ye sleep'. The Two Commandments had been broken and retribution was going to have to be swift and brutal.

Fat Franny burst through the unpainted double-swing doors of The Metropolis, its entrance permanently in the shadow of the dense car-parking levels above.

'Wullie! *Wullie!* Where the fuck are ye?' He shouted into the semi-darkness. A torchlight's focused beam came back and caught him full in the face. 'Turn that fuckin' thing aff, ya cunt!' said Fat Franny, shielding his eyes. It took a few seconds for his vision to re-adjust.

'Who ae ye callin' a cunt, fatman?' It wasn't Wullie the Painter holding the torch. It was Mickey Martin.

'Where's the Painter?' said Fat Franny.

'Aye, ah'd like tae ken that as well,' replied Mickey. Fat Franny was blindsided.

'Ah'm tryin' tae open this fuckin' place at the weekend. Doesnae fuckin' look likely at the minute, does it?'

'We were down here last night wi' your guy Denny. He was fuckin' happy enough *then*.'

'*His* name's no ower the fuckin' door is it? Plus we've lost another day wi' that snidey wee cunt no' turnin' up. Ah've got fuckin' partners an' they're aw kickin' off about us missin' the openin' date.'

'Look, ah've got ma ain fuckin' problems here. Ah don't ken where he is either. In fact, while we were down here yesterday, some bastard wis breakin' intae the house.'

'An' whit the fuck does that have tae dae wi' me? Ye implyin' it was me that did ye ower?'

'Did ah say that?' Fat Franny was struggling to find a positive way out of this conversation. He could recognise that Mickey was holding all the aces, but his blood was boiling and paranoia was his primary driver. 'Though it's a wee bit ae a fuckin' coincidence that we aw get shouted tae an *emergency* meeting here, that isnae really an emergency at aw. An' at the same time the Ponderosie gets fuckin' hit.'

Mickey Martin laughed. He genuinely didn't mean to but *that stupid fucking name.*

'Think it's funny? A big fuckin' laugh, eh?' glowered Fat Franny.

'Hey, watch yer tone, ya prick. Yer in ma' fuckin house now.'

Fat Franny turned to walk out.

'An' aye, ah *dae* think it's fuckin' funny. An' whit's funnier is *you* doin' this work for fuck-all cos' ye think yer gettin' a gig here. Ya stupid bastard.' This stopped Fat Franny in his tracks. 'Why would ah hire a fat walloper like you ower they Heatwave boys?'

Fat Franny turned and walked back towards Mickey Martin. Mickey stood impassively, a smug grin all over his face. Fat Franny was shaking. Mickey could see it. His reflexes were primed for avoiding a thrown punch. But Franny's rage was not so blind as to obscure the consequences of raising fists against Mickey Martin, even with no witnesses.

'Ah'll no forget this, Doc. Ye might no' care too much the now, but we'll be havin' this out in the near future.' Fat Franny poked a stubby finger into Mickey's chest. His stance was aggressive but he was holding back. 'An' when that happens, the fuckin' boot'll be on the other foot!' Fat Franny turned and walked away towards the doors.

'Ah ken ye'll no forget. Elephants *never* fuckin' dae!' shouted Mickey as Franny disappeared through them into the pedestrianised precinct outside.

'Fuck's sake, Doc. That was close. Just as well ah went tae the bog when ah did, eh?'

'Just get on wi' it, eh? Ah wisnae jokin' when ah said that ah'm fucked if we don't get this open for the weekend, so get yer tea down an' get a fuckin' shift on,' said Mickey. 'An' Wullie?'

'Whit?'

'Don't lose ma fuckin' keys, an' stay out ae his way for the next few days, eh?'

2ND JULY 1982: 8:14AM

Hobnail was astonished at the cost of sending a recorded-delivery parcel. He'd never really posted anything before – apart from a severed big toe – but still, £10.98 was daylight fucking robbery, in his opinion. Just as well Fat Franny was paying for it from the £46,763 of which Hobnail had relieved him. Hobnail had kept a small amount for himself, but the vast bulk of this sum was now in the heavily wrapped parcel that sat on the counter of the small post office in the back of the corner shop in Crosshouse. Hobnail had got up early – mainly to avoid detection – but also to walk out to this remote village where there would be far less chance of anyone knowing who he was and therefore of him drawing attention to such a large parcel. He was still amazed that he'd been able to walk around on the night he'd taken it, with all of the money in two double-wrapped Safeway bags that he'd found in Fat Franny's house. The memory brought a smile to his lips and it reminded him of how little he'd smiled in recent years. The thought of that fat tosser trying to interrogate his poor old mum about the identity of 'Andy', whom she was trying to get back into bed, made him go one step further and burst out laughing.

Hobnail couldn't make up for all that Senga thought she had lost by staying with him. He didn't have the vocabulary. He also couldn't connect with Grant in a way that would positively address the dilemma of accepting Hobnail for the person he was, while at the same time persuading the boy that there was a different, better future if he avoided his father's mistakes. Hobnail shared Senga's fears about Grant. He just couldn't articulate them to either. But maybe this pack of twenty-, fifty- and hundred-pound notes could say it for him. It was too late for Senga and him, but perhaps not for Grant and the other kids. Senga would get the money. She'd know what to do with it to avoid suspicion. She'd be savvy enough to know where it came from and would have no scruples at all about utilising this *found* money for the benefit of her family. But she would also get Hobnail's crudely written note, and, although he'd tried to disguise his child-like handwriting, the expressed wishes contained within it that Senga enjoy Vienna would casually betray the identity of the sender. Hobnail took some comfort in hoping that it might also prove to his wife that he *had* been listening after all.

By the time Guardsman Gary Cassidy's four-leg plane journey home from the Falklands had ended, his father, Harry Cassidy, was dead. Somewhere around the equator – as his son slept lightly on a Hercules whose principal purpose was that of repatriation – Harry Cassidy suffered a second attack, which was massive and fatal. His wife was in a ward two floors above, unaware of this or anything else that was going on around her.

Her daughter Hettie had fallen asleep briefly in her room, exhausted from a general lack of sleep and also from the emotional trauma of having both parents in a serious condition in the same hospital. Her brother Bobby was in the hospital café at the time of his father's death. Bobby's Aunt Mary – his mother's sister, to whom he had never spoken, and wouldn't have recognised if she had served him his tea – was on her way to the hospital. Her intention was to come clean with her niece and nephew, and suggest that Ethel come out of hospital to live with her and her husband until Harry was back on his feet. She could afford professional help for her catatonic sister, as her husband had a good job. Meanwhile, her husband – feeling remorse at the stress under which he'd unwittingly put Harry – was dropping off another note at the house in Almond Avenue. This one was a formal card with a single blue flower on the front. On the inside was one word: 'Sorry' in black Monotype Corvisa script. Below this, the initials D and M were written in blue ink. The envelope contained nothing other than the designation 'Mr Cassidy'.

Gary suspected that something was wrong when only Bobby met him at Prestwick Airport, on yet another unusually balmy summer's evening. For weeks it had seemed that the weather was due to break, yet it had held in a way that made Bobby recall the long hot summer of 1976. And there were potentially still a couple of months of it to go.

'Fuckin' hell, Gary. He's dead! Dad's dead!' Bobby's legs buckled and Gary instinctively caught him. Bobby cried in a way that Gary had never seen him do before. Somehow, it wasn't a shock to Gary to hear of his father's passing. When he'd been ordered to gather his pack and belongings together, ready for moving out on the flight from Port Stanley's small airstrip, the unique circumstances had been explained to him. He had been dismissed for a four-week break at home before reporting to Wellington Barracks. The return home at the beginning of this period was being accelerated even further because his father had suffered a heart attack. He said little to Bobby in the car on the way to the hospital. He had no words. He couldn't cry. He had none of those tears left. Bobby just sat in the car, staring out the window into the dark of the moors at Symington, sobbing quietly.

Gary had left to go to war as a boy and come back as a man. The reality of this cliché of warfare was more complex, though. His appearance shocked Hettie, whose numbness about the last three weeks was closer to Gary's than to Bobby's. It had seemed to her that Bobby's head had been completely in the sand during this last month. He had appeared to have the childish expectation that bad things would go just away if you avoided recognising or confronting them. He had run away to Lizzie's or Joey's when dealing with Ethel had got too difficult. It was an uncharacteristically selfish – and sexist – response, but it had made Hettie resent him. It appeared that she was simply expected to care for her mother because that's what daughters did. Hettie had had no outlet to release her feelings of pain, fear, resentment, loss and subsequent joy for Gary. Now he was finally back, she fully expected to feel far more comfortable and safe with her elder brother – the one who had only weeks ago stood trembling next to a friend who was searching in shock for his foot that had been blown off, and another friend whose life he had saved.

Hettie was in her mother's single bedroom – as she had been almost constantly for four days. Ethel was asleep, an induced sleep that she had been in since earlier that day when a doctor had broken the news of her husband's death to her. Her two children had been in the room with her, but her lack of response to the news contrasted sharply with Bobby's reaction; his emotional collapse was as unexpected as it was distressing. Hettie tried to hold it together – tried to listen to the doctor as he spoke directly to her – while it hit home hard how small their family circle actually was. The only current benefit of this was that they had found it easy to conceal Gary's homecoming. They would now have to hide their father's death, to give them time to act appropriately before the press descended on them yet again. Hettie had been suspicious of everyone in the last few weeks and hadn't even spoken to her own small group of close friends since their exams had started.

She looked at Bobby, distraught in the chair in his mum's hospital bedroom, and realised that he was someone who had never given a minute's thought to the passing of his parents. His closeted teenage life revolved around having fun and avoiding anything that might cause him distress. She had once envied such an existence – things that went wrong for Bobby were generally fixed by the opening of his father's wallet, or a girlfriend's sudden change of heart. Now it made her feel more adult and superior, but also a little sorry for him. It was a strange brew of emotions.

3RD JULY 1982: 00:15AM

The three of them returned home, but Bobby changed and headed straight back out to see Lizzie, murmuring that he couldn't stay in the house that night. It was just after midnight. Gary picked up an envelope at the front door and brought it into the living room, sitting it on the mantelpiece. He'd told Bobby to go if he had to, and then eventually calmed his angry sister. It was amazing how mature Gary had become – old before his years. He was only twenty, but he wore the haunted, wrinkled face of a man twice his age. Hettie wanted to talk to him. To soothe him and let him know that he was safe now. At fifteen, she wanted to *protect* him.

'Have ye spoken tae Debbie yet?' asked Hettie quietly, as Elton John's 'Rocket Man' played quietly in the background. It was strange that the first thing Gary had done upon coming home was to put on the record player.

'Naw, no yet,' replied Gary. 'Ah wrote a few times but ah don't think she got them.'

'No, ah don't think she would have,' said Hettie. 'When they came tae tell us you were … y'know, *missing in action*, they brought a load ae letters wi' them. Ah've got them upstairs for ye.'

'Probably too late now. Plus ah'm no great company. Canny sleep. Too many nightmares.' Gary put his head in his hands. There was a long silence following the needle lifting away from the record's run-off grooves. Eventually, he said, 'Ah don't ken whit ah'm gonnae dae, Hettie. Ah thought that if ah could get through the tae the end of it, an' get back an' sort things out wi' Dad, everythin' would be fine after that. Y'know, I could go back tae London, pick up wi' Debs an' have a fuckin' purpose in life for once.' Another long pause passed by. Talking was difficult. They were essentially strangers now – two people who would have to slowly rebuild the close relationship they once had. Hettie felt paralysed by exhaustion.

'Did he say much about me when ah was away?'

'Who, Dad?'

'Aye.'

'He did, Gary. He might no have said it often but he was really, really proud. He sat up watchin' aw the news programmes and even listening tae the World Service radio.'

Gary pondered the comforting thought of he and his father tuning in to the same radio broadcasts each night. He had spent much of the last few years searching for things that they had in common. To have found it in such a tenuous way seemed heartening, but also now incredibly sad.

'D'ye ken one of the most shocking things ah saw?' Hettie's eyes were closed, but Gary wasn't really talking to her. 'On the first day after we landed at San Carlos, ah saw a deid horse – a big fuckin' beautiful stallion, lyin' deid in the middle ae a road. Its eyes were open an' there wis nae visible wounds. It wis jist deid. Ah'd never seen a deid thing before an' ah jist burst oot in tears'. Ah couldnae stop fur ages. Ah thought whit fuckin' chance huv ah got if this big, strong beast cannae make it? The horse had been killed by artillery fire an' it was lyin' on its wounded side. Ah don't ken whether it was Argentine or British fire that killed it, an' for a while it seemed to be really important for me to find out. Ah kept askin' and askin' about the big black horse on the road, but naebody answered. Everybody was just dealin' wi' their *ain* issues.

'Later on, we had marched up a track in the pissing rain an' we heard the first sounds ae battle away in the distance. Ah flicked oan ma Walkman tae block it aw oot. Further on, we passed a coupla guys fae another company. Ah switched off the music. One ae them was hysterical, shouting, "Gerry's deid, Gerry's fuckin' deid", an' the first thing ah thought was, *That's a strange name for a horse*! Then a shell went off about the length ae a fitba pitch away. We aw dived for whit cover there was. Then another yin closer, an' then one about fifty feet behind us. Ah was lying there, in the dark and the wet starin' up the sky, and thinkin' aboot Dad. Ah thought the next fuckin' shell would land right on top ae us, an' that'd be it … an' aw a wanted was ma dad.' Gary wiped away a tear. 'The one thing that kept me goin' aw that week in the sheep shed was the thought ae gettin' home an' tellin' him that.'

Hettie was asleep. Gary got up and pulled a cover from the back of the sofa and laid it gently over her. He then went and put the needle back to the start of the Honky Château LP.

By the time early-morning light emerged, blinking through the edges of the horizontal metal blinds, Gary had listened to the record seven times. It had been the one cassette he'd taken with him at San Carlos. He didn't think he'd really get the chance to listen to many more once he'd left the ship. Gary didn't even particularly like Elton John, but 'Rocket Man' was truly great. When Gary lay in the mud and the blood and the gore, staring up the sky and waiting for death, it was Bernie Taupin's words that were going round in his fevered brain. Mixed feelings about an astronaut leaving his family in order to do a job tens of thousands of miles away: Gary could definitely relate.

Fortunately, Hettie was still asleep. It was almost certainly the first time in weeks that she had slept more than four hours at a stretch. Gary went through to the kitchen. His head hurt and he hunted around for some paracetamol. He found four and took them with whisky. He walked over to the front window and picked up the letter from the mantelpiece. He opened the envelope and read the contents. He then pulled the blinds open, causing Hettie to stir as the sunlight flashed across her face.

'What time is it?'

'It's still only half-seven,' said Gary. 'Ye managed tae sleep for a wee while there, Hets.'

'Is Bobby back yet?'

'Naw. Ah don't think he'll be back today. Let him come tae terms wi' it an' ah'll go an' see him tomorrow. We'll need tae sort out the funeral soon anyway.' Hettie started to sob. 'Hey. Hey, come on. It'll be a'right. Don't cry, Hettie. Ah didnae mean tae upset ye again.' Gary put his arm around his sister.

'Ah'm fine Gary. It's just … it was a bit ae a shock tae see ye standing there,' said Hettie.

'Who's DM?' asked Gary, showing her the card.

'Ah don't really know. A guy called *Doc* or *Don-somethin'* phoned a couple of times a wee while ago.'

'Whit would he be sayin' sorry about?'

'Dunno. Hang on, though, there was also a note ah fished out the bin. Ah kept it somewhere. Try that drawer over there.'

Gary recovered the crumpled note.

'Canny think ae anybody wi' the initials DM,' said Gary. His headache was blinding now. The paracetamol was having no effect. But Gary did go and pour another whisky.

'A bit early for that Gary, Christ!' said Hettie.

'Ah need it, Hets. Ah need it to stop aw the shakin'.'

'I think the guy's second name was Martin. He phoned a few times after we'd heard about you. Ah didnae get a proper message cos' my head was all ower the place that week.'

'Doc Martin? The *gangster*?' asked a surprised Gary.

'Ah dunno. Is he?' said Hettie. 'Ah think Bobby kens him, as well.'

'So whit happened then, after Dad went tae meet him?' Gary held the crumpled note up for reference. He was aware that it was strange to be interrogating her like this, but he felt that something didn't quite add up. Two notes from a local hood in a week, one asking for a meeting. *His dad was a school janny, for fuck's sake!*

'Anything else happen, Het?'

'Gary, ah've been up tae here wi' aw this. Ah don't ken whether ah'm comin' or goin' half the time. Ah huvnae slept properly for about a month an' ma mam doesnae even ken who ah am!' She began to sob again.

'Aw, Hettie look ah'm sorry.' Gary cuddled his sister. 'Look at the state ae us, eh?' Hettie broke away and got up to get a hankie.

'Dad came home wi' a cut face the day he went tae see that guy.' Hettie looked ashamed.

'Why did ye no say that before?' pleaded Gary. 'That makes a difference.'

'Dad said he fell. He said he hit his head off a stone wall. Ah never thought more about it until ye showed me that card there.'

'So why was it no the first thing ye told me?'

'Cos' ah'm worried about ye, Gary. Yer all over the place *yerself*.'

'Whit dae ye think ah'm gonnae dae, Hettie. Mickey Martin's a mental case. Ah'm hardly gonnae go an' take him on when ah'm just back.'

'Right. Well, then, just forget whit ah said tae ye about Dad's face. He died ae a heart attack an' nothin's gonnae bring him back now.'

'Aye.'

But Gary couldn't put it out of his mind. He left the house to go to the bookies, pick up some cigarettes and just wander around the town. He went out the back door and over the school fields. Gary *normally* left the house this way, but on this particular morning, when he opened the front door to bring in the milk, he felt certain he'd seen a long telescopic lens sticking out of a car window further down Almond Avenue. Walking over the fields a backfiring car engine caused him to throw himself instinctively to the turf. He picked himself up, shaken but grateful that the image wouldn't be on a front page somewhere. He also went into the Clansman, and then the Auld Hoose, and then the Kings Arms. He sat drinking whisky, alone. No matter how much he drank, it had no effect. He couldn't blot out the memories, the screams, the flashing lights, the dead … his dad … Mickey Martin.

In the Kings Arms, a mate from his old football team bought him a drink, and asked to meet up at Mickey Martin's new place when it opened at the weekend. It was called The Metropolis. *Supposed to be brilliant.* Under the multi-storey car park. *See you there, then.*

Aye.

3RD JULY 1982: 6:15PM

'Look, ah'm just lettin' ye ken. There might be a real problem wi' the opening. Aye, ah ken … look, listen … Will ye fuckin' *listen* tae me a minute? The work'll get done, ah've sorted that, but it's the permissions. We've got a big problem wi' the fire certificates … Aye … It's because the thing's in a fuckin' concrete bunker, basically … Naw, naw there's nothin' ah can dae about that now, but ah will sort it. I'm goin' away the night for a coupla days up tae St Andrews. It'll be fixed when ah get back … Aye, aye, look, just don't panic, right! Aye, see ye.'

'Who was that on the phone, Mickey?'

'Naebody, Ella, just a bit ae business. Are ye ready tae go?'

'Aye, Mickey. Car's packed. Ye've just tae set the alarm.'

3RD JULY 1982: 8:25PM

'Nae sign, Des?'

'Naw, Boss. Naebody's seen him for days. He's no been goin' intae the Metro an' he's no been home either.' This latest turn of events had flabbergasted Des Brick. 'Ah canny believe Wullie took the cash, Franny. How would he ken the combination?'

'Dae *you* ken it, like?' said Fat Franny.

'Eh, naw … naw, of course no! How the fuck would ah ken it?' Des wished he'd just kept quiet now.

'Well some cunt did, an' there wurny that many folk in the *Inner Circle*.'

'Yer mam no able tae tell ye anything yet?' Des was just tryin' tae be helpful, but failing miserably.

'Aye. She can fuckin' tell me plenty. She can tell me the six wives ae Henry the Eighth, Napoleon had a wee walloper, an' that you're a prick. That any use tae us?'

'Fuck sake, Franny. Ah'm jist askin' seein' as she was here.'

'Well, she told me the guy's first name, that he was wearin' a kilt an' he wis singin' 'Donald, Wher's Yer Troosers'?' So dae ye really think we should fuck off up tae the Highlands an' gie Andy Stewart a right good kickin?' Des said nothing. 'Naw, didnae think so. Right let's get goin'. We've got Grant tae pick up. We're gonny put a right fuckin' spanner in the works ae that cunt Martin. Let's go fur a quick pint wi' Terry Connolly.'

The interior had been ablaze for about four hours before any traces of smoke had been detected. It had been a local baker heading down the Foregate, to begin work at five a.m., who smelled the smoke, although at that point he couldn't see it. The concrete structure of the car park and the lack of any openings into the vaulted basements had kept the fire contained, but the alcohol in the stores had fuelled it. When the Fire Brigade finally penetrated the spaces, the backdraft caused a powerful blast, which – if it had happened during conventional working hours – would've resulted in multiple casualties. As it was, The Metropolis was totally destroyed. The fire took three hours to put out. It had all the hallmarks of an insurance job.

Wullie the Painter knew nothing of the fire, despite being only forty feet above it. He expected to be well rewarded by Mickey Martin for his work at The Metropolis, and if the one condition of that was to keep out of sight, then he'd simply park his van in the car park and head up there to sleep every night. The car park was still accessible by its stairs, but the operator's booth was closed between six p.m. and six a.m., so it was always quiet at night. There was a stair down to the rear metal basement doors that led through the smaller vaults to the club. This was where the alcohol deliveries would come in for the new club and where Wullie let himself in and out every day. The third of July was Wullie's birthday and, although it wasn't the most memorable way to spend it, he'd helped himself to a half-bottle of vodka on the way out and demolished it while listening to some arty-farty rubbish on Radio 2. He'd been deeply out of it the whole time that the fire had raged on and had even slept through the sirens. His shock at seeing the carnage in the morning was threefold. Firstly, his materials were all still in the club, and therefore destroyed. Secondly, he hadn't actually been paid anything yet by Mickey Martin and would be unlikely to be remunerated now. And thirdly, he could see from his vantage point that there was an ambulance in the yard and someone was being loaded into it on a stretcher. One minute past six, Wullie the Painter drove his van out of the car park and away from the scene; his rear registration plate captured on video as the barrier went down.

'Don, ah thought ye should ken first, mate. The guy's jist died in the hospital. Ah ken you've got links wi' Doc Martin.'

'Thanks, Charlie, ah'll no forget this. Ah appreciate it. Who else kens about it?'

'Only me and Dennis. He'll keep quiet. He's a good lad. Auchinleck Masons he is!'

Don McAllister's detective team had done their job well. In fact, the whole Masonic network had kicked into gear, just as it should. The fire chief knew Charlie and had called him first, even before they realised someone had been in the building. The fireman knew an insurance fire when he saw one and later reckoned that, if the guy in the cupboard was the unfortunate arsonist, there was a fair chance that someone in the police department would want to manage that information.

'There's also *this*, Don,' said Charlie, handing his boss a boxed cassette. Mickey had just installed a new camera-recording system in the pub. He had been testing it in the run-up to the opening. It was state-of-the-art technology, but Don had something similar at his home and he knew how to view it.

'Anybody seen *this*, Charlie?' enquired Don.

'Naw, Don. No even me,' replied Charlie. 'It wasnae burnt cos' he had it in his office – the wan room in the building wi' concrete walls and a solid-core metal door. Ah hud tae break in tae get it, mind.'

Don would have to repay Charlie. A promotion could well be on its way. He was an old-school copper, as loyal as the day was long. It would be important to keep him close. Dennis would also benefit.

'Right mate, cheers. Ah'm away oot tae the hospital. Try and track doon Doc Martin. You'll need tae dae that interview, but Martin kens the score. You're in charge though. Ah'll let ye ken once we've goat the identity ae the deid guy.'

'Right, boss. See ye later,' said Charlie.

19

LUCA BRASI SLEEPS WITH THE FISHES

19TH JULY 1982: 10:27AM

The headstone was warm to the touch. It faced east and had been basking in the direct sunshine for two hours. It was a beautiful Ayrshire morning; another in a long line that seemed to stretch back until April. There had been miserable days, but since they had been unseasonably outnumbered by days like today, no-one could really remember them. For Guardsman Gary Cassidy, though, days like this still seemed like gifts. The nightmares remained as prolonged and as vivid. Restorative sleep was a distant memory for Gary, but at least the difficult hours of darkness were relatively short. The heat of the sun on his face felt wondrous. The inevitable descent into winter held real fears for him, but for now the sunshine helped him to forget the chaos.

Gary sat next to the new headstone and drew his fingers across its carved indents. He touched each letter, tracing his fingers over them one-by-one, as if reading Braille. He dwelt over the name 'HAROLD JAMES CASSIDY'. He ran a forefinger over the words 'BELOVED HUSBAND TO ETHEL'. His other fingers stroked the letters of 'MUCH LOVED FATHER TO HEATHER, ROBERT & GARY'. His whole hand underlined the numbers '1933–1982'.

'Thought ah'd find ye here.'

'Are ye goin' tae arrest me, Mr McAllister?' asked Gary, without turning around.

'Ah've told ye son, it's *Don*.' Don looked around. The nearest people were tending the flowers of a grave about a hundred yards away. 'Why would ah want tae arrest ye, Gary?'

'Thanks for sorting out the funeral, an' for gettin' the stone so quickly. Hettie really appreciates it.'

'The least ah could dae, son. Yer dad was a good man.'

'How's ma mum?'

'She's no great, son. But yer Aunt Mary's lookin' after her an' the home help's keeping her stable.' Don dropped down to his haunches. His knees weren't great, and he immediately regretted it, but it seemed important to him to be closer to Gary's eye level. Worse come to it, he'd simply have to kneel. The turfed grass of the grave was dry and full, so at least his favourite Ralph Lauren suit wouldn't get dirty.

'How come wi' kent nothin' about ye till he was deid?' asked Gary.

'Ach Gary, just stupid fuckin' family stuff. We aw fell out ower somethin' daft that happened before you were even born. Seemed important at the time but now ah canny even remember whit. Time went by an' it got harder an' harder for each ae us tae back down. An' ye ken yer dad could be a stubborn bugger. Well, ah was just as bad.' Gary sighed. Don decided to change tack. 'How's Hettie?' he asked.

'She'll be a'right. She wants me to go back tae London, but ah canny.'

'Ah think ye should as well. Ye need tae go and see somebody. Get some help, son.'

'You sound like ma dad.'

'Ah'm only tellin' ye whit *he* would, if he was here. Yer better back wi' folk that ken whit yer goin' through.'

'Ye *ken* why ah canny go back.'

'Naw, actually ah don't. Ye made somethin' ae yerself in the

Army. Ah ken it canny be easy for ye tae confront whit happened at the Falklands but ye did a great thing. Ye saved yer mate's life. Ye *deserve* the medals.'

'Ah killed somebody here. Ah took somebody's life. A complete fuckin' stranger, an' for nothin'. A total fuckin' misunderstanding.'

'Gary, son … ye didnae start that fire.'

'Ah fuckin' did!'

'Naw, ye didnae … an' if ye'll shut up fur a minute, ah'll tell ye whit happened.'

'The version accordin' tae Don McAllister?'

'If ye like, aye.' Don adjusted his posture to shift the weight onto his better left knee. This *was* his favourite suit after all. 'Wullie Blair caused the fire. He'd been working doonstairs and he'd left a lit fag next tae a tin of varnish.' Gary started slowly shaking his head. 'He left the place unlocked, and went up the car park stairs to his van on level four where he slept through the fire being put out. He'd been drinkin' heavily. He was totally unaware that there was an individual sleepin' rough in a back store cupboard of the club. The victim, Robert Dale, was known to Wullie Blair, but had separately broken into the club with keys stolen from Francis Duncan.'

'Aw sounds very official. Well done!'

'That was *his* statement, son.'

'Convenient.'

'Naw, *accident*!'

'It was me that *set that* fire, Mr McAllister.'

'Look, Gary! Listen tae me. Ah don't ken how ye got it intae yer heid that Martin thumped yer dad, an' it disnae matter now. Aw that's in the past. Ah canny turn the clock back, but for yer dad's sake, ah'm no prepared tae see ye mess up yer life completely.'

'How can ye ignore the evidence? That poor bastard's lawyer'll no just accept your version ae events.'

'Ther's *nae* evidence. No any more!'

'Fur fuck's sake …'

'The only evidence left is Wullie Blair bein' the last guy oot before the place went up. Him leavin' the scene after fallin' asleep pished in his van upstairs. Open tins ae paint and varnish, and him admitting he was smokin'. Seems pretty fuckin' cut and dried tae me.'

'Ah killed a guy ...'

'Ah ken ye did. Ye were servin' yer country when it happened. An' they gied ye a medal for it. Ye've been strugglin' wi' aw this since ye came back, ah can vouch for that. Who widnae be a mess after everythin' you've been through? Aw that *yompin'*!'

Gary sneered.

'Whit?' asked Don.

'Everythin' that happened, aw that carnage ... an' aw any cunt wants tae talk aboot is fuckin' *yompin'*!'

Don allowed himself a smile. 'Look, apart fae Bob Dale obviously – an' naebody even kent he was there! – it's no a total disaster. It did Doc Martin a favour. He had committed tae an opening date he could never have made. He didn't have any ae the building consents or the licences in place, an' he would never have got them. His backers will get their money back; he'll reopen it in about six months an' it'll be better.'

'So everybody's a winner then?'

'Life's no a case ae winnin', mate. For folk like us, it's more about scraping a score draw wi' the last kick ae the gemme.' Don stood up. 'Go down tae London, son. Get help, sort yerself oot an' get back intae the job. Phone that lassie Hettie was tellin' me about.' Gary stood up. 'On ye go, son. Ye deserve another chance, an' ah owe it tae yer dad tae help gie ye it. We'll look after yer mum, an' ah'll keep an eye out for Hettie and yer brother as well.' Don held out his hand. It hung there for a few seconds. Eventually Gary reciprocated and shook it. He noted the power and the unusual grip of Don's handshake.

'Aw the best, son,' said Don. 'See ye sometime.'

EPILOGUE

13ᵀᴴ JUNE 2007

'The Falklands War was a great national struggle. The whole country knew it and felt it. It was also mercifully short. But many of our boys – and girls as well, of course – are today stationed in war zones where the issues are more complex, where the outcome is more problematic, and where life is no less dangerous. In these circumstances, they often need a different sort of courage, though the same commitment.

So, as we recall – and give thanks for – the liberation of our Islands, let us also recall the many battle fronts where British forces are engaged today. There are in a sense no final victories, for the struggle against evil in the world is never ending. Tyranny and violence wear many masks. Yet from victory in the Falklands we can all today draw hope and strength.

Fortune does, in the end, favour the brave. And it is Britain's good fortune that none are braver than our Armed Forces. Thank you all.'

Radio message from Lady Thatcher broadcast on British Forces Broadcasting Service to mark the twenty-fifth anniversary of the liberation of the Falkland Islands

SONGS THAT BROUGHT ABOUT
THE LAST DAYS OF DISCO

'Heat Wave'
The Jam
(Written by Holland-Dozier-Holland)
Available on Polydor Records, 1979

'Ghost Town'
The Specials
(Written by Jerry Dammers)
Available on 2-Tone Records, 1981

'The Adventures of Grandmaster Flash on the Wheels of Steel'
Grandmaster Flash
(Produced by Sylvia Robinson and Joey Robinson, Jr)
Available on Sugarhill Records, 1981

'Heart of Glass'
Blondie
(Written by Debbie Harry and Chris Stein)
Available on Chrysalis Records, 1981

'Don't You Want Me'
The Human League
(Written by Phil Oakey, Jo Callis and Philip Adrian Wright)
Available on Virgin Records, 1981

'Up the Junction'
Squeeze
(Written by Chris Difford and Glenn Tilbrook)
Available on A&M Records, 1979

'Maybe Tomorrow'
The Chords
(Written by Chris Pope)
Available on Polydor Records, 1980

'Plan B'
Dexy's Midnight Runners
(Written by Kevin Rowland and James Paterson)
Available on EMI Records, 1981

'Party Fears Two'
The Associates
(Written by Billy MacKenzie and Alan Rankine)
Available on WEA Records, 1982

'Big Bird'
Eddie Floyd
(Written by Eddie Floyd)
Available on Stax Records, 1967

'Get Out My Life, Woman'
Lee Dorsey
(Written by Allen Toussaint)
Available on Bell Records, 1965

'Picture Me Gone'
Madeline Bell
(Written by Taylor and Gorgoni)
Available on Philips Records, 1968

'The Magnificent Seven'
The Clash
(Written by The Clash)
Available on CBS Records, 1981

'Good Times'
Chic
(Written by Bernard Edwards and Nile Rodgers)
Available on Atlantic Records, 1979

'Inside Out'
Odyssey
(Written by Jesse Rae)
Available on RCA Records, 1982

'Best of My Love'
The Emotions
(Written by Maurice White and Al McKay)
Available on Columbia Records, 1977

'Rocket Man'
Elton John
(Written by Elton John and Bernie Taupin)
Available on DJM Records, 1972

'Shipbuilding'
Robert Wyatt
(Written by Elvis Costello and Clive Langer)
Available on Rough Trade Records, 1982

'The Story of the Blues'
The Mighty Wah!
(Written by Pete Wylie)
Available on Warner Brothers Records, 1982

ACKNOWLEDGEMENTS

Writing this book began as a personal dream, the day after my fortieth birthday, along with running the New York Marathon and playing for Glasgow Rangers.

I've all but given up on the other two. They just seem to require far too much training and personal dedication – or a time machine. Maybe someday, who knows?

I'm grateful to my family and friends for encouragement, but especially to Elaine, for her love and support.

Also thanks to Mark Stanton (Stan) for advice and assistance. I'm indebted to Kevin Toner for his countless re-reads. I also thank my lucky stars that I had the very good fortune to meet the effervescent Karen Sullivan, who gave me belief and kept me on track.

Finally, and although he'll probably never be aware of it, I'm grateful to Paul Weller for continuing inspiration. Anyone who reads this book, and then listens to the *Setting Sons* LP will be immediately aware of the place it has in my heart.

Joey Miller will return in *The Man Who Loved Islands*.